NAUGHTON'S *Secret*

USA TODAY BESTSELLING AUTHOR

HEATHER SLADE

ISBN 13: 9798886490770

MORE FROM AUTHOR HEATHER SLADE

BUTLER RANCH
Kade's Worth
Brodie's Promise
Maddox's Truce
Naughton's Secret
Mercer's Vow
Kade's Return
Butler Ranch Christmas

WICKED WINEMAKERS FIRST LABEL
Brix's Bid
Ridge's Release
Press' Passion
Zin's Sins
Tryst's Temptation

WICKED WINEMAKERS SECOND LABEL
Beau's Beloved
Cru's Crush
Bones' Bliss
Snapper's Seduction
Kick's Kiss

ROARING FORK RANCH
Roaring Fork Wrangler
Roaring Fork Roughstock
Roaring Fork Rockstar
Roaring Fork Rooker
Roaring Fork Bridger

THE ROYAL AGENTS OF MI6
Make Me Shiver
Drive Me Wilder
Feel My Pinch
Chase My Shadow
Find My Angel

K19 SECURITY SOLUTIONS TEAM ONE
Razor's Edge
Gunner's Redemption
Mistletoe's Magic
Mantis' Desire
Dutch's Salvation

K19 SECURITY SOLUTIONS TEAM TWO
Striker's Choice
Monk's Fire
Halo's Oath
Tackle's Honor
Onyx's Awakening

K19 SHADOW OPERATIONS TEAM ONE
Code Name: Ranger
Code Name: Diesel
Code Name: Wasp
Code Name: Cowboy
Code Name: Mayhem

K19 ALLIED INTELLIGENCE TEAM ONE
Code Name: Ares
Code Name: Cayman
Code Name: Poseidon
Code Name: Zeppelin
Code Name: Magnet

K19 ALLIED INTELLIGENCE TEAM TWO
Code Name: Michelangelo
Code Name: Reaper
Code Name: Typhon
Code Name: Rogue
Code Name: Hornet

PROTECTORS UNDERCOVER
Undercover Agent
Undercover Prince
Undercover Infidel
Undercover Savior
Undercover Assassin

THE INVINCIBLES TEAM ONE
Decked
Edged
Grinded
Riled
Smoked

THE INVINCIBLES TEAM TWO
Bucked
Irished
Sainted
Hammered
Ripped

THE UNSTOPPABLES TEAM ONE
Furied
Married
Vexed
Inked
Jagged

COWBOYS OF CRESTED BUTTE
A Cowboy Falls
A Cowboy's Dance
A Cowboy's Kiss
A Cowboy Stays
A Cowboy Wins

Table of Contents

1

"Who are you?" Naughton asked the woman he found wandering through the winery at Butler Ranch. "Sign says staff only."

He looked her up and down, taking in the way the snug, sleeveless dress hugged her tight, curvy body and the way it fell just above the knees of her longer-than-shit legs, which were neatly tucked into suede ankle boots.

"You must be Naughton." The woman approached and held out her hand to shake his.

Naughton folded his arms instead. "I asked you a question. Who are you?"

She dropped her hand and scowled. "I'm your three o'clock appointment." She looked at her watch. "And you're twenty minutes late."

Naughton felt the tension building in his chest. He clenched his fists against the imminent growl forming in his throat.

The stare he leveled didn't appear to faze her. Her hazel eyes, which had the same green hues as the grape leaves in his own vineyards and were dusted with golden specks the color of the Paso Robles' hillside, didn't blink.

"Got a name, sweetheart?"

Mirroring his pose, she folded her arms. "Bradley Saint John, and you were expecting me."

Naughton could swear he heard "asshole" at the end of her sentence, even though she hadn't said it.

"Very funny. You his girlfriend or somethin'?" Who brought their girlfriend on an interview? This guy didn't have a chance in hell of getting the job.

"You must be hard of hearing. *I'm* Bradley Saint John. Me. The woman standing in front of you."

There it was again. She hadn't said it, but Naughton definitely heard "asshole" at the end of that sentence too.

"Oh, yeah?" he smirked. This was gonna be good. He envied this Bradley guy. Not only was his woman crazy-ass pretty, with the kind of body his fourteen-year-old self had spent many nights dreaming about, she was funny too. "Come on, tell me. Where's he hiding?"

Instead of answering, the woman turned on the heel of her boots and walked out the winery door. Naughton watched her leave, willing his feet to stay firmly planted where they were, so he didn't do something stupid, like follow her outside.

"Wait!" Naughton heard his brother Maddox shout as he followed whoever she was outside. "Where are you going?"

Naughton stood next to Mad and watched as the woman he'd been talking to climbed into what appeared to be a completely restored, early-seventies, Ford F100 Ranger.

"What did you say to her?" Maddox asked as they watched the tail end of the green and white truck speed down the ranch's main road.

"I asked where her boyfriend was hiding."

"What kind of interview question is that?"

"The kind someone asks when they're lookin' for the person they're supposed to be interviewing. Where the hell is he anyway?"

"Where is who?"

"Jesus, Maddox, follow along. Bradley Saint John!"

"That was Bradley Saint John, asshole."

Naughton may have imagined the woman Maddox insisted was a guy named Bradley call him an asshole, but he didn't imagine his brother calling him one.

"I'm serious, Naught. That was Bradley."

"That woman was Bradley?" Naughton smirked.

Maddox walked away.

"Where are you goin'?"

"To chase her down and beg her to come back. You just pissed off the hottest up-and-coming winemaker on the central coast of California. One we'd be damn lucky to have work for us. She learned to make wine at the knee of her uncle, who just so happens to be Charlie Jenson."

Mad was right about one thing—that woman was hot. Whether she could make wine or not remained to be seen. But that she was Jenson's niece meant something. He was a legend in Paso Robles.

"Come on," Maddox shouted at him.

"Where?"

"You're goin' with me, dickhead, and you're gonna get on your hands and knees and beg her forgiveness if it comes to that."

"There's no way I'm apologizing to her."

Maddox shook his head and opened the door of his truck. "Yeah, you are. What's more, you better pray she accepts your apology and comes back to the ranch with us."

Naughton shrugged his shoulders.

"In about a month, you're gonna rethink your crappy attitude, Naught. Then you'll wish to hell you hadn't pissed Bradley off, because at that point, you're gonna be all on your own for harvest."

Naughton rolled his eyes, something that didn't go unnoticed by Maddox.

"I swear, Naught, we either hire her, or we hire no one. No one else has come close to good enough, and she far exceeds it. God, you're such an asshole."

That name was rolling off his brother's tongue a little too easily today, and it was beginning to piss him off.

—:—

Maddox had warned her that Naughton could be abrasive. He hadn't warned her, however, that he was an arrogant, sexist asshole.

Bradley was used to people being surprised by her name but not having someone insist she was lying about it.

"What are you doing back so soon?" her uncle asked.

"Naughton Butler is a…jerk." There were about a hundred other things she could call him, but her Aunt Jean and Uncle Charlie had always been good to her. She wouldn't disrespect them just because Naughton was pond scum.

Her uncle laughed. "You got that right."

"What happened, honey?" her aunt asked.

"He asked where I was hiding my boyfriend."

"What an odd thing for him to ask."

"He refused to believe I was Bradley Saint John. Evidently, the last thing he expected was a woman applying for a job as winery manager."

Her uncle was chuckling and pointing to the road. "Here comes Maddox now, and it doesn't look like he's alone."

"I'll be inside."

"Bradley."

That was all it took—her Aunt Jean saying her name in that way that reminded Bradley of her mom. "Okay," she murmured and stayed where she was.

Naughton was the first to get out of the truck. He nodded at her aunt and uncle, and approached her, holding out his hand. Instead of shaking it, Bradley folded her arms in front of her.

"Why are you here?" she asked.

"Evidently, I owe you an apology," he said, quietly enough that only she could hear him.

Bradley took a step back. Naughton was a little too heart-stoppingly good-looking to be standing so close to her. "Nice apology. Wait, you didn't actually apologize, did you?" she smirked.

"I'm sorry, Bradley," he whispered, taking another step forward.

God, his voice. It wasn't just his rockin' hard body, but his gravelly voice was sexier than all get-out too.

"Forgive me?"

Bradley hadn't moved, but Naughton had. The step forward he took brought him close enough that she could smell the vineyard on him. She breathed in and instinctively closed her eyes. The vines had a certain smell that lingered on the clothes of someone who spent their day in them. It was like the smell of a campfire to those who loved to camp.

"Bradley, I asked you a question." It came out almost like a growl, but a damn sexy one.

"Yeah," she muttered. Why had the fight she had in her only moments ago abandoned her?

"Can we begin again?"

She nodded, still unable to find her voice.

"Good. How about we walk?"

Instead of turning around, Naughton went forward, and Bradley followed.

"Mad says you're the new rock star."

"Is that what he said?"

"No, but I thought you might take it the wrong way if I told you he said you were gonna be the hottest new winemaker on the Central Coast."

Bradley smiled. At least he was trying to be nice, however misguided his attempt might be. "I give credit for whatever I know to my uncle."

"Where'd you go to school?"

"Cornell."

Naughton raised his eyebrows.

"My father lives on the East Coast."

He nodded. "And your mother?"

"My mother passed away when I was twelve."

"I see. I'm sorry I asked."

"Jean is my mom's sister."

"Why'd she name you Bradley?"

Interesting that Naughton asked why her mother had named her Bradley, instead of her father or both her parents.

"It was her maiden name."

"No brothers?"

"No siblings."

"I like it."

"What? My name?"

"Yeah."

They walked in silence through her uncle's vineyards, the ones she'd walked every summer of her life since she was five years old.

"What do you think of Butler Ranch wines?"

"They're good…"

"But not as good as your uncle's."

—:—

Bradley smiled again. It was the second time he saw her smile after they'd started walking.

He knew what she meant by "good." The wines Maddox made were very good, albeit very traditional.

Charlie Jenson, on the other hand, was on the cutting edge of winemaking, always trying new varietals or different spins on old blends or techniques. Naughton envied that kind of freedom. It was exactly what he and Maddox planned to do at Demetria.

When she got a few steps ahead of him, Naughton stopped and watched. Her hand trailed as she walked through the rows of vines, barely touching the leaves and berries, yet if you looked closely—and he did—you would see her fingertips slide across the surface of both, like they were absorbing the information the vines held. She got lost then, in the Sauvignon Blanc grapes.

"Close," she murmured.

"Three weeks out at least," he answered.

It was her turn to raise her eyebrows. "Two. Tops."

"Wanna wager?"

"When Uncle Charlie will harvest?"

Naughton nodded.

"Sure. What's the bet?"

"What do you want, Bradley?"

She smiled and looked away but not before he saw the pink flush in her cheeks. "Let me get back to you on that."

"How old are you?"

She turned back then. "You're not supposed to ask me that."

"Why not?"

"Because it's illegal."

"I'm not the one hiring you."

"Then why did I have an interview scheduled with you?"

"To see if I liked you."

She smiled again but didn't ask whether he did or not.

"When did you graduate?"

She kept walking. "When did you graduate?"

"A long time ago. Years before you did, I'd guess."

"May," she answered.

"Master's?"

"Dual. Enology and vit."

Naughton was stunned. Even Maddox hadn't gone that far. Mad's master's was in enology, the science of winemaking. Naught had a master's in viticulture, the science of grape growing. Bradley had both.

"Where have you worked?"

"A couple of the Finger Lake wineries, and for my uncle, obviously."

"Why do you want to leave?"

"I don't, or I didn't. Maddox came to me and asked if I'd consider taking the job."

Interesting. She must be a damn good winemaker, then. Maddox wouldn't have gone after her if she wasn't.

"When do you start?"

"Next week."

Naughton's turn to smile. "Mad already offered you the job."

Bradley nodded.

They walked almost to the edge of the vineyard, not far from Adelaida Trail, the road that separated Jenson Vineyards from the outer edges of Butler Ranch.

"It's beautiful," she murmured.

He liked to think so.

"Where are you going?" she asked when he threw his leg over the split-rail fence.

"Home. I'll see you next week, Bradley Saint John."

—:—

The farther he walked from her, the more rounded his shoulders looked. He put both hands in his pockets and didn't look back.

There were a lot of rumors swirling around about the Butler family. The oldest brother, Kade, had been killed in action in Afghanistan, and since, it sounded as though the family was in turmoil.

The youngest brother got involved with the woman Kade had been dating before he was killed. That brother—Brodie, she thought his name was—was almost killed himself in a plane crash in Argentina. Naughton and Maddox were the ones who found the crash site and brought their brother home. She'd also heard the woman was pregnant and that she and Brodie were getting married.

When Maddox had come by Jenson Vineyards the other day, Bradley thought he was there to meet with her uncle. Instead, he'd wanted to talk to her.

He explained that Kade had given him and Naughton property on Old Creek Road. It had been part of the Hess estate, and they were in the midst of replanting the vineyards. Given he planned to live there as well as make a first label on the estate, Maddox was looking for an assistant at Butler Ranch.

His offer intrigued her, not only because of the salary the job paid but because of the other carrot he'd dangled in front of her. If she took the job, she'd be head winemaker at Butler Ranch within three years. After that, he'd also make her second label winemaker at what he and Naughton had named Demetria Estate.

She'd worked hard to get where she was, between getting her graduate degrees and learning as much from her uncle as she could, but it was still an extraordinary opportunity.

"Naughton can be difficult," he'd said. "Once he recognizes your abilities, he'll back off."

The burning question now was, would she want him to?

2

Maddox's phone pinged, and he pulled it from his back pocket.

"I forgot to tell you. Alex called a meeting of the collaborative."

"When?"

"Next Thursday. We should make sure Bradley plans to attend," Maddox suggested.

Naughton agreed, not only because she would, one day, be a representative of Butler Ranch but also because he hadn't seen her since they'd met, and not for lack of trying.

Bradley had spent the last four days in the winery at Butler Ranch with Maddox while Naughton had been working the vineyards at Demetria Estate.

By the time Naughton got back to Butler Ranch each evening, Bradley was gone. Since he had no good reason to see her, he was left at fate's mercy. So far fate hadn't been on his side.

"I requested a meeting with Bradley this afternoon."

"What for?"

"To discuss some ideas she has for the harvest."

The harvest? Was double-master Bradley flexing her academic muscle? Better that she put her head down and spend the next year learning rather than thinking she could come in and make suggestions for the winery that he and Maddox had been working since they were kids.

Other than being there to receive the grapes once Naught's crew picked and delivered them, there wasn't anything he would need her to do this year.

Naughton and Maddox walked the vineyards every year, taking measurements and discussing when to harvest each varietal, but the final decision had always been, and would always be, Naughton's. It had been that way since their father retired.

"You hear me?" Mad asked.

"Yeah. Whatever. Let me know when."

Maddox looked at his phone. "She'll be here in an hour."

"Here?" Naught and Mad were at Demetria. Why would they meet here instead of Butler Ranch?

"I asked her to meet us here, so she and I could walk these vineyards."

"Why?"

"Never know, maybe she'll take over winemaking here too."

Was Maddox jerking his chain? "She really meeting us here, or are you bullshittin' me?"

"She's really coming here."

Naughton studied Mad's face, but his brother wasn't giving anything away.

"There's something else I want to discuss with you."

"Yeah?"

"It's about Lena Hess."

Jesus, what now? The last thing Naughton wanted to think about was the mess his brother Kade had left in his wake. Finding out he'd been married to Lena shocked him to his core. Not just him, it hit Maddox and Brodie damn hard too.

It had been almost two months since Maddox uncovered Kade's secret, and he and his brothers still hadn't decided when or how to tell their sisters or their parents. Whenever he heard Lena's name, his hurt, anger, and questions resurfaced.

It wasn't as though Naughton didn't think about Kade every day. How could he not? Every step he took on this property reminded him of his brother. One of the last times he saw Kade was on this very land.

Eighteen months ago

Kade was leaning against the split-rail fence when Naughton got to the end of the row of old vine Zinfandel. "Let's go for a drive," he'd said.

Naughton didn't ask where, because he didn't care. Kade would be shipping out in a couple of days and any time he could spend with him, he'd take.

They didn't often talk when they were together; they didn't need to fill the silence with unnecessary conversation. It was only one way Naughton was a lot like his oldest brother.

At first, Naughton thought Kade was taking him to Moonstone Beach in Cambria, but when he turned off the highway and onto Old Creek Road, he was baffled.

Ten miles later, Kade pulled up to an unmarked set of gates and waited while they swung open. He drove through and stopped near a grove of trees.

"What's that?" Naughton pointed to a house not far from where they were.

Kade's reply had been vague. "Previous owners lived there."

"Who's the current owner?"

"You are."

Working in a vineyard didn't require much of a wardrobe. Jeans, short or long-sleeved shirts, and boots were the daily standard. So, the fact that Bradley gave any thought to what she was wearing because she was going to see Naughton Butler, was stupid.

Not to mention that her on-and-off boyfriend of the last four years was driving in from Napa later this afternoon. Since they were currently "on," the last thing she should be doing was dressing to impress her boss, or the brother of her boss, or whatever he was.

If it weren't for his eyes, she might not have realized it was Naughton who had stalked into the winery earlier in the week, demanding to know who she was and what she was doing there.

They were the same steel blue as Maddox's. Instead of dark brown like his brother's, Naughton's hair was blond, as though it had been bleached by the sun, and his skin was tan and weathered from his days spent out in the vineyards. Every muscle on his body was rock hard, yet Bradley doubted he'd ever been inside a gym. He'd caught her looking as he walked away the other day, but she hadn't been able to resist. His butt filled out his snug pair of jeans in a way that almost made Bradley drool.

It was the way his shoulders curved forward as he'd walked away, though, that haunted her. She recognized the stance; she'd seen it often enough with her father.

For him, it had been the stress and sadness of losing his wife, Bradley's mother, far too young. A drunk driver was responsible for the car accident that took her life, and after that horrific night, her father swore off any and all forms of alcohol.

The fact that she'd mastered in enology and viticulture at Cornell caused endless arguments between them, but Bradley refused to give in. Winemaking was in her blood. Even though her Uncle Charlie wasn't a blood relative, it was as though she was born to walk among the vines. She'd felt their magic the first time he took her into the vineyard, and every time after.

Her mother had brought her along every July when she visited her sister. Work at the winery was slow during the summer, which meant her uncle had time to show her the different varietals and teach her how to look for veraison, when the grapes started to turn the harvest color and the berries went from hard to soft. There wasn't a more beautiful or colorful time in the vineyard.

The summer after her mother died, Aunt Jean had begged Bradley's father to let her spend July with them, like she had the previous seven years, but he'd refused. Bradley hadn't made a fuss, but instead spent most every day in her room crying.

The following summer, her father agreed to let her visit California, and instead of staying for the month of July, he'd arranged for her to fly out shortly after the school year ended and to fly back a few days before the next school year began. Every year after, it became harder to leave so close to harvest.

Once she started college, her summers grew shorter, until finally, she was able to arrange to work at Jenson Vineyards for the fall semester, as part of her thesis research.

She'd loved everything about the harvest, even getting up at three in the morning to pick grapes. From sorting bad fruit from good to punching down the cap—Bradley was in heaven.

There were machines that looked like giant potato mashers that were used to punch down the solids—grape skins, seeds, stems, pulp—that rose to the surface during fermentation. In order to extract the most color and flavor, the floating cap had to be broken up and resubmerged into the juice every few hours. It was tedious, grueling work, but Bradley never complained.

The vineyard staff admired her work ethic and stamina, and soon invited her into the tight circle of assistant winemakers, winery managers, and occasionally, head winemakers from other estates.

From them, she learned everything she couldn't sitting in a lecture hall at Cornell. She'd been tempted to drop out more than once, but Aunt Jean convinced her to stick it out.

"The years pass much more quickly than you think," she'd said. "Stay with it, get your degrees, and make your father happy."

Bradley heeded her aunt's advice, and shortly after she graduated, her uncle gave her a job. It was nowhere near as good as the one Maddox had offered, though.

Uncle Charlie encouraged her to take it. "This is how you learn," he'd told Bradley. "Work with as many winemakers as you can. Learn how their crafts differ from winery to winery, particularly region to region."

The Paso Robles wine region had many different subregions. Jenson Vineyards and Butler Ranch were on the west side of the valley, but not as far west as Demetria Estate, where she was headed this afternoon.

The east side had its own set of growing conditions, which often resulted in earlier veraison and earlier harvesting. How far north or south the vineyards and wineries were located gave additional sets of variables. Bradley could spend most of her career working in Paso Robles and never stop learning.

"Bradley," her aunt shouted up the stairwell. "Are you leaving soon?"

She checked her phone, ran down the stairs, and kissed her aunt on the cheek. "Be back later," she smiled and waved as she walked out the door.

—:—

"About Lena…"

"What about her?"

"I haven't been able to track her down."

Naughton shrugged. "And?"

"There was something else she was hiding before she left town. Any idea what it was?"

How in the hell would he know, and why would Maddox even ask? Maddox had had more interaction with Lena than he did.

It still bugged the shit out of him that he didn't know how his truck got to Demetria the night Maddox had met Lena here, and she told him she was leaving town.

When Maddox confronted him and asked why he'd been at Demetria that night, Naughton had no idea what his brother was talking about. Maddox wouldn't relent, and followed Naughton to where he'd parked in the hospital lot. While not definitive, there was enough fresh mud on the tires that Naughton had to accept his brother's insistence that someone had driven it to Demetria and returned it to Butler Ranch without his knowledge.

It was common knowledge that most vehicles on the ranch were kept unlocked, typically with the keys left in the ignition. Trustworthiness had never been an issue.

Since, he'd kept his truck locked up tight. He'd also installed a motion alarm that only he, Maddox, and his father knew how to disable. That way, if anyone attempted to take it, even if they had a key, the vehicle's starter would be disabled, and Naughton would get an alert on his phone.

His bike was another story. His vintage BMW motorcycle had always been locked up tight, and if anyone tried to take it, they wouldn't get five feet from where he kept it parked.

Naughton looked at his phone. "She's late."

"Bradley? We didn't have a set time. I just told her to give us about an hour."

Just as Naughton thought he might be able to get away with a disappearing act, Bradley's green and white Ford pickup pulled through the gate.

It was time they started keeping the gate closed, so Naughton could keep out those he didn't want to let in, not that he'd keep Bradley out. At least not yet.

"Stop it." Maddox nudged him.

"Stop what?"

"Scowling."

He wasn't scowling; it's just how his face was. Nothing made him scowl quicker, though, than someone telling him to stop.

"I have work to do. I don't have time for some bullshit—"

"Hi, Naughton," Bradley said, walking up behind him. What was she, some kind of freak ninja that could walk into a conversation without making a sound?

"Bradley."

"I was telling Naughton that I wanted us to walk the vineyards this morning. I was intrigued by some of your ideas for Butler Ranch and thought we might be able to make use of them here."

—:—

That explained the ice-cold shoulder Naughton gave her when she'd said hello. What was Maddox thinking? He knew better than to suggest to a vineyard manager that an assistant winery manager might have ideas for his vines. She glared at Maddox, who smiled and shrugged his shoulders.

Worse, it appeared Maddox was doing it on purpose.

"Hey, Mad." A tall and very beautiful woman came walking out of the woods and kissed Maddox loudly on the lips.

"Hey, Naught." She smiled and looked at Bradley. "You must be the new kick-ass winemaker. I'm Alex."

"Hey, Alex." Bradley smiled. "It's great to meet you."

"You, too. Although I think we met once before. You were about this tall." Alex put her hand near her elbow. "You're Charlie and Jean Jenson's niece, right?"

"I am."

Alex linked her arm through Bradley's. "We need to get you over to Stave to meet Peyton."

—:—

If anyone would understand Naughton attempting to sneak away unnoticed, it would be Alex. She did it all the time, or at least she used to. Since she and Maddox had finally admitted to each other, and everyone else, that they were a couple, and in love no less, he hadn't seen her pull a Houdini.

"We should all have dinner." Alex was looking at him as though she was waiting for him to answer.

Naught looked at Maddox and Bradley, who also looked like they were waiting for his response.

"Sure, whatever," he finally said.

"Great. I'll set it up."

Bradley was still staring at him. "What?" he asked.

"Nothing. Sorry." She turned and walked away.

"Smooth, Naught. Real smooth." Alex nudged him. "I like her."

"You have dinner with her, then," he muttered, hoping Bradley didn't hear him.

It wasn't usually his intention to be an asshole—he just rarely tried not to be one.

"When's the last time you went on a date, Naught?" Alex asked.

"Are you kidding me right now?" he growled at whisper volume, once again hoping Bradley wasn't listening to their conversation.

"She likes you."

"Stop it."

Alex turned her attention back to Maddox and Bradley. "What's happenin' today?"

"We're walking the vineyards here, and then Bradley has some ideas to run past Naughton."

Alex laughed. "You're a wily coyote, Mad-man."

—:—

There was nothing wrong with Bradley's hearing, which meant she didn't miss any of the conversation, nor the laughter following. Whatever Maddox had hoped would happen by bringing her here today, clearly wasn't working out.

"I can see the timing is off for us to do this, Maddox. Okay if I meet you back at Butler Ranch later?"

He shook his head and glared at Naughton and Alex. "Okay, you two. Enough. We have work to do today."

"Hey, Mad. There's something I need to talk to you about before we walk the vineyards."

"We'll be right back," Maddox said before following Alex back into the woods, leaving Bradley alone with Naughton.

"She's just being stupid. Alex likes to yank my chain," Naughton muttered.

"I'll keep that in mind," Bradley snapped.

"Come on, lighten up." When Naughton took a step toward her, Bradley took a step back.

"I don't bite."

"This was a bad idea."

"What? Maddox asking you to walk the vineyards here?"

"Obviously."

He laughed, which only pissed her off more.

"I get it, Naughton. You think I'm a joke. Tell you what, I don't need to set foot on these vineyards ever again. I work for Butler Ranch, not Demetria."

"What? No. You've got this all wrong. No one thinks you're a joke, Bradley. Least of all me."

"Yeah, right." She wanted to smack the arrogant grin off his mouth-wateringly handsome face.

"You don't know me very well, but if you decide to stick around, you'll learn that I don't bother talking when there isn't anything to say."

"Whatever, Naughton. You got your wish, I'm outta here." Bradley stomped off in the direction of her truck but could feel him following behind her.

"Don't go."

She had her key out to open the door of her truck when he rested his hand on her shoulder.

"Why not?" She turned around. Her breath caught in her throat, and she almost forgot why she'd wanted to leave. With Naughton so close, it was hard to remember her own name.

"Because I asked you not to." He stepped forward, not that there was enough room for him to do so, and Bradley melted. There was no other word for the way his being so close made every one of her muscles go lax.

What was he doing? Worse, what was she doing? She worked for him, *and* she had a boyfriend.

She put her hands on her hips, and he took a step back.

"Listen, Naughton, I work—"

"For my brother. You will never work for me."

"Understood. But—"

"You don't understand anything."

Naughton walked away, leaving her standing next to her truck, unsure what to do next.

3

"Come on," he hollered. "They're waiting for us."

While they walked, Naughton pointed out it would be three years, at least, before the vineyards at Demetria Estate would produce enough fruit to make wine, which had been obvious.

Taking it all in, she figured their initial investment in rootstock had to have been significant, even if the bulk of it came from Butler Ranch, which Bradley doubted. She hadn't learned the entire makeup of the vineyards at the ranch, but she knew enough about the wine they made to guess Demetria Estate's production would be vastly different.

"Bradley, have you met Hawks Martinez?" Maddox introduced the man standing near a row of vines. "He'll be field manager at Demetria."

"Nice to meet you. What's your name? Bradley?" Hawks asked.

"Yeah."

"We gotta come up with a nickname for you. Anybody ever call you something besides Bradley? Brad doesn't seem right either."

"Her name is Bradley," Naughton snapped. "She doesn't need a nickname."

"It's okay." She put her hand on Hawks' arm, which only made Naughton's scowl worsen.

"Bradley will work primarily at Butler Ranch," Maddox explained to Hawks.

He winked. "I'm sorry to hear that."

"What are your ideas? Isn't that why we're here, to hear your ideas?" Naughton grumbled.

Bradley nodded and looked at Maddox.

"Go ahead, tell them what you told me yesterday," Maddox urged.

"Okay. As you all know, twenty-three percent of wine consumers are between the ages of sixty and seventy. Of that, fifty-seven percent are women. Millennials account for less than eighteen percent of consumption."

"What's a millennial?" Hawks asked.

"Someone born between twenty-two and forty years ago."

"And?" If Maddox had a stick, he'd be poking her.

"They have a short attention span but tend to be know-it-alls who respond well to premiumization."

"Therefore…"

If Maddox wasn't smiling at her, she'd kick him.

"Aren't we all millennials?" Naughton asked, not smiling.

Bradley nodded. "We are, and for that target, it's all about under eight and over eighty."

"What does that mean? You know what she's talkin' about, Naught?" Hawks rubbed his chin.

"Price point. Under eight bucks and over eighty," Naughton answered for her.

Bradley went on. "There's considerable volume at both ends. The under eight price point will always account for the bulk of sales. However, it's the over eighty dollar price point that's climbing the quickest."

"And varietally?"

"You already know the answer to that question too, Naughton."

"Tell me anyway."

"Rosé followed by sparkling, but the challenge is, the hottest wines in those categories are not domestic.

French imports account for seventy percent, and we're sitting at thirty."

"So we plant the hell out of Grenache, Syrah, and Pinot Noir. That ought to do it." Hawks winked again.

"Plus Sangiovese, Petit Verdot, Roussanne, and Pinot Gris," Naughton added.

"And add relatively small crops of Mourvedre, Viognier, Carignan, and Cinsault." Bradley looked at Maddox, who smiled at her like a proud papa.

"What do you think, Naught?" Maddox asked.

"Covered."

"All of it." Maddox hadn't asked a question, but Naughton nodded anyway.

"And Butler Ranch?"

—:—

Naughton was getting tired of Mad's schoolmarm tone. "Cabernet Sauvignon, Merlot, and Chardonnay," he muttered.

"What do we do, then?"

"Ask Bradley." Naughton's gaze moved from his brother to her.

"Combine production. It's the only solution, long-term anyway."

Naughton agreed, but accomplishing it wouldn't be easy. It would take years to transition the Butler Ranch vineyards, which meant they'd need more land or they'd never have enough volume to produce two primary labels, let alone secondary.

Inside, Naughton swore; outside, he kept his poker face intact.

"What'll it take, Naught?"

"Land." He was getting close to wiping the smug look off his brother's face.

"What kind of money are we talkin'?"

Naughton shrugged.

"Four mil, at least, right?"

Sometimes Naughton thought Maddox just liked dicking with him.

"Naughton?"

"I'm thinkin'." Jesus, did Maddox really expect him to answer here and now, in front of Hawks and Bradley? Even talking about it in front of Alex made him uncomfortable.

"You're still three to five years out, whether you add acreage or not."

Bradley was right. They couldn't just stop production at the ranch; they'd have to wait to ease out and replant after Demetria was at full production, otherwise neither winery would survive.

Maddox nodded as he studied Bradley.

Why? This had nothing to do with her. It didn't take a Cornell grad or anyone else to tell him or Maddox everything she had. They knew it as well as she did. Maybe the whole exercise was simply for Maddox to prove she knew what she was talking about.

It wasn't necessary, though. Naughton hadn't doubted it. He saw it the first day they met, when he'd followed her through the vineyards. One day she'd make a great winemaker, probably one of the best. Maddox had been smart to seek her out, but ultimately, wouldn't her loyalties always be with Jenson Vineyards?

"Alex and I need to get up to the winery. You two okay on your own?"

Naught looked around. Where had Hawks gone? "I think we're done here, aren't we?"

"Can you show Bradley the way back to her truck?" Mad asked.

"Not necessary," she answered for him. "I know my way."

—:—

Famous last words. Once she went back through the woods, she got completely turned around. She didn't remember passing a pasture or seeing horses. Bradley turned back to take a different path, when Naughton came through the woods.

"Know your way, huh?"

"Shut up," she mumbled.

"It took me a long time to learn this land, too." Naughton walked over to the post-and-rail fence, and Bradley followed.

"Whose are they?"

"Mine, and Mad's too. At least that one." Naughton pointed to a heavily-spotted horse. "That's Shazam. He's a bay Leopard Appaloosa."

"He's beautiful. Who's that?" she pointed at the other horse.

"Huck."

"He's huge."

Naughton laughed. "He's a draft horse, so yeah."

"Do you ride him?"

"All the time."

Bradley looked from man to horse. It wasn't surprising. They both seemed to hold equal power. Naughton made a noise, and Huck walked over to where they stood.

"Go ahead, say hello."

Bradley wasn't sure who he was talking to, her or the horse.

"I'm not really a horse-person," she admitted.

"Sure you are. Look." Naughton motioned behind her, where Shazam stood.

Bradley looked over her shoulder. "Uh, hi."

Shazam nudged her with his nose.

"Give him a rub."

Bradley put her hand up for the horse to smell, like she would with a dog. Shazam pushed at it until she petted him.

"Don't ride?"

"I've never had occasion to.

"We'll fix that. Lotta ground to cover, especially if you're walking here and Butler Ranch on a regular basis."

"I don't think I'll be here that often."

Naughton shook his head.

"What?"

"Mad wouldn't have brought you here if that was the case."

"Can I ask you a question?"

"Shoot."

"I guess it really isn't a question."

"What is it, then?"

"I'm trying to figure out why you don't like me."

—:—

Nothing could be further from the truth. Something about her pretty face, sweet curves, and long brown hair spoke to him. It wasn't as dark as Alex's, whose hair was almost black. It was something between bay and sorrel, and changed whenever the light hit it. All he knew is he longed to run his fingers through it.

"How old are you, Bradley?"

"I told you before, you can't ask me that."

"I know, but tell me anyway."

"It isn't difficult math, Naughton."

"Twenty-six."

"Twenty-seven, but I don't see what that has to do with why you don't like me."

"I like you too much," he muttered.

"What?"

"You heard me." Naughton stepped forward, closing the space between them. He reached up and trailed two fingers from her cheek to her chin.

"What are you doing?" She put her hands against his chest.

"I want to kiss you, Bradley, and what's more, you want me to."

"I don't," she whispered.

"Yeah, you do." No point in letting her lie.

Bradley shook her head, but he felt her tremor right before her fingers curled into his shirt.

"Don't lie, sweetheart." He wound his fingers through the soft waves of her hair and wrapped it around his hand. Instead of taking a taste of her beckoning lips, Naughton kissed the side of her face, down to just below her ear, and then backed away. If he hadn't, his mouth would have trailed down farther, to where his hands longed to cover her breasts.

"You want this as much as I do," he whispered.

When he released his hold on her and stepped back, she grasped the wooden fence.

"Stay away from me, Bradley. You get this close to me again, and I won't stop like I did today."

With wide eyes, she nodded and tightened her grip on the fence.

"Follow that path back through the woods. When you come to the next clearing, go left. That path will take you straight to your truck."

When she nodded again, Naughton walked off in the opposite direction.

—:—

Her legs were shaking too much to walk. She let go of the fence and looked at her palm. She'd grasped it so tightly, she had splinters.

Instead of watching Naughton walk away, she closed her eyes against her humiliation. He knew how much she wanted him to kiss her. Her denial had been a lie, and he'd seen right through it. But getting involved with Naughton Butler would mean she'd lose her job with his brother, and she couldn't let that happen. He warned her away from him? Not a problem. She'd give him the same warning.

—:—

The trees gave him cover as he watched Bradley walk away. It was all he could do not to follow. She intoxicated him in a way no other woman ever had. It didn't matter that he hardly knew her. His body knew everything his brain hadn't learned yet.

He'd wanted to kiss her, but if he had, he wouldn't have stopped. He doubted Bradley Saint John was the type of woman who could handle the kind of storm he'd like to rain on her body. He wanted her hard and fast, right out in the open. She'd let him take her too, but then when the reality of what they'd done hit her, she'd hate herself for it. Naughton wouldn't care if she hated him, but she wasn't that type of woman either.

When he'd looked into her hazel eyes, he saw every single thing he'd wondered if he could ever have— love, a family, a future. Would it ever be possible, or was he too much like his oldest brother, Kade?

4

Bradley's phone pinged and she took it out of her pocket.

Where are you?

New winery in PR. Where are you?

Be at JV in a couple hours.

Bradley met Guy Deveux III, who everyone called Trey, the week after she completed her bachelor's degree. A month in the Northern California wine region had been her graduation present to herself. He sought her out at an industry tour of Mumm Napa Valley, intrigued—he'd told her at the time—when he noticed she was there on behalf of Jenson Vineyards.

She'd spent the rest of June on his arm touring the wineries of Napa, Carneros, Sonoma, Alexander Valley, and the Russian River. Trey was handsome, and funny, and knew everyone in the industry, or so it seemed. He introduced her to many of the winery bigwigs and never failed to mention her connection to Charlie Jenson.

Trey had been born in the United States, but his upbringing was heavily influenced by the French customs and traditions of his father and grandfather. He was a perfectionist and expected those around him to live up to his exacting standards. While he told Bradley he loved her just the way she was, her lack of self-confidence when she was around him, often left her feeling as though she fell short. There had been many times over the years, she wondered what Trey saw in her that kept him interested.

Trey's grandfather, Guy Deveux, Sr., had come to the States in the mid-seventies in search of a place to grow traditional Champagne grapes on behalf of GH Mumm, who, at the time, was the largest producer of Champagne in the world. He'd settled on Napa Valley and founded the winery that released its first vintage in 1983, under the name Domaine Mumm.

Trey's father, Guy, Jr., took the helm at Mumm Napa when Trey's grandfather passed away in the mid-nineties, just as Trey would be expected to do when his father either retired or passed away.

When Bradley told Trey she'd decided to pursue her master's at Cornell, rather than take a job right away, she and Trey had their first argument. First he had tried to talk her out of it, saying it was a waste of time when she had a job waiting for her at Jenson Vineyards.

When she wouldn't relent, he pushed for her to transfer to Cal Poly San Luis Obispo or Fresno State for the same reason. If she pursued her degree closer to Paso Robles, she'd still be able to work for her uncle.

When she told him her decision was final, he threatened to break up with her, saying they obviously had a different set of priorities.

She'd been back at Cornell less than two months when he showed up and told her he forgave her, and wooed himself back into her life. She still got a bad taste in her mouth when she thought about his word choice. He *forgave* her?

It was one of those seemingly little things that she'd let go, but when she graduated in May, the first thing Trey wanted to know was whether her uncle had offered her a job.

"He has, but I haven't made my final decision yet."

"Where else would you work?" he'd asked.

She told him she had offers from wineries in Northern California that she was considering.

"You have to work for Jenson. It's your heritage."

While Aunt Jean and Uncle Charlie didn't have children, it was never implied or assumed that she'd take over the winery the same way Trey was expected to take over Mumm Napa.

When Bradley called Trey to tell him about the offer she'd received from Butler Ranch, he was congratulatory, but the conversation made her uncomfortable.

He'd said he wanted to come and spend the holiday weekend with her so they could celebrate, but a familiar feeling of dread had immediately settled in her stomach. She didn't doubt he'd try to convince her to stay at Jenson.

A couple of hours after Bradley had returned to her aunt and uncle's from Demetria, she got a call on her cell from a number she didn't recognize. She thought about letting it go to voicemail, but since it was from a local area code, she hit the accept button instead.

"Hey, Bradley. It's Alex."

"Uh, hi, Alex."

"I'm on my way over to Stave. I thought you might like to join me. I'm really anxious for you to meet Peyton."

"That sounds great—"

"I'm at Los Cab now, but I'm leaving shortly. I'll swing by and pick you up."

"Are you sure it isn't an inconvenience? I can meet you there."

"Nah, I'll be by in a few minutes."

Since Trey wouldn't arrive for at least another hour and a half, she could text and ask him to meet her at Stave, and then she could ride back with him.

Bradley knew of the Los Caballeros Winery, it was down Adelaida Trail from Jenson Vineyards. She'd never seen their facility though. She should make a point of visiting some of the other wineries and introducing herself. The timing was perfect considering most would be open for Labor Day Weekend, even the ones that were usually by appointment only.

There wasn't anything in her closet that she felt like wearing. It was either too east coast college, or too vineyard field worker. Finally, she settled on a sundress she hoped still fit.

She pulled on her favorite pair of ankle boots and studied herself in the mirror. Maybe she was overdressed. She didn't want Peyton or Alex to think she was trying too hard.

Just when she was about to pull her dress over her head and put on a pair of jeans, she saw a car pull into the driveway. When she peered out the window and saw Alex was wearing a dress too, she decided not to bother changing her clothes.

Alex was in the kitchen, talking to her aunt and uncle when Bradley came down the stairs.

"Sorry I didn't tell you, Alex invited me to go to Stave. Oh, and Trey is on his way down for the weekend." She still hadn't texted him to ask him to meet her there instead of at Jenson.

"How nice," muttered Aunt Jean, rolling her eyes.

"Ready?" Alex asked.

"Sure. Uh, I don't know when I'll be back."

Her aunt shook her head and smiled. "It's fine, Bradley. We'll see you when we see you."

"Thanks for picking me up," Bradley said once they were in the car.

"Peyton can't wait to meet you. I'll warn you, it might be a madhouse given it's the last weekend of summer, but more because it's the last few days we have to let loose before harvest."

Bradley nodded. She understood. Once the first varietal was ready to pick, it would be non-stop work for weeks.

"So, uh, the guys will be there too."

"The guys?"

"You know, Mad, Naught, and Brodie. You haven't met Brodie yet, have you?"

"No, not yet."

"He's Peyton's boyfriend. Well, not really her boyfriend, he's her fiancé. They're engaged."

"Oh, that reminds me. I need to text my boyfriend and ask him to meet me there. He's driving down from Napa."

"Boyfriend? Napa? This sounds interesting. Who is he?"

"Trey Deveux. His family—"

"Say no more. I know of Trey's family, although I hadn't heard he and you were dating. How long has this been going on? I take it your aunt isn't a fan."

Bradley laughed. "I've been seeing him four years, on and off, and no, she's not a fan."

"That's too bad. I mean, it's not too bad for him; it's too bad for Naughton."

"Why?"

"Naught's head over boots, girlfriend. He's got it bad."

"What are you talking about?"

"Come on, Bradley. Really? You don't think we noticed? It wasn't just Naughton."

"I can't…I mean…I work for him."

"No, you don't. You work for Maddox."

"That's what he said."

—:—

"Alex asked me to let you know she's picking Bradley up on her way here," Naughton heard Peyton tell Maddox.

He thought about going back out the way he came in, getting on his bike, and going home, but he wanted to see Bradley more than he didn't want to see her.

Maybe he'd stick around until she got there, and then find a reason to leave after he had a chance to see her smile, and maybe get close enough to breathe in the scent of her. She smelled as good as she looked, like sunshine, and fresh herbs, and grape vines.

"What're you drinkin'?" Mad asked.

"What's open?"

Maddox rattled off a list of wines Peyton and Alex were pouring tonight. "I'll have a glass of the Hoffman Pinot."

"Yum," Alex said, sneaking up behind him. "Me too, Mad-man."

Naughton looked behind Alex, where Bradley stood.

"Would you like a glass?" Alex asked her.

"Sure. That sounds good. Thanks."

She had the same look that a deer in someone's headlights would probably have. Naughton didn't know for sure; he'd never seen a deer almost get run over by a car. She looked terrified, though, and it was his fault.

Alex went farther into the tasting room, leaving Bradley standing near him in the hallway. When he stood to offer her his seat, she took a step back, bumped into the wall behind her, and smacked her head.

"Ow," she groaned.

"Be careful. Here, have a seat." Naughton moved so she could take the stool he'd been sitting on.

"That's okay. I'll just…" Bradley looked left and right, as though she was looking for a place to escape, but the tasting room was packed.

"Sit down."

"Sorry," she said when she brushed against him as they shifted places.

"What for?"

Bradley shook her head and looked away.

Did all men make her this skittish, or was it just him? He had warned her to stay away from him, although now, he had no intention of letting her.

"Here you go." Alex came back with two glasses of wine and handed them both to Naughton. "I'll be right back. I'm gonna go wrestle Peyton away from your brother."

When Naughton handed the glass to Bradley, he let his fingers brush against hers. "Unlike you, I'm not sorry," he murmured. "At least not for touching you."

"Naughton, I have a—"

"Here she is." Alex stepped in front of Naughton. "Peyton, this is Bradley. Bradley, meet Peyton."

Naughton watched as Peyton and Bradley exchanged pleasantries, wondering what she'd wanted to tell him before Alex interrupted her.

"Peyton, you remember the Deveux family, right? From Mumm? Well, Bradley here has been dating Trey—for how long did you say?"

When Bradley answered, she looked everywhere but at him. "On and off for a while."

Naughton leaned forward. "What's a while?"

"Four years, isn't that what you said, Bradley?" Alex nudged Naughton with her elbow. "He's meeting her here later."

Bradley nodded, looking more like a deer in headlights than she had earlier.

"I don't think I've ever met him…anyway, it's so nice to meet you." Peyton ran her hand over her stomach, and Bradley jumped off the stool.

"I'm sorry, you should sit. I can stand."

Peyton smiled. "I was on my way out front anyway. It's so much less crowded out there. Alex, why don't we all move?"

Naughton watched Bradley follow Alex and Peyton outside. Maybe he should leave now, before the boyfriend arrived, and save himself the discomfort he knew he'd feel when he saw another man's hands on her.

—:—

At Stave in Cambria. Meet me here? Bradley texted Trey, realizing he was probably getting close.

Almost at JV.

You're about 30 from here then.

"Everything okay?" Alex asked.

"Yeah, I just forgot to text Trey. He's almost at Jenson." It would be just like him to stop in and try to engage her aunt and uncle in conversation, maybe even pretend he didn't know she wasn't there. She hated to put them in that position, knowing they weren't fond of Trey.

"You don't look very happy."

"It's just that he's driven all the way down from Napa. Asking him to drive another thirty minutes…"

"What did he say?"

Bradley looked at her phone. "He hasn't answered."

It was another one of those little things he did that irritated her. If he could use voice-texting to answer that he was almost at Jenson, why couldn't he respond, saying that he'd meet her at Stave? He'd tell her it was assumed, and she'd counter that it was assumed until it wasn't.

—:—

Naughton finished his glass of wine and had another when he decided not to wait around to see the boyfriend. The name sounded familiar, but then a lot of vineyard owners from Napa had been contacting him lately.

He'd walked out the back door and was on his bike when he saw the red convertible Alfa Romeo Spider pull up and park.

"Nice bike," said the guy driving the car.

Naughton nodded his head. "Nice car."

"My baby. Early sixties, had it restored myself. You?"

Naughton wasn't sure what the question was but didn't care enough to ask.

"You look familiar," the man said.

"Lived here my whole life," Naughton muttered.

"Trey Deveux, nice to meet you."

Instead of shaking the man's extended hand, Naughton put on his helmet, climbed on his bike, and started it up. He was out of the parking lot before the boyfriend went inside.

—:—

"Hey, Brad." Trey walked up behind her, put his arm around her waist, and kissed her cheek.

She tried to keep from stiffening under his touch or look to see if Naughton was anywhere near. Instead, she smiled. "Hi, Trey."

Bradley took his hand and led him to where Alex and Peyton waited with Maddox and Brodie.

"This is Trey," she said, and then stepped back as they shook hands and introduced themselves. Bradley looked behind her, and then in the direction of the tasting room.

"He left," Maddox said.

"You startled me."

"And you didn't deny you were looking for him."

"Who?" she smirked, but there wasn't any point in lying. "Does he always leave without saying good-bye?" As soon as the words had traveled from her thoughts to out loud, she regretted saying them. Maybe he had said goodbye, just not to her.

"No, that's me." Alex laughed.

"Not anymore, baby." Maddox wound his arm around Alex's waist.

Even though Trey was standing in front of her, talking to Brodie, Bradley still felt like a third wheel.

"Be right back," Maddox said before kissing Alex's cheek again and going inside.

When Alex whispered, "He's a hottie," Bradley watched Maddox walk away, wondering if Alex expected her to respond.

"Not him, although he's a hottie, too. Him." Alex pointed at Trey.

"Oh, right." He was, although she no longer looked at him the same way she did when they'd first met. She'd gotten used to him, or maybe she knew the personality beneath the hotness too well. Trey was well aware that his good looks opened doors for him. He wanted everyone to like him and was happiest when he was the center of attention and the life of the party. Sometimes it was too much.

Naughton, on the other hand, seemed completely unaware of his hotness. The man was comfortable enough in his own skin not to care what anyone else thought of him.

"He's bigger than life," Alex commented, and Bradley nodded. "Easy to get caught up in."

"Yeah," she murmured, not wanting to get started on how she sometimes felt invisible when she was with Trey.

Maddox came back out to the patio with an unmarked bottle of wine and four glasses.

"Got somethin' I want you to try, baby."

One of the tasting room employees followed with another unmarked bottle and three more wine glasses.

Maddox opened the bottle and winked at her. When he poured, she knew what it was. But where had he gotten it? One bottle would be hard to get, but two?

Maddox swirled the wine he'd just poured into his glass. "Surprised to see you this far south, Deveux. Don't you have grapes to harvest?" He tilted the glass to its side, studied the hues, and spoke again before Trey had a chance to respond.

"Five, six transitions of color, nice age on the edge, great legs. On the wine, that is." Maddox smiled and glanced at Bradley's legs. "Although yours aren't bad either, Saint John."

Alex laughed. "What are you up to, Mad-man? You gonna pour for anyone else?"

Instead of answering, Maddox handed Alex his glass. "Taste, sweetheart. Close your eyes and take a little trip to bliss. I'll pour for everyone else in a minute."

Alex didn't bother swirling but, instead, stuck her nose in the glass and took a deep breath. "*Damn.* What is this?"

"Taste," Maddox said, eyes twinkling.

Alex closed hers, sipped, let the wine linger, swallowed. "Oh. My. God. What *is* this?"

"I'll let the winemaker tell you." He looked straight at Bradley.

"Brad—" Trey began, but Alex raised her hand.

"No talking."

They watched Alex take another mouthful, chew on it a bit, and swallow.

"Cab, Cab Franc." She took another mouthful and swallowed. "Merlot, Petit Verdot, and what? I can't figure it out." Maddox reached behind him to pour more wine from the unmarked bottle.

"Dang, girl," she moaned. "If you made this, Maddox needs to quadruple your salary, because no matter what he's paying you, it'll never be enough. This wine is priceless."

Alex sipped, closed her eyes again, and then opened them and looked at Bradley. "I'm rarely stumped, girlfriend. There's something I'm missing."

"What's this? Alex Avila is giving up?" Maddox stood behind her and put his arms around her waist, mirroring Brodie's hold on Peyton. "Not even a guess?"

"Give me a minute."

"Vintage?" Peyton asked, rubbing her hand over Brodie's, and looking as though she was having a hard time keeping her eyes open.

Alex tilted the glass and studied the color transitions the same way Maddox had. "That part's easy. Gotta be a two-thousand and seven."

Bradley smiled and nodded.

"Tell her what it is. It's Jenson, right?" Trey nudged Bradley.

Alex glared at him. "When I want Bradley to tell me, I'll say so, Three." She took another sip.

Only knowing Trey didn't find it funny kept Bradley from snickering. *Three.* She loved it.

"It isn't Carménère."

Bradley smiled and nodded again.

Alex looked at Maddox. "What am I missing?"

Maddox shrugged. "This is your superpower, Al. Not mine."

Maddox studied Alex, his eyes full of pride and such pleasure. Brodie's fingers were woven with Peyton's, and when she leaned back and closed her eyes, Brodie kissed the side of her face and closed his eyes too. She couldn't imagine ever being loved as much as Alex and Peyton were.

"Tastes like a Meritage blend," Alex commented.

Bradley laughed when everyone else did.

"As if she's going to take that bait, sweetheart."

Alex smirked at Maddox, and then looked at Bradley. "I'm stumped."

Maddox turned to Brodie and held out his hand. Brodie put a folded bill in it, but Bradley couldn't see what denomination it was.

"You bet against me, Mad-man?" Alex slugged him.

"I've tasted the wine, Brodie hasn't."

Alex set the glass on the table.

"Is it yours? Tell them what it is," Trey nudged.

"I told you before, Three, when I'm ready for her to tell me, I'll say so. This is my game, in my tasting room, by the way. You don't make the rules here, Mumm-man." Alex was smiling, but her tone was anything but.

"Do you want me to tell you?" Bradley whispered to Alex, who didn't answer right away.

"Nope. I'm loving the mystery. Congratulations by the way, not for besting me, but for making a truly remarkable wine."

"Thank you," Bradley murmured and looked away, unaccustomed to such praise or to being the center of attention.

"Is this why you went after her, Mad?" Alex asked.

Maddox nodded.

"Getting late, Brad." Trey wove his fingers through hers. She hated the nickname, and he knew it, but his grasp was tight enough that she couldn't pull her hand away without anyone noticing.

"You aren't leaving already. Are you crazy? Do you know what tonight is?"

Trey sighed. "I give up. What's tonight?"

"It's our night to officially welcome Bradley Saint John to Butler Ranch, *Three*. Where are you staying, by the way? Not at Jenson, am I right?"

"It's okay," Bradley began. "It's been a long day."

Maddox spoke up. "It isn't okay. What it is, is tradition. Don't know what it's like up in your part of the world, Trey, but down here, we take our harvest traditions very seriously. We're superstitious that way."

"Trey's exhausted from the drive, and I—" Bradley said again.

"I'll give you a ride back to Jenson." Bradley hadn't seen Naughton come back out to the patio.

—:—

"You're the guy with the bike," the boyfriend turned to Naughton, who nodded. "I didn't catch your name."

"This is my brother, Naughton," Maddox spoke up.

Trey's eyes opened wider. "Naughton Butler?"

"That's right." Naughton looked at Trey briefly, before his eyes settled on Bradley.

"I've been trying to get in touch with you." Trey pulled a business card out of his wallet. When Naughton didn't take it, Trey set it on the table in front of him.

"You must know how sought after you are in Napa."

"What's this?" Maddox clapped Naughton's shoulder.

"Your brother is quite elusive."

Maddox laughed. "Is that a fancy way of saying playing hard to get?"

Naughton glared at his brother. "You gonna share that wine or let it sit in the bottle all night?" he asked instead.

Maddox jumped up. "Shit, I almost forgot."

Alex opened the second bottle while Maddox poured from the first. She swirled and breathed in its aroma before pouring the remaining glasses.

"Here you go, girlfriend." Alex handed a very short pour to Peyton, and then stood next to Bradley.

"She doesn't have to—" Naughton heard Bradley whisper to Alex.

"It isn't that big of a deal. She just tastes and spits, although she wouldn't taste if there were customers here."

Bradley nodded and peered at the crowd still lingering on the patio.

"Only locals left," Naughton muttered.

"I'm pretty sure my mama drank a glass of wine with dinner every night when she was pregnant, and she gave birth to seven perfectly healthy children. It's all about moderation. Hey, Mad-man, you want to handle the toast?"

Maddox stood and raised his glass. "A toast to Bradley Saint John. Welcome to our family. May the wine we make together be at least half as good as the wine you made on your own."

"Hear, hear," said Alex, and elbowed Naughton.

Naughton raised his glass and watched Bradley. He caught only the slightest grin as her cheeks turned a lovely shade of pink, like a fine rosé.

He studied the wine Maddox had poured. He swirled and stuck his nose in the glass, breathing in the aroma. As he took a drink, his eyes drifted closed. Alex hadn't been blowing smoke; Bradley's wine was damn good. When he opened them and found her watching him, he walked over to her.

With his back to the rest of the group, he whispered, "Carignan and Cinsault," and then took another sip.

She didn't need to respond, he knew exactly what else was in her blend.

He turned around far enough to see the boyfriend talking to Brodie, and then back to look in her eyes.

"It's incredible."

"Thank you." He loved that, with him, she didn't look away like she had when Alex had talked about her wine. Instead, her eyes never left his.

"You and I are going to make amazing wine together, Bradley Saint John."

"What gave it away?"

"Cardamom on the palate for the Cinsault. Carignan was tougher. A little rose petal on the nose, smoke and vanilla on the palate. But I cheated."

"You did? How?"

"You gave it away today at the vineyard."

Bradley's cheeks turned that perfect shade of pink he was quickly coming to crave. And then she smiled. "You were listening."

"I'm always listening, Bradley. Watching too."

"So…" The boyfriend approached and rested his hand on Naughton's shoulder.

When he shifted away from the man's grasp and closer to Bradley, his arm grazed hers. Naughton could feel the tremor move from the place they'd touched, and flow throughout his body like an electrical current.

"We need you in Napa."

"Can't help ya."

"What's bad for Napa is good for the Central Coast. That it?"

"Trey!" Bradley gasped.

The boyfriend ignored her. "Or did someone else get to you first? Whatever their offer was, we'll double it."

Naughton shook his head. "Excuse me."

"Trey, what's wrong with you?" he heard Bradley ask as he walked away.

5

"You were rude to him," Bradley said as she waited for Trey to open her door.

"Yeah? From my perspective, he was the rude one."

She shook her head and got in the car. It was too chilly on the coast to drive with the top down, but Trey insisted. "What's the point of having a convertible if you don't take advantage of it?" he'd say.

He had just started the engine when Bradley's phone pinged. Before she had the chance to dig it out, the back door of Stave flew open.

"Fire at Butler Ranch!" someone yelled.

Trey was about to back the car up when Maddox smacked his hand on the trunk. "Hold up—"

Bradley jumped out of Trey's car and ran over to where Alex was getting into her BMW.

"Wait! Bradley—where are you going?" Trey yelled.

"Go with Naughton!" Alex shouted. "He's taking Mad's truck."

Naughton was already on the phone when she opened the door and climbed in. All Bradley could glean was that the fire was in the vineyards.

"We're on our way." Naughton disconnected the call and dropped the phone on the center console.

"How bad is it?" she asked.

"The northwest vineyards are burning, and the front is moving south, which puts structures in danger."

"What can I do?"

"Call Alex and see if she and Mad have heard anything else."

Bradley nodded.

Alex's phone went to voicemail, but she called back moments later.

"Call your aunt and ask her to call the Far Out wineries. She'll know what to do."

"Got it. Anything else?"

"Hang on." Bradley could hear Maddox speaking but couldn't decipher his words. "Mad says that's it for now."

Aunt Jean answered before Bradley heard the phone ring. She told Bradley she'd already called most of the wineries in what was known as the "Far Out" region in the collaborative, which was the area north of the fire. She also told Bradley that Uncle Charlie and all of Jenson's employees were already on their way to Butler Ranch.

"Mad and I will probably get up in the air right away," Naughton told her when she hung up.

"The air?"

"We're USFS carded."

Bradley had no idea what Naughton was talking about, but it didn't matter. A fire in the vineyard was the worst thing she could imagine.

Depending on the heat levels and how quickly the fire moved through, the vines could survive, if the cambium layer just beneath the bark survived. If the cambium layer burned, there'd be no way to save the vine. The financial losses could be staggering.

Naughton's jaw was strained, and the muscles in his arm were corded. As if it had a will of its own, Bradley's arm reached over, and her hand rested on his forearm.

"I don't know what to say…"

Naughton rested a hand on hers. "I'm glad you're with us, Bradley."

He said it so quietly, Bradley wasn't sure she heard him right. When she tried to move her hand, he grasped it tighter. They rode the rest of the way to Butler Ranch in silence.

They were still at least twenty miles from the ranch when the smell of smoke assaulted his senses. It grew more pungent the closer they got, until the overwhelming stench made him sick to his stomach.

The only thing keeping his panic at bay was Bradley's hand beneath his. Her warmth spread from his hand and arm through the rest of his body, her presence inexplicably calming him.

An orange glow lit the sky, visible from miles away, which meant the fire was spreading rapidly. It wasn't just Butler Ranch that was in immediate danger, Los Caballeros and Dunning Estate Wines were too. If it crossed the road, Jenson Vineyards would be threatened, along with several other wineries.

Most of the central coast of California had experienced severe drought conditions for the last decade.

If this fire spread, the majority of Westside Winery Collaborative would be in the fire's path. The potential devastation was more than he could wrap his head around.

As they got closer to the ranch, Naughton could see the vineyards ablaze through the thick gray haze of smoke. It was as though the vines had been lit with strings of bright orange lights.

When he pulled up to the gate and opened the truck's window, the warm summer breeze combined with the heat of the fire came at him in suffocating waves.

"That you, Naughton?" another vineyard owner standing near the gate asked.

"Know where Maddox is?"

"Waitin' on you."

Naughton pulled out his phone. "I'm at the gate," he said when Mad answered.

"He'll meet me here," Naughton told Bradley after he disconnected Mad's call. "Will you be okay driving the truck in?"

"Of course."

"I'll drive her in." Naughton hadn't seen Hawks approach.

"I can—"

"Hawks knows this land better than you do."

She nodded. "Of course."

Instead of opening the door and getting out, Naughton leaned over and wrapped his hand around the back of her neck, pulling her close to him. When her eyes met his and she didn't resist, Naughton leaned over and covered her lips with his. He didn't have time to linger or even think much beyond the feel of her tongue when she opened her mouth to let him in.

This would forever be their first kiss, and it was under the worst circumstances he could imagine. Not knowing what the next few hours would bring, he had to kiss her. He needed it to sustain him.

"You stay out of harm's way, you understand?" he said, reluctantly pulling away from her.

"You, too."

—:—

When Naughton got out of the truck, Bradley's eyes filled with tears. She had no business getting emotional. She was trained to know how to handle vines after a fire. It was experience she got firsthand as part of a team who flew into California's Lake Country when a wildfire destroyed almost ten-thousand acres of crops.

The impact of a fire in vineyards could manifest itself in several different ways. The amount and type of damage would determine the best approach to treating the vines. Some effects would be obvious, such as dehydrated leaves and burnt bark, but others would not.

They wouldn't know anything until the fire was out. The longer it raged, the more danger they'd face in terms of crop loss. It wasn't just Butler Ranch whose harvest was in jeopardy. Every grape grower for miles could face devastation from the smoke alone.

She wiped at her tears. If Hawks saw her crying now, he'd think she wasn't cut out for the task ahead.

"Where are Naughton and Maddox going?" she asked as Hawks put the truck in gear.

"Heliport. They're both certified pilots, trained by the USFS for aerial firefighting."

Hawks turned off the main drive.

"Where are we going?" she asked.

"Vehicles are safer behind the main house. That sucker will never burn."

Bradley prayed he was right. "Why not?"

"Naught's grandpa put concrete all around the outside of the house, and then covered it in stone. Nowadays that's common, especially in California, but back then it was unheard of. Old Grandpa Butler learned as much as he could from Julia Morgan."

Bradley knew well that she had been the architect William Randolph Hearst hired to construct *La Cuesta Encantada* in San Simeon. However, she didn't know the Butler family had a connection to it or her.

When they pulled closer to the house, Hawks pointed to the roof that was barely visible through the smoky haze. "Beneath the slate is galvanized steel. The castle's roofs are tile, but over the same steel."

"Did Naughton's grandfather work for Julia Morgan?"

"Sure did. In fact, so did his grandmother. That's where they met."

She and Hawks climbed out of the truck and went through the courtyard that led to the house. Her lungs burned, and her eyes stung from the smoke-filled air and oppressive heat.

"Almost there," he said, his eyes watering like hers were. "The main house is command central. We'll get our marching orders here."

Alex and Brodie were both on their phones when she and Hawks came inside. "Got it," Bradley heard Alex say.

"Maddox wants me to talk Laird into staying in Cambria," she said after she disconnected the call. "He took Sorcha and my mom to my place at the beach."

Brodie ended his call and walked over. "Da is staying put for now."

"You talked to him? Thank God. Maddox asked me to call him, but—"

"It's okay, Al. He gets it."

"Who's moving the horses?" Alex asked.

"A few of my guys loaded 'em up. They're taking them to Demetria," Hawks answered.

"What can I do?" Bradley asked.

"Not much right now. The fireline is about two miles north of where we are now. Since it's shifted and moving this way, they're saying it'll be easier to contain than if it was spreading north," Alex told her. "I'm staying as long as they'll let me, or Maddox gets word to me that he wants me to do otherwise." She looked at her watch. "He and Naught should be in the air soon." When her phone buzzed, she stepped away to answer it.

"Not like the old days when we'd be out there with buckets and brooms—right, Brodie?" said Hawks.

"Is what Naughton's doing dangerous?" Bradley asked.

"They have to get close because they're dropping water, unlike the planes that'll either spot for them from above or drop the retardant. Naught knows what he's doing, though. He started volunteering for aerial fire-fighting shortly after he got his pilot's license. Maddox hasn't volunteered for as many fires, but he's a good pilot. They'll be fine," Brodie assured her.

Bradley turned around to look for Alex and caught Hawks watching her. He had to have witnessed her and Naughton's kiss, and under any other circumstances, Bradley would be mortified. Right now, though, she didn't care.

She saw a tanker make one pass, dropping retardant on what Brodie explained was the southernmost fire-line. To Bradley, it looked like they'd all landed in hell.

It occurred to her that she left Stave almost an hour ago and hadn't heard a word from Trey.

At Butler Ranch, she texted, and waited to see if he'd respond. After five minutes, he still hadn't.

"I just talked to Mad," Alex reported. "He said from the air it looks pretty bad, but his spotter told him the fire was already fifty percent contained. Thankfully someone called it in before it spread out of control."

"Who called it in? Your da?" Hawks asked Brodie.

"He said he didn't. He and Ma were asleep."

"Must've been one of the other vineyard owners spotted it, or smelled the smoke."

Alex didn't comment, but the look on her face worried Bradley. When Hawks and Brodie stepped away, Bradley asked, "Obviously you're worried about the fire, but is there something else you're not saying?" She said a silent prayer that whatever it was, wasn't about Naughton.

"It's something someone told Maddox about who called the fire in."

"Who was it?"

"I'm sure it wasn't who he thought." Alex looked over at Brodie, who was walking back toward them. "I'll tell you more later."

"Naught is still dropping water, but he's saying they're optimistic about the containment. We might be able to get out in the vineyards in two or three hours, at least the ones outside the fire's main path. The command chief said we can access the winery now to set up cold storage." Brodie held up a radio. "He gave me this in case we have to evacuate. Ready?"

Bradley was thankful to finally have something useful she could do. If there was any fruit to salvage, timing was crucial, even on the vineyards that didn't burn. Work to minimize or eliminate smoke taint had to begin almost immediately, otherwise, any wine Butler Ranch produced from this harvest would smell and taste like smoke. Setting up cold storage now would save them precious hours later, when they were able to get to the vines.

Once they were given the go-ahead, they'd check every accessible vineyard for fruit. If any was left hanging, it would be hand-harvested as quickly as possible. After that, any remaining leaf material would be removed. Leaves held the most smoke marker compounds, which would threaten any vines still alive.

The harvested fruit would be put into cold storage and held below fifty degrees Fahrenheit in order to minimize or eliminate smoke taint. Until they were able to get into the vineyards, they wouldn't know the volume of fruit they were dealing with.

Every available body would be needed to pick. Aunt Jean told her word had gone out for help, but where was everyone?

Alex got on the phone again once they got to the winery. "I'll let you know the minute we can go in," Bradley heard her say before she disconnected the call.

"The natives are restless."

"Huh?"

"Gabe said there must be more than five hundred people at Los Cab, waiting for word we can get out in the field."

"Tell your brother we may need more," replied Brodie.

—:—

It was after eight in the morning when Naughton drove along Adelaida Trail on his way back to the ranch. The fire was over ninety percent contained, and most of the active burning had been extinguished. As much as he wanted to close his eyes for a few minutes, he knew he'd never sleep.

Brodie had promised to let him know the condition of each vineyard they inspected. They hadn't got through many yet, and worry was eating away at him. From the sky, the land looked charred.

He drove past Los Caballeros and saw the grounds and parking lots full of vehicles. Every person who had parked on the Avila's property was at Butler Ranch, doing their best to salvage his vines. The enormity of the number of people the vehicles represented filled him with gratitude. His exhaustion made him emotional, but it was more than that.

Shortly after he'd made his final water drop and landed, Naughton walked into the command station for an update. He knew most of the guys who worked for the forest service, and the local firefighters, so he wasn't surprised when a guy Kade went to school with approached him.

"Naughton Butler, I'd ask how the hell you are, but under the circumstances, I already know. What's it been, fifteen years?"

"At least." Naughton shook his hand. "Thanks for all you're doing, Jay." He looked at the station name on the man's uniform. "You're in Livermore now?"

"I am, but coincidentally, I was here conducting a training session. I took the call reporting the fire."

"Who called it in?"

"Damn, strange thing. I could've sworn it was Kade, but before I had a chance to ask, the guy hung up."

"What number did he call from?"

"Blocked. How is your brother anyway? Still out saving the world and protecting the freedom of innocent guys like us?"

"Kade was killed in action over eighteen months ago."

The glimpse of a smile that had been on Jay's face quickly vanished. "I'm so sorry, Naught. I hadn't heard."

Naughton shrugged. "You didn't know."

"Sure sounded like him." Jay shook his head. "Again, I'm real sorry, Naughton. Please give my regards to your family."

So who had made the call? That's what Naughton wanted to know now. It wasn't his father, which would've explained why Jay thought the caller sounded like Kade, but his dad would've never just hung up, and when they asked, he said that he and their mother were asleep when they got the call alerting them. As much as he wanted to get to the bottom of it, Naughton had bigger things to worry about, like whether any of the Butler Ranch vines had survived the fire.

6

They only had access to a few vineyards, none of which had been in the direct path of the fire. They couldn't assume those vines had survived, though. Radiant heat from the blaze could kill them in the same way burning would.

Bradley and Brodie went row by row, cutting the T-buddings to check the cambium layer of each vine. If the tissue beneath the bark was creamy white with tinges of green, and moist, then the cambium was still alive, and there was a chance the vine would survive. So far all the vines they'd checked were still viable.

Hand-harvesters followed behind them, picking every remaining cluster they could. When to pick was no longer a factor. They needed to salvage fruit regardless of its ripeness. At the end of each row, runners waited to carry full bins into cold storage. Following the grape pickers were pruners, who were tasked with leaf removal.

Access had been granted at three in the morning, and thankfully, Butler Ranch had big overhead lights already on premise for the upcoming harvest. Soon they'd have to decide whether to continue picking in the heat of the day or take a break until temperatures dropped when the sun went down.

When she asked Brodie, he wanted to know what she'd do if they were harvesting Jenson grapes.

"I'd keep picking," she told him.

"Then we'll pick until one of my brothers tells us otherwise."

—:—

After he drove through the ranch gates, Naughton texted Brodie, who told him which vineyard he and Bradley were in. When he parked the truck and walked toward the vines, she was the first person he saw.

The feeling of calmness he experienced when she had put her hand on his arm earlier, filled him again. When he got closer, the calm turned to worry, not for the vines, but for her.

She was covered in the soot and ash that filled the air, and she looked exhausted, like they all were. Even from where he stood, he could see Bradley's hands were raw and bleeding. Before she moved to the next vine, she wiped her brow with her sleeve, looked up, and met his eyes with hers.

"Naughton," he heard her say as she dropped her knife into the dirt. She walked into his arms, and he held her close to him. When he saw Brodie walking over, he squeezed her tight, let her go, and stepped back.

Brodie embraced him. "Man, am I ever glad to see you."

"Likewise," Naughton said, tightening his hold on his brother.

"Where's Mad?"

"He's with Alex. He said he'd be out shortly. How's it progressing?"

"Slow, but steady."

"About time you got your ass back here," he heard someone say.

When Naughton spun around, the boyfriend was walking toward him, now barking into a hand-held radio rather than at him.

"Get into vineyard twenty-two." Naughton didn't catch the answer the person gave, but the scowl the boyfriend leveled at Bradley made Naughton clench his fists.

"I don't care what she told you. Go to twenty-two."

Bradley walked away, back to checking vines. Naughton would've followed her, but first he needed to quell his desire to pummel her boyfriend into the ground.

"What the hell?" he asked Brodie, who motioned for Naughton to follow.

"He swept in here an hour ago and took over. Bradley had everything organized and running smoothly until he decided she didn't know what she was doing."

When Naughton saw the boyfriend approaching out of the corner of his eye, he raised his hand. "I need a minute with my brother, and then I'll get to you," Naughton barked right back at him.

He and Brodie walked farther away. "What else?"

"Bradley was sending out crews as soon as they arrived. I think even you'd be impressed with how organized she was."

"I'm impressed by everything she does," Naughton murmured. "What about him?"

"From what I can tell, she and most everyone else ignores him. She pulls her cell out every few minutes to either answer a call or send a text."

"Where are we?"

"Ask her," Brodie motioned toward Bradley. "And get her to take a break. She hasn't left the dirt since three this morning."

Still ignoring the boyfriend, Naughton approached her. "How's it going?" he asked.

Bradley looked over at Trey.

"I asked you, not him."

She pulled folded papers out of her back pocket. "Here's where we are."

Bradley explained that Hawks had gone out with fire command to identify which vineyards they'd have access to and when. Then she'd put them in order by varietal. The Sauvignon Blanc needed to be picked first, followed by Chardonnay, and so on.

She pointed to one of the crumpled pages. Through the smudges of soot, Naughton saw each vineyard was labeled with a crew lead and their cell number.

"Good work."

"I thought so, but Trey…well, the two of you should decide what to do next."

"It isn't his decision."

"I know, but—"

Bradley's phone buzzed and she took it out of her pocket. "Yeah?" she answered, her voice heavy with fatigue.

"Vineyard seventeen," she said to Naughton. He sifted through the papers again, found it, and handed it to her. She held the phone between her shoulder and her ear, and leaned over to make a note on the paper, using her knee as a writing surface.

"Head over to eighteen next. Thank you so much."

She disconnected the call, wrote something else on the paper, and handed it to him. She smiled through her tears. "Sorry, I don't know why I'm so emotional."

"It's called exhaustion." Brodie rubbed her shoulder.

Naughton read what she'd written and smiled too. *One hundred percent ALIVE. Ninety percent picked.*

"I'm having my crew bring down a crush pad. It should be here in an hour."

Naughton hadn't seen Trey approach. "Why?"

"Flash boil. It's—"

"I know what flash boil is, and it's too early to even consider it. Turn your crew back."

"If I were you, I'd take the help that's offered and say thank you," he snarled.

Naughton shook his head, reigning in the rage that continued building. "Appreciate the help. However, now that Maddox and I are back, you can hand over the radio and head out."

Trey more thrust the radio at him than handed it over. "Are you serious?"

Naughton turned toward Bradley, not answering.

"You unappreciative bastard."

Naughton spun back around. "As I said, I appreciate your help."

"You're too stubborn to take help from people who can afford to bring in the kind of machinery you'd never be able to? Suit yourself—"

Naughton clenched his fists, so close to leveling the asshole, and gritted his teeth. "Like I said, you can leave."

"Brad," the boyfriend called out. "Let's go."

She raised her head and looked back and forth between the two men, as though she was waiting for Naughton to tell her what to do. He wouldn't though. This was her decision.

He figured she made it when she turned away and went back to work.

—:—

Bradley was too tired to care about the fight brewing between Trey and Naughton. She had a job to do, and she intended to keep doing it until she couldn't stand any longer, and then she'd take a break.

She'd been hired as an assistant winery manager, but in times like these, everyone was expected to be in the vineyards, doing everything they could to salvage the harvest.

The pissing match between Trey and Naughton was eating up time they couldn't afford to waste. It disgusted her when she looked out at the people who had been here with her for seven hours straight, and probably hadn't slept any more than she had before that.

Watching Naughton block Trey's path when he attempted to walk over to her was the last straw.

"Stop it, both of you, and either get to work or get the hell out of the vineyard," she spat.

Alex was clapping as she walked over. "Well said, but instead of them, I'm getting you out. Time for a break, Bradley."

"I can't," she wiped at the sweat dripping from her forehead into her eyes.

"You have to. If you don't, you're going to pass out from heat exhaustion."

Bradley looked at Naughton. "You have a decision to make about whether to keep picking."

He nodded.

"When you make up your mind, tell them." Bradley waved her arms toward the vineyard and tossed her phone at Alex.

"What's your password?"

"I disabled it."

She pulled the papers out of her back pocket, thrust them at Naughton, and stomped out of the vineyard.

He caught up to her when she got to the main drive.

"Where are you going?"

"Home."

"I'll drive you over there."

"No thanks." She kept walking, hoping Naughton would let her be.

Alex was right, if she hadn't gotten out of the scorching heat of the vineyard, she would've passed out. Only the shade of the big oak trees kept her from doing so now. As soon as she got back to her aunt and uncle's, she'd take a shower and get some rest.

Naughton and Maddox were back and could make their own decisions about their own damn vineyards.

Naughton grabbed her arm. "Quit being so stubborn and come back to the cottage with me."

Bradley spun around and wrenched away from him.

"Me? You're calling me stubborn?"

"Damn straight."

"Trey tried to help you, but you refused to even listen to him."

"We don't need his help."

"Of course you don't."

"You and everyone out in the vineyards were ignoring him. The workers looked to you for guidance, not him."

She kept walking but spun around when she heard his footfalls getting closer. "Quit following me."

"No."

She shook her head and kept walking.

"Do you agree about the flash boil?"

She wasn't sure. The process was extreme. Flash boiling the skins and juice, at temperatures up to two hundred degrees, followed by putting them through a vacuum chamber to extract the volatile compounds that contributed to smoke taint, hadn't been proven. In fact, it could do more harm than good to fruit that was already compromised. Had it been her decision, she would wait until fermentation, and test the juice.

She doubted Trey was suggesting an immediate crush though, not that Naughton had given him a chance to say what he was thinking.

"We have our own crush pad, Bradley."

"Instead of telling him that, you tell him to turn his crew around. You wanted to pick a fight with him when you should've been thanking him."

"You're defending him after he ran roughshod over you?"

"He has more experience than I do—"

"Bullshit."

"I don't care what you think, Naughton."

"Yes, you do. You wouldn't have kissed me back if you didn't care."

"How dare you?" she said through tears she didn't think her body had enough hydration to produce.

He grabbed her again, and this time, she didn't have the strength to pull away from him.

"Let her go." Neither had seen Trey's red Spider pull up, or him get out of it. "Let's go, Bradley." When Trey took her other arm, Naughton dropped his hold on her.

"Don't leave," she heard him say, but she had to.

—:—

"Where is she?" Alex asked when Naughton walked back into the vineyard.

"Gone."

"With him?"

"Yep."

"You're such an asshole."

"Not now, Alex."

"I wouldn't be surprised if she quit."

Naughton walked away.

"Go get some sleep," he heard her say as he left the vineyard.

"What's goin' on?" Maddox asked when Naughton walked past his brother's cottage on his way to his own.

"Gettin' some rest. Isn't that what you're supposed to be doing?"

"Can't sleep."

Naughton understood. His body needed rest, but he was past the point where he could force it. "Bradley left."

"Good. She needed a break."

"Maybe for good."

Maddox shook his head and went back inside.

Naughton followed. "Don't you want to know why?"

"No, I don't."

"Why not?"

"Because I know she'll be back."

"She left with him."

"Yeah? Why wouldn't she?"

"Because he's an asshole who treats her like shit."

Maddox put his hand on Naughton's shoulder. "Go sleep. Take something if you have to."

"I can't. I have to talk to her—"

"I'm gonna stop you right there. The only thing you have to do is leave Bradley Saint John the hell alone before your words become a self-fulfilling prophecy and she never comes back. I need her at the winery, now more than ever. If you do anything to jeopardize that…"

"What are you going to do?"

"I'm not going to do a fucking thing, Naughton. But I'm asking you, as your brother, to just do this one thing for me. Leave Bradley alone. Walk away. Do what you know is the right thing."

"I can't," he said, but Maddox didn't hear him. He was out of his brother's cottage and in his own before he admitted the truth. He couldn't leave her alone, and what's more, he knew she didn't want him to.

When Trey drove out of Butler Ranch, he didn't take Bradley home. Instead, he took her to Adelaida Inn, where he always stayed when he came to visit.

"We need to talk," he began.

"Before you say anything more, I need a break, Trey. It's trite, I know, but it isn't you, it's me. I appreciate you trying to help—"

"Are you sleeping with him?"

"*What?* How could you ask me that?" she gasped.

"Settle down. Either way, there are things I need you to do."

Bradley's exhaustion was at a level where she thought maybe she wasn't hearing him right. "What things?"

"I want to know exactly how much of Butler Ranch's juice is tainted. And since you're in so thick with Alex Avila, I want to know what other wineries in the area are having issues with their production levels. If you hear of anyone whose production is compromised, I want to be the first to know."

"You're asking me to spy on them?"

"Don't be melodramatic. I'm asking you to pass on information."

Bradley had always hated his condescending tone, but mixed with lack of sleep and debilitating fatigue, she was beginning to hate him as much as the way he talked to her.

"No."

"Do you understand what's at risk, Bradley?"

"I guess I don't, and honestly, I don't care."

"Twenty-six billion dollars a year is at stake, and I can tell you, the wine conglomerates will stop at nothing to get what they want."

"I don't understand—"

"It's called climate change, Brad, and it threatens everyone in our industry."

"I'm leaving." Before she could walk out the door, Trey grabbed her arm.

"Davis, Fresno, hell—even your precious Cornell have been courting Naughton Butler."

She jerked her arm away from him. "For what?"

"To head up their climate change research departments."

"Why him?"

"Because he's the goddamn vine whisperer. Drought, pest infestation—he's the master. What he's done here in Paso Robles is groundbreaking." Trey scrubbed his face with his hand. "You know viticulture, you've got a damn degree in it. What comes with temperatures that average five, even ten degrees above what we previously considered normal?"

Bradley stood with her arms folded, but nodded. Trey's question was rhetorical.

"That's what we've experienced over the last ten-year period. No one paid much attention at first. Just thought it was warmer than average, but when, summer after summer, the warming trends continued, the winery owners started paying attention. If these trends continue to affect the valley's winter climate, grapevine moths, mildews, even red blotch virus, thrive. Without temperatures cool enough at night to kill them off, they spread, year after year, and there's no end in sight."

"You came here to convince Naughton to come work for you."

"Mainly."

She laughed, and not because she thought it was funny. "He won't help you, Trey."

"Maybe not, but he'll do whatever you ask."

"I have no influence over Naughton Butler."

"Bullshit."

"What's that mean?"

"He wants to fuck you."

She slapped Trey's face with every ounce of strength she could muster.

He brought his palm to his cheek. "You don't think I saw that display in the vineyard when he got back? You owe me."

"*I owe you?* For what?"

"You're someone in this industry because of me, otherwise you'd be just another marginally pretty girl, who thinks she knows how to make wine."

Bradley's head was reeling. She was someone because of him? What exactly did Trey believe he'd done for her? She opened the door and was on her way out when Trey's next words made her stop.

"Don't say you weren't warned."

She spun around. "About what?"

"What will happen if your lover doesn't play nice."

"He's not my—"

"The economic impact of this region is less than ten percent of what we do up north. Without us, their wine production doesn't mean jack shit. They need us to survive, and the sooner they figure that out, the better it will be for all of us."

"I can't help you."

"You'd better. Even I won't be able to step in and save Jenson if you refuse to do what I asked."

"Is that a threat?"

"Accidents happen, don't they?"

Bradley slammed the door behind her, letting Trey's words sink in. Had her exhaustion made her delirious? Had she heard him right? Was he threatening her family's winery?

When she rounded the corner of the building, she almost ran into Jim, whose family had owned the inn for over fifty years.

"Whoa, slow down there, Bradley—"

Jim's words cut short when he saw she was crying. "What's wrong?"

"I left my phone…"

"Tell me what you need, sweetheart."

"A ride home."

"Come with me."

Jim dropped her off, but neither her aunt nor her uncle was home. They were probably still at Butler Ranch, helping in the vineyards. She should've asked Jim to drop her off there instead of here. Her reflection, when she walked past the downstairs bathroom mirror, made her gasp. Black soot, streaked from her tears, covered her face, even her hair was matted in it. She had to shower and put on fresh clothes, but then she'd go back to Butler, and tell Naughton and Maddox everything Trey had said.

After her shower, she put on a robe and sat on her bed, intending to rest for just a minute but, instead, slept through to the next morning.

—:—

Naughton heard Bradley was back this morning, but so far he hadn't seen her. They needed to talk, and soon, to finish the conversation they'd started before she left last night.

Did she really believe he was in the wrong? The boyfriend had been showing off, flexing his muscle where it wasn't needed. He was a pompous ass who didn't deserve Bradley's defense.

It was only Maddox's plea that kept him from seeking her out as soon as he heard she was back. His brother had asked him to leave her alone, and he knew Maddox was right to ask. This thing between them burned as hot as the vineyard fire had.

She felt it too; he knew she did when she kissed him back. He'd never forget the way her body melted against his or the way her breath quickened when she opened her mouth to his.

It had been their first kiss—he remembered thinking that when it happened—but it sure as hell wouldn't be their last.

—:—

When Bradley got back to the ranch, she went in search of Maddox, who asked her to come into the winery so he could fill her in on what they'd done since she left.

"It wasn't as bad as we thought it might be," he told her. "Your work yesterday saved us, Bradley. I don't know how we can ever repay you."

"It's my job," she murmured, hating that Trey's words echoed in her head.

"I'd say you went far beyond the job."

She hated to ask, but she had to. "Do you know how the fire started?"

"My guess is heat lightening, although it's too early for anyone to know for certain."

Maybe Trey was the one who was being melodramatic yesterday, but after her unintentional several hours' sleep, questions about what he'd meant and where he'd been were spinning in her head.

"Bradley, are you listening?"

"Yes. Sorry, thinking about yesterday. What did you say?"

"I said that Naughton had been planning to pick Sauvignon Blanc in the next few days anyway, and Chardonnay was close enough that we'll get a decent amount of juice at crush."

"That's good news."

"As you know, the bulk of the Cabernet vineyards were left unscathed, so Naughton decided not to pick yet."

That didn't surprise her. It was only the first week of September, and harvest would go well into the first week of October, fire or no fire.

"Not sure how we'll be affected by smoke taint, but the good news is, grapes are less susceptible after veraison. The other contributing factor is time. The fact they were able to contain and extinguish the fire as quickly as they did is what will save the juice of the fruit that survived."

"So, no flash boil?"

"Naughton doesn't think it's necessary at this point. We'll reevaluate after we get the numbers back from the lab."

It was standard procedure to send fruit to a lab that could better determine what compounds were found that shouldn't be there. Bradley assumed they'd pulled from every batch that had been picked, and would continue to do so.

"We're leveling everything that burned, and we'll replant, implementing what we've been discussing."

Bradley didn't kid herself into thinking she'd played any part in that decision, after all, according to Trey she was just a marginally pretty girl who thought she knew something about making wine.

Whether she worked for Butler Ranch or not, Maddox and Naughton would have come to the same conclusions she had. For the winery to remain viable, they had to diversify and experiment. It's what Maddox told her the day he had offered her the job.

"We need new blood, fresh ideas. I want time to focus on Demetria, but more importantly, I want someone who is willing to shake things up around here," he'd said. "You'll have my full support, I promise you that."

Bradley had questioned his decision then. There was financial risk involved that, now, no longer mattered. Their hand had been forced.

"Naughton is bringing in overhead irrigation today. In fact, the process has probably already started."

Maddox's cell buzzed, and he looked at the screen. "It's the fire marshal; I need to take this."

Bradley stood to give him some privacy, processing what he had told her. He and Naughton had to have been up all night, making decisions, and getting the field workers refocused. Everything appeared to be back under control.

Her job now would be to focus on the fruit that was being held in cold storage and wait for Maddox's instructions for the crush. It would likely begin later today or tonight. Holding the fruit past a couple of days, could result in spoilage.

"Jesus!" Maddox exclaimed. She spun around to see he was still on the phone, his hand gripping the

back of his neck. Before she turned away, he hurled a bottle of wine at the opposite side of the winery, shattering it. He stormed out of the building without another word.

Not knowing what else to do, Bradley went into the cold room and began an inventory of what was there. She couldn't focus, though. She hadn't seen this side of Maddox before and could only assume that whatever the fire marshal told him was bad. Her hands shook, making it near impossible for her to write the numbers she'd just counted. She was about to give up when she heard the winery door open.

"Are you okay?" Alex asked, meeting her halfway between the main door and the cold room.

"Me?"

Alex nodded.

"I'm okay. Maddox got a call."

"Come with me." Alex led her out of the winery and into the vineyards.

"Why are we here?" Bradley asked.

"I want to be sure no one can hear us." Alex looked around. "There's news."

"About?"

"The fire."

"What about it?"

"The fire marshal thinks it may have been set intentionally. Maddox and Naughton are meeting with the investigators now."

Bradley felt her knees give way, and she gripped Alex's arm to stay upright. "Jesus," she murmured.

"I thought about canceling the collaborative meeting, but now I'm glad I didn't. There's a lot of shit happening in the valley, but this was the worst of it. It wasn't just the vineyards or Butler Ranch at risk, people could've died. The entire westside could've been devastated if they hadn't gotten the fire under control so quickly."

Bradley felt sick to her stomach, recalling Trey's words. *Twenty-six billion dollars a year is at stake, and I can tell you, the wine conglomerates will stop at nothing to get what they want.*

"You're pale, Bradley. Do you need to sit?"

Bradley shook her head. Her mind raced, trying to remember every detail of what Trey had said.

"Is there proof?"

"Not officially."

"What does that mean?"

Alex looked over Bradley's shoulder. "Here comes Naughton. We'll talk more about this later."

"Got a minute?" she heard him say, and was about to leave when Alex gripped her shoulder. "You sure you're okay?"

"I'm fine. I'll just head back to the winery."

"He wants to talk to you, not me."

When Bradley turned around, Naughton was right behind her.

"Is there something you need?" she asked, not sure what else to say.

"Damn right, there is."

He said it loudly enough that Alex turned around and glared at him. Bradley felt as though she was going to be sick to her stomach.

—:—

He was done waiting for her to make the first move to talk to him. Maddox thought; he and Bradley had a lot to discuss, and he told his brother so. Especially now. If what the marshal believed was true, everyone in the valley needed to be on high alert.

"Come with me."

"I can't. I mean, Maddox—"

"He knows you're leaving."

"Are you firing me?"

Naughton stopped so abruptly, Bradley almost ran into him. He spun around and faced her. "Why in God's name would you think you were being fired?"

Bradley chewed at her fingernails, and Naughton gripped her wrist.

"You're trembling. What's going on?"

"Alex told me, you know, about the fire."

"Good. I mean, I'm glad you know."

"I'm so sorry…"

She looked as though she had more to say, so Naughton waited. He let go of her wrist and pulled her to him, soothing tears that turned into something worse. Bradley's body shook against his.

"Hey, now," he said, pulling back to get her to look at him. "Come on, let's get out of here."

He took her hand and she followed, but her shaking didn't stop. "Where are we going?" she asked.

"For a ride."

"I told you, I'm not a horse person."

"Not that kind of ride."

He stopped in front of the barn, punched his code into his phone, and waited while the doors swung open.

"Here," he said, handing her a helmet. "Put this on."

"There's something I need to tell you, Naughton."

"Yeah? There's something I need to tell you too, and both can wait."

Bradley looked at the helmet, and then at him. "I'm not a motorcycle person either."

"You will be," he said, taking the helmet from her hands and putting it on her head. He adjusted the chin strap, and then put his hands on her shoulders. "Wiggle it around a little. Is it comfortable?"

When she nodded, he put on his own helmet and started the bike. "Get on."

For a minute he didn't think she was going to, but then she rested her hand on his shoulder and threw her leg over.

"Scoot closer and put your feet on those pegs," he said, pointing behind him.

She moved a little closer and rested her feet where he told her to. "Put your arms around my waist." She had to move closer to do so, and when she did, she was right where he wanted her. It may not have been the best idea to get her on the bike when she was upset, but riding always helped him get out of his head. Maybe it would do the same for her.

"Ready?"

She nodded, and Naughton eased the bike out through the barn door and onto the ranch's main drive.

"Hold on tight," he said when they reached Adelaida Trail. "If I lean, go with me, okay?"

She nodded again.

He took a right, and they rode under the canopy of the big oak trees. When he picked up speed, he felt her hands grip his waist tighter. He loved the feel of her behind him, her body sliding closer until there was nowhere else for her to go. Bradley's body tight against his felt like heaven.

Instead of going out to the highway, Naughton took a couple of turns and followed the back roads, eventually arriving at the front gate of Demetria. He stopped the bike, dug out his phone, and punched in the gate code. A moment later, it swung open and he pulled the bike through. He stopped near the creekside and killed the engine.

"Climb off, and I'll help you with your helmet," he said.

As soon as she let go and put her foot on the ground, he missed the feel of her against him and regretted not riding farther. He had things to tell her, though, and this was the best place for him to do it.

He took his own helmet off first, and moved her hands that were fiddling with the chin strap. "Here," he said, easily releasing the buckle.

"That was amazing," she said once she'd pulled the helmet off her head.

"You can set that here." He patted the seat. After she'd set it down, he put his next to hers.

They walked over and sat on the bench of the picnic table next to the creek.

"You're quiet," he said after a few minutes.

"I don't know what to say."

"Just listen, then."

"Okay."

"Alex told you there's evidence the fire was set intentionally."

Bradley nodded, and the stress he'd seen on her face when she was talking to Alex in the vineyard returned.

"I think I know who set it," he said.

Bradley stood from the table, walked a little ways away, and bent over, her hands on her knees. "So do I, Naughton."

8

Her response stunned him. How could she? Had her uncle filled her in on what had happened with Rory Calder and Los Caballeros? Even if he had, no one outside of the Butler and Avila families knew the whole story. They knew enough to be cautious, but that was all.

Naughton had a lot of thinking to do about what he should tell Bradley, especially given her reaction.

"Change of plans," he said. "Let's get back on the bike."

"Do we need to go back?"

"To the ranch? No."

"But there's so much work."

"You did a great job yesterday, Bradley, and now Maddox has taken over what you started. What we need to talk about is more important."

"Okay…"

"When's the last time you ate?"

Bradley shrugged her shoulders. "I don't have much of an appetite."

"That's what I figured." Naughton handed her the helmet and helped her fasten the chin strap after she put it on. Since he hadn't put his on yet, it would be so easy to lean forward, tilt his head, and put his lips where they'd long to be since the last time he kissed her. He didn't, though. First, they needed to talk.

He stayed on the back roads as long as he could before riding out to the highway that ran east and west between Paso Robles and the ocean.

When that highway dead-ended, he went south on Highway One, pulled off the main road, and took the access road to Harmony.

"Where are we going?"

"Sadie's."

"Who's Sadie?"

"The woman who owns the diner."

This time Bradley unfastened her own helmet and held it under her arm.

"It'll be safe here," he told her. "We can leave them on the seat."

"Hey, Naught," said Sadie when they walked inside. "Who's this?"

"This is Bradley Saint John. Bradley, this is Sadie."

Bradley shook Sadie's hand and looked around her toward the back of the diner.

"Need a restroom, sugar?" Sadie asked.

"Yes, please."

"Follow me."

When she came back to the table, Bradley sat across from Naughton and looked everywhere but at him. He didn't take his eyes off her, even when her cheeks turned pink.

"Naughton, I…what you said before—"

He stopped her. "We'll have plenty of time to talk about the fire later, after we've eaten. Let's not spoil either of our appetites."

"Is she going to bring us menus?"

"I already ordered."

"For both of us?"

Naughton nodded. Maybe that had been presumptuous of him. "If you want something else…"

"That's okay. I'm sure whatever you ordered is fine."

He hated the awkwardness between them and stood. "Scoot over," he said, sitting on her side of the booth, close enough that his hip rested against hers.

He could feel her eyes on him. Her warm breath against his neck was like a caress, and he swallowed the groan that threatened to escape.

If he turned to look at her, he'd kiss her, and he couldn't do that yet. First, he had a story to tell her.

—:—

"There's a meeting of the collaborative on Thursday. Did Maddox talk to you about it?" he asked.

"Alex did."

"Did she tell you Mad wants you to attend?"

"No, but—"

"He does."

"I can do that. What's it about?"

"How much has your uncle told you about what's been happening in the valley?"

"A little. He said there was some trouble between you and the new owners of Tablas Creek."

"The trouble was with Los Caballeros, not Butler Ranch."

"Right. He did mention Los Cab, too."

"You ever met Rory Calder?"

Bradley thought for a minute. "I don't think so. Does he own Tablas Creek?"

Naughton nodded. "His family does. Steer clear of him if you can."

"What happened?"

"Couple months ago, Calder tried to orchestrate a coup at Los Cab."

"That's right. I remember Uncle Charlie saying that."

"Calder discovered the Avilas had been storing wine in Demetria's caves."

Bradley knew exactly what Naughton was talking about. It wasn't just that they were storing it there, they were hiding it. Her uncle had told her that Los Cab almost lost their bond over it.

Wineries were required to have a bond with the Alcohol Tax Bureau in order to legally make and sell wine. The bond was like an insurance policy against the winery's taxes. Quarterly reports had to be filled, stating how much wine they'd made and how much wine was in on-premise storage versus how much they'd sold.

Evidently, one of Alex's brothers had severely underestimated Los Cab's production, and then tried to cover it up by hiding it in caves that hadn't been used in years.

"The fines Los Cab had to pay were hefty, but they were put on probation and able to hang on to their bond," Naughton told her. "There's more to it, though."

"Go on."

"Calder moved the wine from Demetria's caves in the middle of the night, and then placed an anonymous call to the ATB. The next day, when Los Cab was raided, Calder showed up and told Gabe Avila he had proof that I was the one behind it."

"Surely they knew he was lying."

"Not right away."

Bradley turned to look at him and raised her eyebrows. He was so close, and looking right at her. When she faced him, he ran his finger down the side of her face.

"Why not?" she asked. With him this close, Bradley was having a hard time remembering what they were talking about.

"Family history. Having Gabe accuse me was like goin' back to the days when our families hated each other."

"They hated each other? What about Alex and your brother?"

"Years ago, Alex's father, Alfonso, accused my father of cheating in the Paso Zin competition."

"It's sounding vaguely familiar."

"I understood how Da felt when it happened to me."

"What happened?"

"Then?"

Bradley nodded.

"Alex's father had a heart attack and died. Maddox stepped up and begged my father to let us help them bring the harvest in that year."

"Because of Alex?"

"In part. I was one of the few people who knew that Mad and Alex had been seeing each other on the sly for years. But it was more than that. The vineyard owners in the valley have always worked together, no matter what. None of us could sit by and watch Los Cab struggle. I'm sure Da would've stepped in with or without Maddox asking him to."

"How did they find out it wasn't you?"

—:—

He'd started this story, and now he had to finish it, but the fewer people who knew about Lena and her marriage to Kade, the better, especially given Naughton and his brothers still hadn't told their parents.

"Someone who knew it had been Calder came forward."

"Sounds mysterious."

"It is."

"What happened to him?"

"Nothing. The problem was, there was no legal basis for prosecuting him. He'd moved the wine from the caves and delivered it to its rightful owner. Calling the ATB wasn't illegal either. However, what the Avilas had done was."

"Why, though? I mean, what was Calder after?"

"Land. Any way he could get it. That's the theory anyway. Most of the land on the westside is fami-ly-owned, and will probably never be sold. With what is happening up north, the big wine conglomerates, which Calder's family is a part of, are doing whatever they can to buy land down here. From what I've heard, they're going as far as paying two or three times what the land is currently worth. If that doesn't work, I guess we're learning they'll do something more sinister."

"You're part of what they want."

Naughton shook his head. "I'm no genius, Bradley. Just because I've had success here combating the drought, higher temps, and infestation from pests that we've never had to deal with before, doesn't mean I can help them up north. I don't know why they think I can."

"I heard it was more than that. Universities are trying to hire you."

"The boyfriend tell you all this?"

Bradley nodded and looked away.

"Don't look away from me. Whatever you have to say, say it. Do you agree with him—that I'm refusing to help because I want them to fail?"

Bradley turned to face him again. "No. I'd never think that."

"Good. That isn't the kind of person I am."

"I know that, Naughton."

—:—

"Who's hungry? Mind my reach." Sadie handed Naughton a plate. "Thanks, sugar," she said when he set it in front of Bradley, and then set the other plate in front of him. "Be right back with your toast."

Bradley studied the plate of food in front of her. Naughton had ordered the same for himself, but how did he know it was exactly what she wanted when she wouldn't have known it herself? Even the eggs were just the way she liked them.

"Everything okay?" he asked when Sadie walked away from the table.

"It's perfect. Thanks."

Naughton half-smiled and dug into his own food. "Where's the boyfriend now?" he asked between bites.

"I don't know."

Sadie came back with their toast and set it between them. "How's your brother these days?" she asked.

Naughton shook his head. "Big a pain in the ass as ever."

"I heard he and Alex are getting married."

"Haven't heard, but won't be surprised if they do."

Sadie laughed. "You're so much like Kade," she added before she walked away.

"Why don't you know?" Naughton asked.

"What?"

"Where the boyfriend is."

Bradley took a deep breath, wishing she had a good reason to change the subject. "We had a fight."

"Good."

Bradley pierced her egg with a piece of toast, dipped it into the bright orange yolk, and took a bite.

"Did he go home?"

Bradley shrugged. "I hope so."

"I hope so too. He's not at Jenson?"

"No, he never stays there."

"If you're not going to eat that last piece of bacon, I'll take it." Naughton's hand was halfway to her plate when she swatted it.

"I'm good at sharing," she told him. "Except when it comes to bacon."

"Woman after my heart," he murmured.

Bradley knew what he meant, it was just an expression, but she liked hearing the words anyway.

"I know you said you didn't want to talk about the fire, but…"

"Soon as Mad told me he'd heard arson, Calder was the first person that came to both our minds."

"There were other people here, when the fire started, who are also associated with the conglomerates."

—:—

Naughton almost dropped his fork. Instead, he squeezed the hell out of it. "Don't go there."

"But—"

"No, Bradley. Don't put yourself in the middle of this. If they're thinking arson this soon after the fire is contained, there's evidence. If there's evidence, then I believe we'll find out who's behind it."

"He asked me to gather information on the members of the collaborative."

Naughton raised his eyebrows. "Yeah? And what did you tell him?"

"I told him I wouldn't."

"Good girl. My guess is he didn't let it go that easily."

"No. He didn't." Bradley looked away again.

"What else did he say?"

"He pushed me to try to change your mind about helping, but I told him I didn't have any influence over you."

"He didn't buy it."

She shook her head.

"That's because he's right."

"Naughton, I would never."

He set his fork down, wiped his hands on his napkin, and put his arm around her. "Look at me." When she did, he leaned forward and kissed her. "I know you would never; that's not the kind of person you are."

"You hardly know me," she murmured.

"I know enough." He kissed her again, and this time she opened her mouth to his. Naughton held her chin with his fingers, keeping her where he wanted her. Everything he couldn't do when he had kissed her in his truck, he did now. He wanted to linger then, but he couldn't. He wanted to capture her tongue with his and take every breath from her. When she tried to pull back, he went deeper, and she let him.

He stopped only when they heard the diner door open and felt her tense up.

"There hasn't been a minute I've been with you that I haven't wanted to do that," he said, pulling back far enough to look in her eyes.

"Me, too."

"I'm glad to hear it."

Naughton saw something out of the corner of his eye and looked around her.

"What is it?" she asked when he slid out of the booth.

"I'm not sure. I'll be right back." He ran out the door of the diner and looked down the street. He was quick enough to catch sight of the man who went inside one of the houses.

Bradley came out of the diner door. "Naughton? What's wrong?"

"My da."

"What about him?"

Naughton shook his head. "It looked so much like him, but what would he be doing in Harmony?"

9

Naughton pulled his phone out of his pocket and called Maddox.

"Have you seen Da?" he asked when his brother answered.

"Not since this morning, why?"

"Wondering if he's home. Where are you?"

"Walking up to the barn now."

"Can you see if his truck is there?"

"Sure is. What's goin' on, Naught? Where are you?"

"I'm at Sadie's, and I swear I saw him walk into a house down the street."

"Let me check something."

Naughton watched the house while he waited.

"Shit," he heard Maddox say. "His old truck is gone. Bradley still with you?"

"Yeah."

"Bring her back."

"But what about—"

"Just bring her back, Naught. We'll talk more about this when you get here."

Naughton walked a little farther down the block and held up his hand for Bradley to wait. "What are you thinkin'?"

"That whatever is goin' on, isn't something she needs to know about."

"What makes you think something's going on?"

"Because no one drives that truck except him, and he hardly ever does." Maddox paused and Naught waited. "There's more."

"Go on."

"I thought I saw someone the last time I was in Harmony, too."

"Who?"

"I'll tell you when you get back."

Naughton disconnected the call and rubbed the back of his neck. As much as he wanted to go pound on the door of the house he had seen his father go into, what would he say if he did?

He walked back to the diner and saw Bradley hadn't moved since he motioned for her to wait. "Naughton, are you okay?"

"Yeah, just seein' things, I guess."

"It wasn't your father?"

"Nah. He's home," he lied, not knowing why exactly, other than his fear there was more to his father being in Harmony than met the eye.

It didn't look like she believed him, or maybe he was just being paranoid. When he went back inside the diner, she followed.

"You done?" he asked when they got back to their table.

"Sure. I'm done."

Naughton pulled his wallet out and threw some money on the table. "Ready?"

"You don't want to wait for the bill?"

"Don't need to, I eat here all the time."

"It's a wonder you can afford it," she mumbled.

"Why's that?"

"You just left a hundred on the table for a meal that shouldn't have cost more than twenty dollars."

Naughton shrugged, went outside, and handed Bradley her helmet.

—:—

He was lying to her, but whatever was going on really wasn't any of her business anyway. From the moment Naughton thought he saw his father, his whole demeanor changed. When she climbed on the back of his bike and put her hands on his waist, she felt his muscles tighten. She wanted to let go, but what else could she hold onto?

They drove back in silence, not that talking would've been easy on the motorcycle. He took a different way back, which brought them to Adelaida Trail from the other direction. When they came to Jenson Vineyards, he pulled in.

"My truck is at Butler Ranch," she told him after she climbed off the bike and took the helmet off.

"I'll bring it over later."

"Is there a reason you don't want me over there?"

He shook his head. "Long couple of days. Take the rest of the day off."

That just made her mad. "I don't work for you, remember?"

Instead of answering, Naughton started the bike, waved, and left.

Bradley stood with her hands on her hips and watched him drive away.

"What's going on?" her aunt asked, coming out the back door.

"I have no idea."

"Was that Naughton?"

"Yep."

Her aunt shook her head and laughed.

"What?"

"You two are a pair."

Bradley followed her back inside. "What do you mean by that? Naughton and I aren't…aren't…"

"A pair?"

"We're not."

Aunt Jean rested her palm on Bradley's cheek. "Of course you are, sweetheart."

"But I work for him."

"No, you don't. You work for Maddox."

"Why does everyone keep saying that?" she mumbled as she climbed the stairs to her room.

—:—

Maddox had been right; his father's old truck wasn't at the ranch, and he didn't need to look in the barn to confirm it. He saw it when he drove by the house he thought he had seen his father go into. Worse, there was another Butler Ranch vehicle sitting in the driveway in front of it.

"You're back," Maddox said when Naughton parked the bike and killed the engine. "Let's go inside."

Naughton followed his brother, took off his helmet, set it on Mad's kitchen table, and sat down.

"Who'd you see?" Naughton asked.

"Not wasting any time, are ya? I said I *thought* I saw someone."

Naughton really wasn't in the mood for this shit. "*Who,* Maddox?"

"Someone who looked like Kade."

Naughton slammed the chair against the wall when he stood up. He rubbed the back of his neck and paced Mad's kitchen.

"Sit back down."

Naughton spun around. "Are you serious, Mad?"

"It wasn't—"

"When?"

"The day before we went to talk to Lang."

"That was over two months ago." Naughton willed away the rage he felt building. "Why are you only saying something now?"

"I thought I was losing my mind. It was right after a fight with Alex, and I honestly thought I'd lost it."

"Why didn't you mention it when Lang said Kade had paid him a visit?"

"Because I thought he was crazy too."

"What do you think now?"

Maddox stood up and walked to the refrigerator. "Beer?"

"Hell, no. Something stronger."

Maddox took two glasses off the shelf, dropped a couple of ice cubes in each, and opened the cupboard where he stashed the booze. "What's your poison?"

"Bourbon. And lose the ice."

Mad tossed the ice in the sink and poured a couple of fingers in the glass.

"More."

Mad shook his head, poured as much again, and handed the glass to Naughton.

"Answer me. What do you think now?"

"It wasn't Kade. Let's start there. Kade is dead."

"Who was it?"

"You remember what Alex said when all that went down with Lang? She said she didn't mean any offense, but all those guys look alike. She was right, to a certain extent. From that distance, it could've been anyone."

"There was someone else from Butler Ranch there today."

"Who?"

"Don't know, but it wasn't just Da's truck I saw. The old Silverado was there too."

"Which house was it?"

"Third one down, same side of the street as Sadie's, tan siding. Is that where you thought you saw Kade?"

Maddox nodded. "Not Kade, someone who looked like him."

"Why is Da at the same house, and who else was there with him?"

"No idea."

"Do you think he was the one who drove my truck to Demetria that night?"

Maddox didn't answer right away. He stood, dumped his ice in the sink, poured himself more bourbon, but didn't turn around. "I had some time to think while I waited for you to get back."

"And?"

"There's a lot going on that doesn't add up, Naught."

When Maddox turned to face him, Naughton saw Mad was fighting against the tears just as much as he was. They may have gotten word Kade had been killed over a year and a half ago, but that didn't mean the pain of losing him was any less raw.

"Talk to me, Mad."

"I can't get the day out of my head, when Da gave me Kade's letter." Maddox gripped the back of his neck with his hand. It was something all of his brothers did when they were stressed.

"It didn't make sense then, and it still doesn't. Why did the attorney ask our parents to come to the office instead of me? You're the one who told me Peter Wendt didn't know anything about us owning the property before that. How did you know?"

"Because Kade told me where the deeds were."

"What else, Naughton? It's time you told me all of it. Every single thing you've been keeping from me. *Now!"*

Naughton understood Mad's frustration, but there wasn't all that much he knew, except about the deeds and how Kade had wanted Maddox given the news. "I'm the one who asked Wendt to call Da. I'm the one who gave him the envelopes that he passed on to our parents, who gave them to you."

The glass Maddox held in his hand shattered in his grip. *"And you're telling me this now? What the fuck, Naughton?"*

"I told you then, it was the way Kade had wanted it."

"*You goddamn hypocrite.* Not five minutes ago you railed at me for not telling you I thought I saw Kade in Harmony." Maddox went out the door of his cottage, letting it slam behind him. Instead of following, Naughton poured himself another couple of shots of bourbon and cleaned up the glass scattered on the floor.

He stood with his back to the door but didn't flinch when Mad came back through it a few minutes later, slamming it behind him again.

"*What else?*" he demanded.

"That's it."

"It was up to you, and you alone, to decide when to tell me Kade left us the land?"

Naughton nodded.

"Why?"

"Why what?"

"Why you?"

"Because I was the one who knew about you and Alex. For years, I was the only one."

"This is bullshit." Maddox slammed his fist on the counter.

"*You're getting sidetracked with things that don't matter!*" Naughton yelled.

"*How can you say they don't matter?*"

"Because that's in the past."

Naughton sat back down and finished the bourbon in his glass. "Because you know about the land. Because you and Alex are together and happy. And that's what Kade wanted for you. For you and Alex to be happy."

Naughton's eyes filled with tears he couldn't hold back any longer. He silently cursed both of his brothers. The one who stood before him, and the one who had left them both behind.

Maddox grabbed the bottle from the kitchen counter and sat down too. "What did he want for you, Naught?"

Naughton put his head in his hands. "I wish I knew."

"I wish I knew too. I wish I could understand why all this shit is happening—why Da was in Harmony, who was with him, who I saw that day when I was at Sadie's, and who the fuck set the fire. Because I gotta tell you, I feel like there's someone out there who wants to take us down."

Naughton agreed. It felt like there was more to it than Calder and his cronies from up north wanting more land on the Central Coast. If there was anyone who would be able to get to the bottom of all that was happening around them, it was Kade, and he was gone.

"I miss him so much," he murmured.

Maddox nodded. "Me, too."

They sat at the table in the kitchen until after the sun went down. When one emptied their glass, the other filled it, and neither spoke.

"What the hell?" Alex said, walking into the kitchen and finding them sitting in the dark. When she hit the light switch, both he and Mad covered their eyes. She picked up the bottle that sat empty on the table.

"Are you drunk?" She looked back and forth between the two of them until Maddox finally nodded.

"Pretty sure."

"Oh, Lord." She tossed the bottle in the trash, filled the pot with water, and scooped coffee into the filter. While she waited for it to brew, she washed out their glasses and put them in the dishwasher, and then picked up the phone Mad had left near the sink. "Just as I thought. Ringer's off."

She looked at Naughton. "Yours too?"

He shrugged. "Don't know where mine is."

Alex walked around him. "It's right here, on the counter behind you." She set it on the table in front of him.

"I've been calling you both for the last two hours."

"I'm sorry, baby." Maddox tried to pull Alex into his lap, but she swatted his hand. "Let me get your coffee first, and then you can tell me what the hell happened."

Naughton put his head in his hands, wishing he could stop the room from spinning.

"Drink this." She set a glass of water in front of him and another in front of Mad, and put her hands on her hips. "All of it." When they had, she refilled their glasses.

Naughton watched Alex open the refrigerator, get out the milk, and add a little to Mad's coffee and more to his. Alex had been a part of their lives for so long, it wasn't just that she knew how Mad liked his coffee, she knew how he liked it too.

"Thanks, sweetheart," Maddox said when she set the coffee in front of him. "I'm sorry."

"It's okay. I get it. Now tell me, what the hell happened?"

"You wanna tell her?" Maddox asked.

"What happened today or all of it?"

"She knows everything that happened up to today."

"Even about thinking you saw Kade in Harmony?"

"Oh, Lord," Alex said for the second time. "Damn, I wish you hadn't killed that bottle of bourbon. Did you see him too, Naught?"

"Not Kade. Da," Maddox answered for him.

"Okay, start at the beginning."

Naughton looked at his phone. "Crap. I can't believe it's after nine. I told Bradley I'd bring her truck over."

"I still had her phone. When she came to pick it up, she got her truck."

"Was she mad?"

"Should she have been?"

Naughton shrugged. "Hell if I know."

"I'll say this again when you're sober, but Naught, don't screw this up. Bradley is worth the effort."

"I know," he murmured.

She laughed. "That's how I know you're really drunk. Now tell me what happened this afternoon."

Naughton skipped over the time he spent with Bradley, and cut straight to thinking he saw his father in Harmony.

"Are you sure it was him?"

Naughton shrugged.

"Why didn't you go knock on the door and ask why he was there?"

"Bradley was with him," Maddox answered.

"And that made sense when you were both sober?"

Naughton nodded. "Whatever this shit is, she doesn't need to get swept up in. She's already feelin' guilty about the fire."

"*Why?*" Maddox and Alex asked at the same time.

"She thinks the boyfriend might have something to do with it."

Alex looked at Maddox, who looked at Naughton.

"What?"

"They questioned him."

"About the fire?"

"Yeah."

Naughton knocked his chair over when he jumped up from the table. "Where the hell is he? Where's she?"

Alex stood and put her hand on Naughton's arm. "Settle down. Bradley is with her aunt and uncle."

"Where's the boyfriend?"

Again, Alex looked at Maddox.

"*Just tell me!*"

"He checked out of the inn this morning, so we assume he's back in Napa."

"You assume? What if he's not?" Naughton rubbed the back of his neck. "I can't drive, I've had too much to drink. You gotta take me over there."

"What? No. She's fine. I told you she's with her aunt and uncle. You can't go over there now. You're too drunk."

"I'll walk then." He stormed out the door, letting it slam behind him. He hadn't gotten very far before Alex was on his heels.

"We'll call her, okay? Let's go back to the cottage, and I'll call her. I'm telling you, you can't go over there like this."

"Like what?"

"Drunk off your ass."

"What if he hurts her?"

"Naughton, stop and look at me." When he stopped walking, Alex stood in front of him and put her hands on his shoulders. "He isn't going to hurt her."

"Do Charlie and Jean know?"

"They know Trey was questioned about the fire, but not why. The marshal made it sound like they questioned him more about what he'd seen than where he was or if he had any involvement."

He couldn't decide if that was a good or bad thing, but it made him feel worse either way. "She's gonna blame herself."

—:—

"No, Naughton. I'm not blaming myself."

Alex jumped and Naughton stumbled backwards.

"Sorry, I didn't mean to startle you."

Alex put her hand on Bradley's arm. "Startle me? Jesus, girl. You scared the crap outta me."

Naughton leaned up against her. "Bradley, God. I'm so sorry." When she caught a whiff of his breath, she waved her hand in front of her face.

"He's shitfaced," Alex explained needlessly.

"What are you doing here?" Naughton asked. "I was so worried." He put his arm around her shoulder and rested his head against hers. "I'm so glad you're here."

"Let's go back, Naught. Now that you know Bradley's safe, we'll get some more water in you, and you can call it a night."

Naughton shook his head. "Only if you come with me," he said to Bradley. "I gotta keep you safe."

She put her arm around his waist. "I'll come back with you."

"Why are you here anyway?" Alex whispered.

"Couldn't sleep. Especially after Aunt Jean told me Trey had been questioned."

"I'm so glad you're here, Bradley," Naughton said again. "Let's go home now."

"How much did he have to drink?" Bradley whispered.

"Half a bottle of bourbon far as I can tell. Mad's in no better shape."

When Alex helped Bradley get Naughton inside his cottage, they agreed it wasn't a good idea to try to get him upstairs.

He sat down on the couch and pulled Bradley with him. "You gotta stay here, with me, tonight."

She couldn't help but smile. "I do? Why's that?" The alcohol lowered the wall Naughton kept so carefully constructed around him, and she got a glimpse of how sweet he could be. Tomorrow, though, he was going to feel like death.

"I gotta keep you safe."

"I'm not in danger, Naughton."

"You might be. You never know with all Kade's shit. We all might be in danger." Naughton closed his eyes, and his head fell back against the couch.

"What's he talking about?" Bradley asked Alex, following her into Naughton's kitchen.

"I'm not sure, but whatever it is, you can rest assured he doesn't know either."

"The fire…"

"I have my own theory about who started the fire."

"Naughton told me about Calder."

"He's my number one suspect."

"It's hard to believe this is all over wanting to buy land."

"It's a fifty-six billion a year industry, and that's just in California. Over one-hundred billion in the US."

Bradley nodded. She knew the numbers, and as daunting as they were, she still had a hard time wrapping her head around someone going to such lengths as arson.

"What did he mean by 'Kade's shit'?"

"No clue."

"I thought Kade was dead."

"He is."

"So what does he have to do with the fire?"

"He doesn't. To be honest, I can't figure out any of this. There's one thing Naughton got right in his drunken ramblings, though. There doesn't seem to be an end to Kade's shit popping up when it's least expected."

"Bradley? Where'd you go, sweetheart?"

"Oh, Lord." Alex laughed when Naughton hollered from the other room. "I should be videoing all this. She's right here, Naught. She told you she'd stay."

Alex's shoulders shook as though she was holding in laughter.

"Stop it." Bradley swatted her.

"Any vineyard secrets you want to know, now's the time to ask."

"I refuse to take advantage of a drunk man."

"Oh, sugar, you can take advantage of me all you'd like." Both Bradley and Alex startled when Naughton came into the kitchen, but kept laughing.

"Come on, Bradley. Tuck me into bed." Naughton grabbed her hand and pulled her toward the stairs.

"If this is too much, say so," Alex told her.

"I'm okay. Maybe just help me get him up the stairs. I'm guessing that's where his bedroom is."

"You think you'll like my bedroom, Bradley? Wait until you see my *bathroom.*"

"Oh, Lord," Alex said again as she helped Bradley deposit Naughton on his bed. "He's right, the bathroom is spectacular. Take a peek." She winked. "Mad's is too, although it's really different."

10

Bradley knew she shouldn't be snooping, but Naughton was out cold the minute his body landed on his mattress. His snoring confirmed it.

Naughton and Maddox referred to their houses as cottages, and they definitely had that look, from the outside at least.

They both resembled the ranch's main house, with stone facades and slate roofs. Bradley remembered what Hawks said about how the houses were constructed with concrete underneath the stone and steel beneath the roof's slate. Also like the main house, there were four dormers on the front of Naughton's cottage, embellished with black shutters.

From the outside, Naughton's looked a little bigger than Maddox's, although she hadn't been inside either until tonight.

She tiptoed down the hall and found two other bedrooms on this level. Both looked unused but had beds in them. Each had a sloped ceiling, and all the walls were painted a taupe color, except one. The accent color in the first of the smaller bedrooms was a dark, sage green. In the second, it was a warm gray.

Bradley tiptoed back to the room where Naughton was sleeping and sneaked into the bathroom. Alex hadn't been kidding, and neither had Naughton. It was spectacular.

One wall of the spacious room was stone, and the floor was too. The finish was natural, like what was used on the outside of the cottage.

Two glazed sinks sat on top of individual and very cool pedestals that were made from tree trunks, and the tub, plenty big enough for two, sat back in an alcove also surrounded by stone.

Three doors were inset in the opposite wall, which was covered in what looked like reclaimed barn wood. The first door had a one by two foot window and a control panel to the left of it. Bradley peeked in at the two-person sauna.

Behind the second door, made of tempered glass, was a steam shower, which, like the tub and sauna, was plenty big enough for two. Behind the third door, made of the same reclaimed wood as covered the wall, there was a toilet.

Relieved to hear Naughton's continued snoring, Bradley crept back into his bedroom. The accent wall in this room was painted a cool, grayish blue that complemented the wall of stone the tufted, dark leather headboard of his bed sat up against.

On the gray-blue wall, a series of black and white lithographs were hung in such a way that the angle of the grouping matched the slope of the ceiling. She wasn't certain, but if she had to guess, each of the lithographs was produced by the same artist, and the scenes depicted in the simple drawings were of places in Scotland.

On the third wall, ten rustic wood planks, each looked to be two by eight, were hung one above the other with their ends staggered slightly. On those boards was a large drawing of a grapevine that spanned from the highest board to the lowest. Bradley didn't see an artist's name anywhere on it, but she'd remember to ask Naughton. She'd love to see more of whoever's work it was.

The last wall held a massive arts and crafts-style armoire that was easily over ten feet tall. Celtic designs adorned the inlaid stained glass panels on each side of the piece, which held eight drawers. Next to it was another door, which led to a well-organized walk-in closet. She expected nothing less of Naughton.

A tufted-leather oversized chair, which matched the bed's headboard, sat near a window. Bradley couldn't imagine a better spot to cozy up with a good book. When she saw a fisherman's knit throw and a basket of books on the floor near it, she switched off the light near Naughton's bed, turned the floor lamp on by the chair, and settled in to read.

—:—

That's the way Naughton found Bradley a few hours later, with a book open on her lap and her head resting against the arm of the chair.

He didn't remember a lot from the night before, other than asking her to stay with him, which he felt like a complete ass for doing. He should wake her, but he couldn't bring himself to. She looked like an angel with the glow of the soft light streaming through the window, resting on her.

The headache he'd anticipated didn't materialize, and he vaguely recalled her or Alex giving him a couple of pills before they helped him climb the stairs. He wondered how Mad was faring this morning; his brother had as much bourbon as he'd had.

Bradley stretched her arms above her head, opened her eyes, and sat up in the chair. "Hi," she murmured.

"You caught me staring. Good morning, beautiful." Naughton ran his hand over her silky hair. "Doesn't look like a very comfortable place to sleep."

Bradley set the book back in the basket and scooted forward like she was going to stand. "How are you feeling this morning?" she asked.

"Stay where you are. I love how you look with the light coming in the window. If I had a sketchbook, I'd draw you this way."

"Do you draw?"

"Not as much as I used to." Naughton pointed to the grapevine drawn on the wood planks. "I did that one about five years ago."

"It's gorgeous. I was looking for an artist's signature. I love it."

"Thank you. Maybe I'll show you some of my other work one day."

"I'd like that."

When she tried again to stand, Naughton knelt in front of her and ran his fingers down the side of her face. "You stayed."

"You asked me to."

"Not exactly the way I imagined us together in my bedroom for the first time."

When she closed her eyes, leaned against his hand, and her cheeks turned that perfect shade of rosé, he leaned forward and covered her lips with his.

"Maybe you'll come back again sometime," he whispered.

She smiled. "Maybe."

"How about if I cook a big breakfast to make up for last night?"

"You don't have to do that."

"I want to."

He caught her sneak a glimpse at her phone.

"Work's a no-go today. It's Labor Day, and the winery is closed."

"But there's so much to do."

"Not today, there isn't. We're not even opening the tasting room."

Bradley looked from him to the bedroom door.

"Come on, sleeping beauty. Let's get some breakfast." Naughton took her hand and walked down the stairs and into the kitchen. He pulled the chair out from the table and motioned for her to sit.

"You don't have to do this. I can go home."

"I don't want you to go home."

"I can help."

"That's an offer I'll take you up on."

Naughton showed Bradley where he kept the coffee and pointed to the coffeemaker. "You can use that, or there's a French Press in that cupboard." She opened the cupboard, took out the press, and filled the tea kettle sitting on the stove with water.

He smiled. "My preference too."

"Are you sure about not working today?"

"Mad and I talked about it earlier yesterday, and we aren't crushing until tomorrow. Butler Ranch employees, along with most of those from other wineries, have been here, working around the clock as it is. We all need a day off."

"Okay, well…"

"Say it. Whatever's on your mind."

Bradley shook her head. "It's nothing."

"If it's nothing, it's something."

"I don't want to intrude."

Naughton set the pan he'd gotten out to cook bacon on down and stood with his hands on either side of her, trapping her between him and the counter. Instead of reassuring her with words, he used his lips first, and then his tongue. He kissed her lips, and then each of her eyelids, the tip of her nose, her cheek, and her neck, beneath her ear. When he felt her arms circle his waist, he pressed his body into hers, letting her feel exactly how much he wanted her there with him, in his arms, his kitchen, and soon he hoped, in his bed.

The kettle on the stove whistled, and Naughton stepped back to turn the burner off. Bradley moved from where she was so her back was to him.

"You're quiet this morning," he said.

Bradley turned around. "You're not."

"No?"

"You've said more words between last night and this morning than you've said since I met you."

"There's a lot I want to tell you."

Bradley turned back toward the counter.

"What just happened? And don't say nothing."

Bradley shook her head, and Naughton walked over to her. "Turn around and look at me. Tell me what upset you."

Bradley turned around and looked everywhere but at him. Naughton bent his knees and leaned over until he was in her line of vision. "Tell me."

"It isn't any of my business."

"Sleeping with me changed everything. Now it's all your business."

That made her smile. "I didn't sleep with you."

"I was asleep. You were asleep. Both in the same room. That's sleeping together."

She smiled again. "You really can be charming when you want to be."

"I feel as though that wasn't all you wanted to say."

When Bradley tried to turn away again, he held her tight. "Just say it."

"Okay, I will, but you asked for this."

"I'm ready. Give me your worst."

"You lied to me yesterday, and then you were cold, and distant, and…rude."

"The trifecta."

"Why? If it's none of my business, just say so, but don't lie."

"You lied, and I didn't like it either."

"When?"

"At Demetria. When you said you didn't want me to kiss you."

"It's not the same, and don't change the subject."

Naughton let her go and went back to the bacon. "I saw my father in Harmony yesterday, and it threw me."

"Enough that you lied to me."

"Yep."

"You said some other things last night. Alex said you wouldn't remember, but…"

"Go ahead. Tell me."

"You said we might all be in danger because of your brother."

"It's hazy, but I do remember saying something like that."

"And?"

"I'm going to be very honest with you now, Bradley, so pay attention."

"Okay."

"A lot of shit has happened in the valley in the last few months, not just with Calder, but with our family too. There are secrets that have come to light, but none of us—not Maddox, Brodie, or I—believe we've uncovered all of them."

"Kade's secrets?"

"Yes. And when I saw my father yesterday, I realized it isn't just Kade's secrets. There's something else going on that I know nothing about."

"And neither does Maddox?"

"He doesn't know any more than I do, or that Brodie knows."

"Why didn't you just ask your father?"

He wasn't sure how to answer that question. Fear maybe. Or not wanting to open up the wound of Kade's death again.

"If you saw your father out, somewhere you'd never expect him to be, and there was evidence he was hiding something, would you knock on the door and ask?"

Bradley thought it over. "No," she said after a couple of minutes. "I guess I wouldn't."

"Let's not talk about this anymore. We'll have breakfast, I'll take you home, and then come back around one, and we'll go wine tasting this afternoon."

"I'd like that. I was thinking, the other day, that I should make a point of visiting some of the other wineries. I haven't had much time to do it in the past."

"It'll give me the chance to thank some of them for their help the last couple days."

"Do you think Alex and Maddox might like to go along?"

Naughton smiled. This would be a first. In all the years Mad and Alex were together, he'd gone out with the two of them, but he'd never brought a date. This was a date, wasn't it? He pulled out his phone and sent a text to both of them. Within seconds, Alex answered.

"Did you ask?"

"I did, and she answered. They're in."

—:—

"Tell Naught your idea, Al," Maddox said as they walked up the steps to the entrance of Pear Valley Winery.

"I think we should host a dinner at Los Cab, to thank everyone who came out to help after the fire. It needs to be this week, before we get into the thick of harvest."

"That's a great idea," said Bradley. "I'll help. When are you thinking?"

"Wednesday. It won't be hard to get the word out. Stave has been getting calls from people who want to know what they can do to help. That's where I got the idea. To be honest, it was more Peyton's idea than mine."

"That's not much time."

Alex put her arm around Bradley's shoulders. "Not to worry. Here in the valley, we know how to get it done."

"What do you think, Naught?" Maddox asked.

"Sounds like a lot of work, but then we owe them, don't we?"

Maddox shook his head. "Come on, ya big grump. Let's get these pretty young things some wine."

"I'm glad we did this," Alex said while she and Bradley waited outside on the patio. "We needed a break from all the bad juju swirling around us."

"Good way to describe it."

"It's like it blows in and then blows away, and as soon as you think it's gone, it blows back."

Bradley could see Naughton standing near the bar inside. She watched as he stepped back while Maddox talked. He smiled and nodded his head, but it didn't look like he said much.

"Whatcha' thinkin' about?" Alex nudged her.

"How quiet he is."

"Our Naught isn't much of a talker."

Bradley shrugged.

"You don't agree?"

"Sometimes he is."

"Ooh, I'm going to enjoy this. Tell me more," Alex teased.

"There's nothing to tell really…" Bradley's eyes hadn't left Naughton, so when his expression changed—even his whole body—she watched it happen. "Uh, oh."

"What?" Alex asked, following Bradley's line of sight. "Oh, shit. What the hell is he doing here?"

"Who?"

"Calder."

"Should we go in?"

"I'm not sure. Let's wait a minute. Naughton won't want you in there, that I'm sure of. Maddox knows I can't stand Calder, and probably worries I'd make an even bigger mess of it."

Both Bradley and Alex gasped when they saw Naughton reach back and throw a punch at Calder. When she jumped up, Alex put her hand on Bradley's arm. "Just wait," she said.

The next thing they saw from their outdoor vantage was a group holding Calder back, and then moving him away from the bar. No one seemed to be holding Naughton back.

"What's happening?" Bradley asked.

"I think they're throwing him out."

"Who?"

"Calder. Definitely not Naughton."

At that moment, Naughton turned and looked at Bradley. The look he had on his face was the same one she'd seen at Sadie's. It was like a curtain had lowered on the Naughton she was with this morning, and when it went back up, a different man was standing in his place.

"I should go," she said to Alex.

"What? Why? Naughton is—"

"He doesn't want me here anymore."

"Where is this coming from, Bradley?"

"Look at him."

He'd turned his back to them, but Bradley could see his shoulders slowly round. Something haunted him, and whatever it was, he wouldn't want her to see.

11

The internal war raged inside him. In the last twenty-four hours, Bradley had seen him at his worst. A drunk first, and now, a brawler. Those weren't the only two demons he kept buried inside.

The day Kade first took Naughton to see the property on Old Creek Road, his oldest brother had called him out on those demons.

"Feed the white wolf," Kade always said.

Naughton had heard reference to the Cherokee legend from his brother so many times while he was growing up. So often that he confronted Kade about it.

"I don't ever hear you say this shit to Maddox or Brodie. Why are you always on me?" he'd said.

"When I look at you sometimes, I feel as though I'm looking in a mirror. You hold it all inside."

"What's wrong with that?"

"To hold it in, you have to keep yourself closed."

"What keeps you up at night?" Kade had asked.

"What do you mean?"

"When you're lying in bed, unable to sleep, what haunts you?"

"I don't know."

"I'll tell you what haunts me if you want me to."

"Go ahead," Naughton had prodded him.

"The day the man I am meets the man I could've become. That's my private hell, Naughton."

"There's nothing wrong with the man you are."

"But what of the man I could've been?"

But what of the man I could've been? He'd never truly understood those words until this moment—looking out from where he stood at the woman who made him want to be a better man.

He saw her fear, her worry, but what else? Disdain? Or was he imagining it? He turned his back to her, afraid of what else he might see.

You hold it all inside. Isn't that what he was supposed to do? Keep the anger inside, where he couldn't hurt anyone with it? It had escaped moments ago, when Calder got in his face and taunted him.

If Kade had been with him today instead of Maddox, his oldest brother would've sensed his turmoil and stopped him. It wouldn't have been the first time Kade prevented him from letting his anger loose.

Feed the white wolf. The white wolf is filled with peace, love, hope, courage, humility, compassion, and faith. That's how the legend went.

When he felt a strong hand on his shoulder, Naughton closed his eyes and wished, for just a moment, that it was Kade's hand. He missed him so much that sometimes he felt as though his chest would open from the pressure of his broken heart.

"Naught," came Mad's voice. "He's gone."

"I hate that sonuvabitch."

"You're not alone in that."

"I'm alone in letting him provoke me to the point that I hit him."

"I'm sorry. What he said is complete bullshit. I should've stepped in."

Naughton turned to look at Maddox. "Why?"

"I don't know…because I'm the big brother. Because Kade would've."

"Kade wouldn't have let me hit him."

"No, he wouldn't have. Instead, he would've had some cut-him-off-at-the-knees comeback that Calder wouldn't have figured out until days later."

"He was a smart bastard, wasn't he?"

Naughton was afraid to turn around and look outside. "Is she gone?"

"Who?"

"Bradley."

"Of course not. She and Alex are waiting for us."

"You sure?"

"I don't know why you think they wouldn't be, but turn around and see for yourself."

Naughton turned slowly and saw Maddox was right. Bradley's back was to him, and Alex was talking to her. He knew Alex well enough to be able to read her expression. It was some kind of lecture; he'd been on the receiving end of enough from her to know. Bradley nodded and turned when Alex pointed in his direction.

When their eyes met, Naughton raised his hand and waved. Bradley waved back. Neither smiled.

"Go," Maddox nudged him.

Naughton picked up two glasses that had been filled with the first wine on the tasting list and walked toward the patio, and Maddox followed.

"I'm surprised you two feel like drinking today." Alex took a glass from Maddox and winked.

"Water and acetaminophen does the trick every time. Thanks for taking care of me, Al." Maddox put his arm around Alex's waist.

Naughton handed Bradley a glass and motioned for her to follow him to the other side of the patio.

"I'm sorry you saw that," he said. "The guy knows how to get under my skin."

"How long have you known him?"

"I don't know him, which is why I don't understand why he tried to frame me for the Los Cab incident."

Kade had asked him what kept him up at night, and right now, it was Calder. It had to be personal, but Naughton had no idea why.

"My uncle doesn't like him either."

"Not surprising."

Bradley swirled and smelled the wine. "Holy cow," she commented. "Perfumey."

Naughton swirled and stuck his nose in his glass. "Yeasty."

"Brioche," she murmured, and Naughton agreed.

"Good nose."

She rolled her eyes and smiled. "I better." She took a sip. "Very different on the palate. I didn't expect so much lime, or the minerality to be so sparse. The stone fruit is expected in an Albariño." Bradley lowered her voice. "It's a little green, though."

Naughton agreed with every comment she made. The wine tasted hurried. Fruit picked too soon; wine released too early. Bradley's palate was highly developed for someone her age, but then Naughton would bet she'd gone into wine tasting with no preconceived ideas. Charlie Jenson probably taught her to trust her instincts, not taste what a wine should be, just what it was.

It was the same way his father had taught his siblings and him about tasting. They had started very young, tasting raw juice. They learned what the fruit of each varietal tasted like before the introduction of yeast or acids—before fermentation. When he was too young yet to write, his da would tell him to draw what he first smelled, and then tasted, in the juice. While his siblings' drawings were rudimentary, Naughton's were detailed, and very specific.

"What are you thinking about?" Bradley asked.

"Nothing."

She smirked. "If it's nothing, it's something."

"Do you remember the first time you tasted?"

Bradley nodded. "Like it was yesterday."

"What was your first?"

"Raw Chard."

Naughton smiled.

"You?" she asked.

"I remember, but not the varietal. I figured you would. Do you remember how old you were?"

"My first memory was when I was five, but Aunt Jean says I was much younger, like two or three."

"Same for me and my brothers and sisters."

"Are you and Maddox the only two that wanted to work in the vines?"

"Brodie, too. But he's more of the salesperson. You know from the fire that he knows his way around the vineyard."

"Right. Of course." Her cheeks pinkened.

"You never have a reason to be embarrassed with me, Bradley."

"What do your sisters do?"

"Skye's focused on her kids; she has two. Spencer is three, and Kade was born in July."

"Two boys? I love that she named the youngest one Kade."

Naughton smiled. "Skye made sure we were all okay with it before she did. And we were, obviously.

Spencer, though, is a girl. I guess she has that in common with you. You'll have to tell her not to let anyone get away with what I did to you."

She smiled too.

"What about your other sister?"

"Ainsley is…I don't know what she is. Still in school, on a business track."

"I don't have any brothers or sisters."

"I remember you telling me you didn't."

"No cousins either."

"What was that like?"

"Quiet. Lonely."

"I like quiet."

Bradley smiled and held up her glass. "What's next?"

"Your choice of Chenin Blanc or Sauv Blanc."

"Chenin Blanc, please."

That was his choice too, although he'd get the Sauv Blanc, just so she could taste both.

"I asked them to pull the Aglianico for later," Naughton said when he came back with the next tastes.

"Oh, good."

—:—

"You haven't really seen the best of me," he blurted after they'd had a couple of sips of wine.

Bradley raised her eyebrows. "I haven't?"

"You've seen a lot of the worst."

"I don't know. I've seen some I guess."

"Kade used to talk to me about the legend of the white and black wolf."

"The conflict of inner forces."

Naughton nodded. "You know it?"

"After my mom died, my father insisted I see a therapist. I talked more about him than my mom."

Naughton listened but didn't say anything.

"My dad was eaten up when my mom died. A drunk driver…" Her eyes filled with tears, something that didn't happen as often anymore when she talked about her mom. Why was she telling him this?

"Go on, Bradley," he whispered.

"His anger scared me more than anything else."

"Understandable. You weren't very old."

"I kept a lot buried so I didn't upset him. The therapist said then that it wasn't up to me to starve his black wolf; it was up to him."

He nodded again.

"He'd get very angry, to the point where he'd throw things…" She had to stop talking about this. Her eyes were already full of tears. If she said anything more, she'd cry right here, on the patio of Pear Valley.

"Come on," Naughton said and took her hand. "Let's walk."

He led her down the steps from the patio to the lawn, where people were having picnics and playing corn hole. Naughton kept walking, leading her into the vineyards. How did he know the peace they brought her?

"The summer after she died, he wouldn't let me come stay with Aunt Jean and Uncle Charlie. It was the only place I wanted to be, and he wouldn't let me. The next year he did."

"What made him change his mind?"

"Now that I think about it, probably the therapist. I was filled with guilt about it though. Leaving him alone, and how I never wanted to come home. I wanted to stay with my aunt and uncle forever. I've never told anyone that, not even the therapist." How had they gotten on this topic? "I'm sorry, I don't know why I'm telling you this."

"Inner turmoil."

"Right."

"Do I remind you of your father?"

Bradley's breath caught. It was obvious he did, otherwise why would she have told Naughton about her dad when all he'd mentioned was the legend? "Sometimes," she murmured. God, he'd cut right to the thick of it, hadn't he?

"I'm sorry."

He held her hand as they walked through the rows and rows of vines.

"You should stay away from me."

It was the second time Naughton had warned her away from him, and part of her agreed with him. There were certainly enough logical reasons why she should.

For her, the most important reason was how unprofessional it was. As everyone reminded her, she worked for Maddox, but that was semantics. She worked for Butler Ranch Winery, and Naughton was their vineyard manager.

As far as her relationship with Trey, that was over. She didn't care if she ever saw or talked to him again.

"Bradley?"

"You're too hard on yourself. There are times you remind me of my father, but you haven't heard all I love about him."

He smiled. "You're too easy on me."

"You're a good man, Naughton."

He pulled his phone out of his pocket. "Sorry," he said before he looked at it. "Maddox has asked us to come back."

Before he put the phone back in his pocket, another text came through. "Sorry," he said again.

Naughton gripped the back of his neck and closed his eyes.

"What is it?" Bradley asked.

"A text from Brodie. They've made an arrest."

"Who?"

12

"He didn't say, but we need to leave."

Bradley nodded and followed Naughton back up the steps to where Maddox and Alex were waiting.

"Brodie text you?" Maddox asked him.

"Yeah, but he didn't say who was arrested."

"He told me the sheriff asked to meet us at the house."

Naughton cringed inside. He wasn't prepared to see his father yet. Instead of getting drunk last night, he and Maddox should've come up with a plan for how and when to confront him. One thing he knew for certain, they wouldn't do it in front of their mother.

Back in March, she'd suffered a heart attack. While it had been mild, it was one of the reasons he and his brothers kept putting off telling their parents about Kade's marriage to Lena Hess.

Whatever his father had been doing in Harmony was something they'd get to the bottom of, without her involvement.

"I hate to ask this," Alex began on their ride back, "But do you think your father is having an affair?"

"No," both he and Maddox answered at the same time, although the thought had crossed Naughton's mind. He wondered if Maddox might have considered the possibility too.

"Sorcha would string him up in the vineyard." Alex laughed, and Naughton turned to look at Bradley. She and Alex were in the back seat of the Tahoe, and Bradley was sitting behind Maddox, who was driving. She was looking out the window, so he couldn't see her face, but he could tell from the set of her jaw that she was tense.

"Where are you going?" Naughton asked when Maddox drove past the Butler Ranch gates.

"Dropping Bradley at Jenson."

"It's okay, Naughton," he heard her murmur.

"It's not okay. I want you with me."

"Naught…" Maddox began, but turned around.

"We'll wait in the winery. Will that work, guys?" Alex asked.

It would be better than having her go to Jenson, although he knew she'd still be stressed, wondering if Trey Deveux was the person who'd been arrested.

"Go to my place instead," Naughton said to Alex, who nodded. "Okay?" he asked Bradley, who nodded too.

—:—

Peyton was waiting on the front porch when Maddox pulled up to the main house.

She walked down the steps and over to Alex, who pulled her into a hug.

"I've felt so far away," Bradley heard her say. "I'm sorry I wasn't here to help with the fire."

Alex patted her belly. "You gotta keep my god-daughter healthy and happy. Come with Bradley and me. We're waiting at Naughton's."

"Hi, Bradley," Peyton said as they walked over to the cottage. "Brodie told me they wouldn't have known what to do if you hadn't come to work for Butler Ranch. He said they might've lost everything if it wasn't for your quick thinking."

"That's right," Alex added. "You should've seen how organized she had it all."

"Just did my job," she murmured and looked back at the house. The sheriff's car was parked out front, along with the fire marshal's. What were they telling the Butler family? If Trey had anything to do with the fire, she'd never forgive herself. Worse, she wasn't sure how she'd be able to live with the guilt of knowing he'd used the excuse of wanting to see her to be in Paso Robles this weekend.

"Come inside." Alex ushered her into Naughton's kitchen.

"Don't know about you, but I could use some coffee."

"Sure," Bradley said, and went to the cupboard where Naughton kept his French press.

"Uh, I didn't mean you should make it." Alex nudged Peyton. "But I am curious to know how you know your way around Naughton's kitchen."

"Me, too," added Peyton.

Bradley felt the heat rise in her cheeks. "He made breakfast this morning."

"Whoa, back up. I'm really out of the loop. He made you breakfast? Alex…" Peyton stood and slugged her. "How come you didn't tell me about Naught and Bradley?"

Alex rubbed her arm. "Jeez, you been workin' out or somethin'?"

"It wasn't what you think. I was here last night because Naughton had too much to drink and asked me to stay. Nothing happened. I slept in the chair upstairs."

"Way to over-explain, girlfriend. But take it from me, Peyton, if Naughton has his way, he'll be making our Bradley a lot more breakfasts."

She smiled even though all she could think about was who had been arrested. If it was Trey, not only would Naughton never make her breakfast, he'd probably never want to see her again.

Alex stood and opened the refrigerator. "Who's hungry? Damn, look at all this food. Maddox never has any food at his place."

"I'm hungry." Peyton stood and looked over Alex's shoulder. "But I'm always hungry. Bradley, what about you?"

"No, thanks. I'm good."

Alex was getting food out of the fridge while Peyton looked around for dishes.

"They're in here." Bradley opened a cupboard and took out plates, and then opened a drawer and took out silverware.

"Sure seems like you've had breakfast here more than once. Brodie used to live here too, and I don't know where anything is in this kitchen."

"That's because he always stayed at your place. Me? Maddox never stayed at my place. He always made me come stay with him."

"Aren't you both living in the house on Old Creek Road now?" Peyton asked.

"Pretty much. It was mostly furnished, so Maddox hasn't moved much out of his cottage, but he needs to."

"Bradley, aren't you living with your aunt and uncle?" Peyton asked.

She nodded. "For now."

"Alex, maybe you should talk to Maddox about letting Bradley move into his place once you're at Demetria full time."

"That's a great idea, although…"

"Although what?" Bradley asked.

"Why would you need to stay at Mad's place when Naughton would happily have you stay here?"

"I don't think Naughton would want me to *stay* here. And as far as me moving into Mad's place—that's silly. I'm just across the street."

"I'll talk to him," Alex said to Peyton. "It's brilliant really."

"Wait. I don't think it's brilliant."

"Yeah? Well, we're older and smarter." Alex pulled her phone out at the same time Peyton did.

"They want us to come up to the house." When Bradley sat down at the table, Alex pulled her back up. "All of us."

—:—

They didn't know any more than they had this morning, except that arson was conclusive. A migrant vineyard worker had been arrested after a tip came in from one of the other workers who said they saw him start the fire.

No one believed that was all there was to it, although the man had been questioned for a couple of hours and hadn't confessed anyone else's involvement.

"Someone paid him," Naughton said.

"The man had no known connection to Butler Ranch, so that seems likely," Laird commented, and then rested his hand on Sorcha's shoulder.

"Da, maybe the two of you go back to the beach for a few more days," Maddox suggested.

"If Alex doesn't mind," Sorcha said as Alex came inside, followed by Peyton and Bradley.

"Mind what?"

"If they stay at your place a while longer," Maddox answered.

Alex walked over to Sorcha and knelt in front of her. "You can stay there as long as you'd like."

Sorcha cupped Alex's cheek with her palm. "Thank you, sweetheart."

"We'll leave after the sheriff is done talking with us," said Laird.

Naughton walked over to Bradley and put his arm around her shoulders. "I was worried you'd gone back to your aunt and uncle's. I'm glad you didn't."

She nodded and turned when the sheriff asked for everyone's attention.

"What was said in this room, stays in this room. "I'll be in touch when we know more."

Once their parents and the sheriff had left, Maddox reiterated what his father had said about agreeing the migrant worker hadn't acted alone, which led to a lot of questions from Alex about that evidence they'd found and what the next steps would be.

"Trey could still be involved," Bradley whispered to Naughton.

"So could Calder."

"I feel so…powerless."

Naughton understood. He felt the same way, knowing there was someone out there who was doing their best to take down Butler Ranch and Los Caballeros.

"What happens next?" she asked him.

"The sheriff's office will hold a press conference saying they've made an arrest, after which, they'll let everyone believe the case is closed."

"So whoever it is acts again?"

"Or they find more evidence."

"Trey threatened my aunt and uncle. I need to warn them."

"Not yet," Naughton told her. "The collaborative will meet this week, and we'll make sure everyone is on high alert, but we have to abide by what the sheriff said. What he told us stays in this room. No one outside of the family can know the investigation is still active."

—:—

"I'm outside of your family, Naughton."

"No, you're not. You're part of the Butler Ranch family, just like Alex and Peyton are."

"It isn't the same. I just work here." And not for very long at that.

"It's the same as far as I'm concerned."

"Do you plan to tell Hawks?"

"No, we don't."

"Why not?"

"Tell her what Calder said to set you off today, Naught," Maddox said.

Naughton shook his head.

"Tell her," Maddox said again.

"What did he say?" Bradley asked.

"It was stupid. I shouldn't have let him get to me."

Maddox refused to budge. "If you don't tell her, I will."

"He told us to mind the new fox in our hen house."

Bradley felt sick to her stomach, a feeling that hadn't gone away completely since she first heard there was a fire at the ranch. "He was talking about me, wasn't he?"

"Who knows what the hell he was talking about. Could've been Hawks."

"Do you really think that?"

Naughton shook his head.

"I have to go." Bradley walked toward the front door, but Naughton wasn't very far behind.

"Don't run," he said.

"I'm not running."

"Then stop."

"I'm going home. I never should've taken this job in the first place."

Naughton went around her and stopped. "Why not?"

There were a thousand reasons, too many of which echoed in her head in Trey's voice.

Naughton put his hands on her shoulders and forced her to stop walking. "No one puts credence in anything Calder says. He'll dig his own grave soon enough."

"I can't keep this from my aunt and uncle. Trey threatened them."

"Tell me what he said. Exact words."

"He said, 'Even I won't be able to step in and save Jenson if you refuse to do what I've asked.'"

"That's what you can tell them. Nothing else about the arrest. Okay?"

Bradley thought it over for a minute. That was enough to warn them, wasn't it? Knowing an arrest had been made, coupled with Trey's warning, would surely lead them to believe there was still a threat.

"Okay."

"Good. Now come back to the house with me."

"I can't. I need to talk to them."

"I'll come with you."

Bradley shook her head. You need to get back to your family, and I need to get back to mine. I'll see you tomorrow."

Naughton's hands were still on her shoulders, keeping her from leaving. He leaned in closer and kissed her, but this time he was gentle, not demanding like the other times they'd kissed. He stroked her hair away from her face as his kiss deepened.

Bradley wanted to cling to him, to let him take her back to his cottage, and make all the terrible stuff swirling in her head go away.

"Let me walk you back," he said, and she relented. His hand that rested on the small of her back felt reassuring. She brought her fingers to her lips still tingling from his kiss, wishing things were different, that there'd never been a fire, and she didn't have to worry about Aunt Jean and Uncle Charlie.

All she'd ever wanted to do was make wine, and not in Napa Valley where there'd be constant pressure to produce something great, but here, where she'd first learned to love it. Why couldn't things stay that simple? Naughton may feel as though someone had it in for Butler Ranch, but she was beginning to feel as though someone had it in for her.

—:—

Naughton kissed her again when they got to the front door of her aunt and uncle's house. She didn't invite him in, not that he'd expected her to. He couldn't help but feel disappointed anyway, having held out hope she'd change her mind. He didn't feel right letting go of the hand he had held as they walked down Adelaida Trail, or saying goodnight to her now.

In his drunken stupor last night, his need to protect her had come to the surface, and now that it had, he couldn't push it back down.

"You probably think I'm crazy," he said.

"Why?"

"I don't want to let go of you. I don't want to be away from you, even for a few hours. Crazy, right?"

"No," she said so softly, he had to strain to hear her. "I don't think you're crazy at all."

When she opened the door and went inside, Naughton felt empty, like he was leaving part of himself here on the Jenson's doorstep.

Maddox was waiting for him when he walked up to his cottage. "We need to talk about Da," he said.

Naughton knew they needed to, but he just didn't have it in him today. His father hadn't said much when the sheriff was at the house. He'd sat, holding their mother's hand, and looked so sad, it nearly broke Naughton's heart.

"He's hiding something, Naughton, and whatever it is, is weighing heavy on him. I'm worried about him."

"Let's wait until tomorrow, Mad."

Maddox shook his head but squeezed his brother's shoulder as he walked by him.

"You and Alex going to Demetria now?"

"Nah. She's with Peyton at her parents' place, and I told her I'd wait until she got back. Think it's better we stay here for a few nights anyway."

"I'll go over and check on the horses, then."

"I can go."

"I want to talk to Hawks anyway."

Naughton had given him a key to the house by the front gate and asked Hawks to stay until they could bring the horses back to Butler Ranch. There wasn't much furniture in it, but enough that Hawks would be comfortable.

He went into the barn to get his bike and missed Bradley even more when he put the helmet she'd worn back into the storage cabinet where he kept it.

He pulled the bike out of the garage and got on the road, the memory of her arms around his waist and her body flush against his, fresh on his mind.

Hawks had heard an arrest had been made, but without Naughton confirming one way or the other, deduced on his own that there was more to it.

"Someone put him up to it," Hawks said, and Naughton shrugged his shoulders.

"I mean it, Naught."

"Migrant farm worker, Hawks. Hard to say what he might've been thinkin'."

"Is that what they told you? They arrested Johnny Vatos."

He nodded, Vatos was the name the sheriff gave them, but he didn't remember the man's first name. It wasn't Johnny though, of that Naughton was sure.

"He ain't no migrant farm worker, Naught. I've known Johnny since we were kids. He got himself in a lot of trouble over the years, but nothin' like this. Been mostly piddly shit. Stole some cars, broke into houses when he was younger. Got hooked on drugs, you know how that story goes."

"How well did you say you know him?"

"Since we were kids, man. We go way back."

"How could a guy you've known all your life be mistaken for a migrant worker? Maybe it's a different Vatos, Hawks."

"Not according to what I've been hearing from my guys."

"You look into it from your end, and I'll do the same. If you're sure it's your buddy, it might be worth payin' him a visit."

"I was thinkin' the same thing." Hawks scrubbed his hand over his face. "Naught, there's something else I need to tell you."

"Yeah?"

"It's about your father."

Shit. What now? "Go ahead."

"I'm not sure how to say this."

"Just tell me."

13

Naughton's head was spinning. Hawks had it wrong. There had to be an explanation for what he told him because Naughton could never believe his father would do what Hawks had accused him of.

He turned into the gates at Butler Ranch and, out of the corner of his eye, saw a red Alfa Romeo headed in his direction. He pulled the bike over, near the trees inside the gate, and cut the engine. The top was up on the convertible, but Naughton could see well enough to recognize the man driving the car and the woman seated next to him.

What the hell? Why was Bradley with the boyfriend? He thought about following them, but why? To deepen the hole he felt forming in his gut?

No wonder she'd been so adamant about going home, saying she needed time with her family.

Had Calder called it correctly? As soon as his back was turned, did Bradley report everything she'd learned this afternoon to a man she told him earlier she believed might be behind the fire in their vineyards?

It didn't make sense. When Maddox hired Bradley, Naughton believed her loyalty would always be with Jenson Vineyards, but maybe he'd gotten it wrong. Maybe her loyalties were with the boyfriend and Mumm Napa. He hated the thoughts churning in his head, echoing the words Calder spoke earlier in the day.

He had to believe there was an explanation. He couldn't accept the woman he felt such a strong connection to, from the moment he had met her—even when he still believed she was some guy named Bradley's girlfriend—could betray him and his family.

The same with his father. Between the two, Naughton felt as though he was losing it. Ever since they got word Kade had been killed, there had been a never-ending stream of strange shit swirling around him and his family.

Earlier, Maddox said he should've stepped in when Calder was taunting him because that's what Kade would've done. Is that what Kade had *always* done? Had he always stepped in to make sure this kind of shit never touched his family?

—:—

This was probably the stupidest thing she'd ever done, but when Trey called and said he was sorry and begged her to let him explain, she agreed to listen. But only because she had her own reason for wanting to see him, and it wasn't to forgive him. If he had anything to do with the fire at Butler Ranch, she had a better chance than anyone of picking up on something he might let slip that would tie him to it.

He said he'd pick her up, and when she offered to meet him instead, he was insistent.

"Where are we going?" she asked when he came to the door.

"Somewhere to talk. I was thinking La Cosecha."

"That'll work. I'm starving,"

Trey closed the front door behind them, and she saw the top was up on his Alfa Romeo. "What's this? I thought there was no point in having a convertible if you drive with the top up."

"I know you don't like it, so I put it up when I got here."

She didn't believe him. There must be another reason, but she didn't care, unless it had something to do with the fire.

They were almost to Butler Ranch when she saw the motorcycle make a left into their gate. There was no doubt in her mind that it was Naughton.

Instead of sliding down in the seat like she wanted to, she turned her body toward Trey. "Thanks for calling today," she began, hoping that Naughton was through the gate and didn't see them drive by.

"I couldn't leave things between us this way."

"I was sure you'd gone back to Napa."

"No."

Interesting that he didn't say a word about being questioned about the fire. Maybe they weren't letting him leave.

"Are you still staying at the inn?"

"Nah. I moved to a place downtown."

A place? Why didn't Trey want her to know where he was staying?

Trey pulled up in front of the restaurant and parked in an area clearly marked as a loading zone. She didn't say anything, because it was the kind of thing he did all the time.

"No one's gonna tow this baby," he'd say about the car he treated like an offspring. She wished, just once, someone would and teach him a lesson.

"I didn't mean the things I said, Brad," Trey began while they waited for the hostess to seat them. "I'd rather sit in the bar, if that's okay with you."

Bradley nodded, not caring where they sat. She wanted to get this over with as quickly as possible and be on her way back to her aunt and uncle's.

The feeling of him resting his hand on the small of her back as they walked into the bar, made her skin crawl. It was so different from the way she had felt earlier, when Naughton's hand reassured her.

"You have no idea the kind of pressure we're under," he said once they were seated. "Everyone in Napa is panicking, grasping at any straw they can. You wouldn't believe the kind of stuff going on up there."

"Or down here," she commented, which made him pause.

"I acted like a jackass and I'm sorry. It's just that…"

"What?"

"You have to understand, there are people who believe Naughton Butler can help us. That he's refused, doesn't sit well."

"You said the wine conglomerates will stop at nothing. Does that include setting vineyards on fire?"

"No, no. That isn't what I meant. Money, they're willing to throw whatever money he wants at him, but he won't even discuss it."

"He doesn't think he can help."

Trey picked up his water glass and took a drink.

"We think he can." Trey waved the bartender over.

"What can I get ya?" he asked.

"Couple of drinks. Brad, what would you like?"

She didn't want anything but to get away from Trey. How had she ever thought she might want to spend her life with him? Once she saw how Maddox was with Alex, and Brodie with Peyton, she realized how different her relationship with Trey was. Not just different, it was so apparent they didn't belong together. Once again, she thought about the time she'd spent with Naughton. They'd known each other a handful of days, yet she believed he cared more about her than Trey ever had.

"Brad?"

"What Cabs do you pour by the glass?"

He rattled off a couple, and when he mentioned Tablas Creek, she ordered a glass.

Trey didn't show any sign of picking up on it. "Same."

When the bartender left, Trey continued. "All we're asking is for him to come up and hear us out."

"And if he doesn't?"

"I can't accept that."

"You may not have a choice."

"That's why I need your help, Brad. I know I was a shit before, and I'm sorry."

Continuing to call her by a nickname she detested wasn't the smartest thing he could do when he was asking her to help him.

"I told you before, I don't have any influence over Naughton."

"He respects you," Trey said, taking a tack she didn't expect.

"He hardly knows me."

"Would you at least try? Do it for me."

It was all she could do not to roll her eyes. "I can try, but I'm not promising anything."

"I can't tell you how much I'd appreciate it."

The bartender delivered their wine and asked if they were ready to order.

"Give us a minute," Trey told him.

While they perused the menus, Bradley stole glances at Trey. He was grayer than she'd noticed before, and the lines on his face were more pronounced. He had dark circles under his eyes, but then she probably did too. Hers were from lack of sleep. Were his from stress?

When he looked up, she looked back at the menu, hoping he hadn't caught her staring. He was facing the door, and she felt a renewed tension seep off him, confirmed by the white-knuckle grip he had on his wine glass.

"What looks good?" she asked, pretending not to notice his change in demeanor.

"What?"

"What are you having?"

"Hmm. Not sure."

When he looked back at the menu, Bradley turned slightly and saw the man being seated in the booth right behind her. She doubted he'd have any reason to recognize her, but she knew who he was.

What was the connection between Trey and Rory Calder—and why did the two of them want her to believe they didn't know each other?

—:—

Naughton waited fifteen minutes for Maddox to answer his text before he knocked on his brother's door. When Alex answered, looking like he woke her, Naughton wasn't sure what to say. Alex was like a sister to him, but it had to be Mad's decision to confide in her once Naughton told him what Hawks had reported about their father.

"Sorry, Alex, but it's urgent I talk to Mad."

"It's okay." When she stepped aside and waved him in, Naughton saw Maddox coming down the stairs, tugging a shirt over his head.

"I just saw your text." Maddox leaned forward and kissed Alex's cheek. "I'll be back soon, sweetheart."

"Is she okay?" he asked his brother once they were outside.

"Yeah. She reads us pretty well. What's up, little brother? Your text said it was urgent."

"Let's walk." Maddox followed Naughton past the vineyards, toward the wine caves.

"It's about Da," he began.

"Yeah?"

"I think Alex may have been right about him having an affair. Hawks saw him at Demetria."

"With someone?"

"Yep."

"*Shit.*"

"He said Da pulled in the front gate, and a few minutes later, a woman walked up and got in his truck. His old truck, by the way."

"Where'd she come from?"

"Hawks said she came out of the woods, on the path that leads to the meadow where we're keeping the horses."

"What did Hawks do?" Maddox asked.

"Nothing, until they left. Once he was sure they were gone, he walked back the way she came but didn't see a car anywhere."

"Does Da know someone saw him?"

"I doubt it. Hawks has been keeping his truck pulled around on the other side of the house, instead of where we usually park near the creek."

"Why?"

Naughton shrugged. "You know how Hawks is, doesn't like anyone to know his business."

"That's right. Didn't he have some trouble with an ex a while back?"

Naughton shrugged. "What about Da, Maddox?"

"Did Hawks give you a description of the woman Da was talking to?"

"Young and pretty were about it."

"Lena young?"

"That was my first thought too, but when I described her, he shook his head."

Maddox walked farther, past the entrance to the caves, and Naughton followed. It was only when he noticed his brother grip the back of his neck, that he released his hold on his own.

"What are you thinking?" Naughton asked.

"I don't think Da is having an affair."

"I don't either, but lacking another explanation…"

"My gut is telling me this has something to do with Lena."

"The other secret?"

"Another one anyway. Hard telling if there are more."

"Da is in on this one."

"It's lookin' that way, Naught."

"What do we do?"

Maddox gripped Naughton's shoulder. "We wait."

—:—

Bradley excused herself to the restroom just to get away from Trey for a few minutes. This had been a terrible idea. She hadn't gotten a thing out of him. He was the one asking all the questions. When he wasn't pestering her about Naughton, he was asking endless questions about other wineries in the area, including Jenson Vineyards. Maybe if she told him she didn't feel well, she could get him to take her home.

She was on her way back to the table when her phone vibrated. Maybe it was her aunt checking in. When she pulled it out of her purse, she saw Trey's name on the caller ID. She hit the accept call button and was about to say something when she heard Trey's voice.

"I don't know," she heard him say. "The land is worth it, always has been, particularly if we can add more along Adelaida Trail."

"Has she *forgiven* you?" she heard another voice ask. Even through the phone, she picked up the dripping sarcasm.

"I gotta tell you, Ror, the last four years have been a real struggle."

"Keep your eye on the prize, brother. And she ain't it."

"I hear ya."

"The stuff will go down at Jenson soon. Next week we'll go to plan B for Los Cab and Butler Ranch."

"You sure about this?"

"Why not? Are you backing out on me, Trey?"

"Hell, no, Ror. I'm just saying there's a lot of heat on us right now."

"Heat but no proof. Listen, if you're not in this one hundred percent, your father's gonna hear about it."

When Trey's phone rustled, Bradley disconnected the call. She'd heard more than enough to know she had to figure out how to get the hell out of this restaurant, and home, so she could warn her aunt and uncle, along with the Butler and Avila families.

She ducked back into the ladies' room, feeling as though her heart was beating out of her chest. When the door opened, every nerve ending on Bradley's body tingled in fear.

"Diane, thank God," she whispered.

"Bradley? What's going on? You don't look good. Are you okay?"

"Shh." She held a finger up to her mouth. "I have to get out of here before the guy I'm with finds me."

Diane rested her hand on Bradley's arm. "Trey? What happened?"

"I can't explain right now. Is there a back way out?"

"There is. Where's your car?"

"I didn't drive. Trey did. *Shit,*" she said, thinking out loud.

"Can you call someone to come get you? Maybe get a cab?"

"Yeah, but I don't have a lot of time. Any second he's going to wonder what's taking me so long. In fact, he's probably outside the door right now."

Diane poked her head out. "Nope. Come with me."

Bradley followed Diane out the ladies' room door and in the door to the men's room. "Where are you—"

"Shh," Diane whispered. "There's a window."

The men's room was empty, and the window was already open, so when Diane gave her a leg up, Bradley crawled through it.

"Thanks," she said when she landed outside, in the parking lot.

Diane looked behind her. "I gotta go."

When she moved away from the window, Bradley had no idea what she should do. She had no car, and Trey would likely come looking for her any minute. She slunk her way through the parking lot that ran the length of the block of businesses. When she got to the corner, she ran across the street and slipped inside another restaurant.

"Table for one?" asked the hostess.

"Um, yeah. Thanks. Is there a restroom I can use first?"

"Of course, it's just down that hall."

Once inside, Bradley took a deep breath. It had to have been at least fifteen minutes since she had left the table at La Cosecha. Trey must be looking for her by now.

More than anything she wanted to call Naughton, but she couldn't. She had to get in touch with her uncle first. What had Trey said? Even he wouldn't be able to step in and save Jenson if she refused to help him. Evidently, her time was up, and whatever he and Calder had planned would be happening *soon*.

Bradley called her uncle's cell, but didn't reach him. She tried the house phone next, and when no one answered that, she tried her aunt's cell. It wasn't late enough that they'd be asleep. She waited a couple of minutes, and then tried again, still without any luck. Soon the woman who greeted her at the entrance would be wondering where she'd gone, and if by some slim chance, Trey came here, looking for her, she didn't want the hostess to tell him she'd disappeared into the ladies' room.

Dreading the conversation she'd have to have, she placed one more call.

"Yeah?"

"Naughton? It's Bradley. I need your help."

14

There was a bottle of bourbon in his kitchen calling his name, but after last night, he decided to skip the booze and get some sleep. He was halfway up the stairs when his cell phone rang.

"Yeah?"

"Naughton? It's Bradley. I need your help." The tone in her voice was just concerning enough that Naughton set his underlying anger at her aside and asked what was going on.

Five minutes after Bradley had explained where she was and why, he was on his way to downtown Paso Robles, working to cool his anger so maybe, by the time he got there, he wouldn't wring her neck.

It took him fifteen minutes to make the drive. When he pulled up, he texted Bradley, who'd told him she'd wait in the ladies' room until he got there.

When she came out the front door of the restaurant, she had the same deer in the headlights look that he'd seen before, and that, coupled with the fact that he could see the relief flood her face the minute she saw him, kept him from railing at her.

He opened the passenger door of his truck, which sat idling. "Get in," he told her when she hesitated, looking left and right.

"Naughton, I—"

He closed the door behind her before she finished her sentence. His patience was paper-thin, and the hold he had on his temper was quickly slipping away.

"Thank you for coming to get me," she said when he climbed in the driver's side and put the truck in gear.

He pulled onto the highway without answering, tightening his already white-knuckle grip on the steering wheel.

"I'm sorry."

"Yeah, what for?"

It took her a while to answer, but that was okay with him. He was having a hard time putting words together anyway.

"That you had to," she finally said.

"What? Come get you?"

He saw her nod.

"You're very angry—"

"Yeah? Got any idea why? And I'll tell ya, it isn't because I had to come get you."

"Why?"

"Maybe because of your harebrained idea. You takin' over for the sheriff now? *What made you think—*"

"*Stop.* I know it was stupid, but when Trey called and told me he was sorry, I just thought…I thought…"

"*Spit it out. What did you think, Bradley?*"

"*Stop yelling at me.* I thought I could help, okay? I know it was stupid, but I thought I could help."

Naughton turned off the highway on a road north of downtown Paso Robles. He drove far enough in, that it was no longer illuminated by the lights from the high-way, pulled over, and cut the engine. He unfastened both their seat belts and brought her closer to him. He gripped the back of her neck and kissed her hard, his mouth crashing into hers without caution or hesitation, just all the heat and anger his body held for her.

He wove his fingers in her hair and ran his tongue over her lower lip, flicking it until she opened to him, and he could plunge his tongue in to do battle with hers. Relief at having her in his arms battled the anger he felt from the time he first saw her in the car with the boyfriend, and then when he heard how she'd put herself at risk, all without telling him.

Naughton pulled back and looked into Bradley's eyes. His fingers grazed her neck, and she shivered.

"Naughton, I…I have to get in touch with my uncle."

He knew she did, and he'd been trying to reach him since they'd hung up. He'd called Charlie, and her aunt, as well as a couple of the guys he knew worked at Jenson. That he hadn't been able to reach anyone weighed heavy on his mind.

She pulled back and looked away from him.

"We're headed to Jenson now. My brothers and Alex's brothers are on their way there too."

"Thank you, Naughton," she murmured.

"But, Bradley—later, after we've told everyone what you overheard, you're leaving with me."

"I am?"

He nodded.

"To harvest?"

"You can use it as an excuse if you need to tell yourself that, but you know damn well we won't be in the vineyards tonight."

Her breath caught. "Where will we be?"

"We'll be in my bed, and you want it as much as I do."

"More," she murmured, her gaze resting on her hands folded on her lap.

"Look at me," he said. "I'm mad at you."

"I know."

"But I can't keep my hands off you."

"I know that too."

When they pulled through the gates of Jenson Vineyards and up near the house that sat dark, Naughton saw Maddox and Brodie's vehicles, along with others that probably belonged to the Avila brothers.

"Look," Bradley pointed to the winery that was lit up like a landing beacon. "What's going on?"

"I don't know." Naughton cut the engine and jumped out of the truck. Bradley was already running toward the winery.

She pulled the heavy door open, and what Naughton heard inside chilled him to his core.

Yelling, even screaming, sounded from the back of the building.

"It's coming from the vat room," Bradley told him.

As they got closer, the devastation seeped out on the floor beneath their feet.

"Oh my God," Bradley gasped, seeing what everyone was trying to do even though they were far too late.

Someone had broken in and gone one-by-one, opening the spigots of the vats that held vintages from the last ten years. The wine that had gushed onto the floor and down the room's drains was Jenson's best.

Naughton caught Charlie's eye and saw the utter hopelessness etched on his face.

"It's all gone," he cried, walking over to put his arms around his niece.

"Where's Jean?" Naughton asked.

"She and your brothers are checking the caves."

"I'll go," Naughton said, and Bradley nodded through her tears.

When he heard her tell her uncle she was sorry, Naughton turned around.

"This isn't your fault," he said to her.

Charlie nodded. "You told me Trey threatened Jenson, but I never dreamed he'd go this far. *You warned me.* What more could you have done, sweetheart?"

"But tonight, he…" Tears ran down her cheeks.

Naughton pulled her hands from her face. "Look at me." He waited until her eyes met his. "It was already done. You couldn't have stopped it."

"What are you talking about?" Charlie asked.

"Trey and Calder," she tried to explain through her tears.

"Bradley overheard them say there was something happening at Jenson. She tried to call you and Jean but didn't reach either of you. I've been calling too."

"When was this?" Charlie asked.

"Less than an hour ago," Naughton answered.

Charlie put his hand on Bradley's shoulder. "Naughton is right. It was already done."

"But—"

Her uncle shook his head. "You did everything you could."

Naughton's phone pinged, and he pulled it out of his pocket. "It's Mad."

"You here yet?" Maddox asked him.

"With Charlie now."

"We got here just in time. There were two of them, but they ran off into the fields, both in different directions. Gabe and Trevino went after them. They'd just gotten started on the barrels. Tell Charlie he lost a couple barrels of Merlot. That's it out here."

Naughton hung up and relayed Mad's report to Charlie and Bradley.

"Gabe and Trevino know this land," said Charlie.

"They do, and they'll do everything they can to run the bastards down."

Their heads hung heavy as they walked out of the winery. Charlie was still inside, talking to the police, who'd told Bradley they'd get a statement from her once they were finished talking with her uncle.

Naughton led her over to a bench, and Bradley let him pull her down on his lap. "You heard your uncle, it was too late. That's why you couldn't reach him; he was already here, trying to salvage whatever wine he could."

Bradley knew Naughton was right, but it didn't change the responsibility she felt. She knew what had been in the vats, and what those vintages were worth. Off the top of her head, she estimated the combined value to be at least five million dollars.

Bradley wriggled from Naughton's hold and stood. "What?" he asked.

"*You're all here!* Trey said Los Cab and Butler Ranch too."

Naughton pulled her back down to sit on the bench next to him. "Think back, Bradley. When I talked to you earlier, you said you heard them say next week."

She nodded. That's right, they had said next week, but what if they stepped up their plan, knowing she'd overheard them?

"There's heavy security in place at both Los Cab and Butler Ranch. When I talked to him while I was on my way to get you, I told Maddox exactly what you'd heard. My guess is he's added more already."

"Okay," she murmured, and looked up when her uncle came out the door.

"They're ready for you now," he told her. When he stood to go with her, her uncle put his hand on Naughton's arm. "Just her," he said.

There were three men seated at a table just inside the winery door, who introduced themselves. Two were detectives and the third was the sheriff, who Bradley recognized.

It took less than a half hour for her to tell them what she'd overheard and to answer their questions. When they told her she was free to go, Bradley hoped

Naughton hadn't left. She breathed a sigh of relief when she saw him still seated on the bench just outside the door. When he saw her, he jumped up.

"You okay?" he asked.

"No, but yes."

"Charlie took Jean up to the house. I'll walk you up and say goodnight."

"Wait. Why?"

"What do you mean?"

"Who are you saying goodnight to?"

"You…your aunt and uncle."

"Oh." She tried to stop the tears that filled her eyes from spilling down her cheeks.

"Why are you crying?"

Bradley shook her head.

"Don't do this. Talk to me. Tell me what's wrong."

"I thought I was going home with you."

"I thought after…well, that you wouldn't want to."

"But, I do. Unless you don't want me to."

"Of course, I want you to." Naughton smiled. "I want *you*, Bradley."

"I want you too, Naughton."

—:—

They were partway up the unlit pathway to the house when Naughton grabbed her and stopped her from walking farther.

His lips were hungry for her skin, but his tongue could not get enough of her mouth. He pulled her close and kissed each corner of her mouth.

When he did, she leaned forward and ground her mouth into his.

Naughton pulled back. "Are you sure this is what you want, Bradley? You and me? With what's happened tonight?"

"More than anything." Even as they walked in the darkness, he could see her flushed skin, the way her eyes drooped with want.

"What about your aunt and uncle?"

"Let's go talk to them, but then I want to leave with you."

When Bradley opened the front door, Naughton saw Charlie and Jean sitting in the kitchen. He recognized the look on both their faces. They were shell-shocked, just as he and his family had been. While the fire could've ruined Butler Ranch, the loss from it was nowhere near what he'd originally feared it would be. They were able to salvage most of the fruit that was in jeopardy, and still had over one hundred acres of vineyards that suffered no damage at all.

What happened here tonight was so much worse. Jenson Vineyards had lost millions of dollars worth of wine, yet that was nothing compared to the ten years' worth of vintages that had literally gone down the drains of the winery floor. Its impact would still be felt twenty years in the future.

"Is there anything I can do?" he asked.

"Not tonight," Charlie answered. "Have you heard whether Gabe and Trevino caught them?"

Naughton shook his head. "Last I heard from Mad, they hadn't, although I don't think they've stopped looking."

Charlie nodded and stood when Jean did.

She hugged Bradley. "I'm going upstairs, sweetheart." Jean looked at Naughton, and then back at her niece. "Will you stay with Naughton tonight?" she asked.

"Unless you need me—"

Jean held up her hand and looked back at Naughton. "Take care of her, you hear me?"

"Yes, ma'am," Naughton answered. "I don't know how to tell you how sorry I am this happened."

"We appreciate that, especially given the trouble you've had at Butler Ranch."

Charlie followed Jean up the stairs. "Get the lights on your way out," he called behind them.

"You sure about this?" Naughton asked her again.

"Please, Naughton."

Bradley walked out after him and closed the front door behind her, making sure it was locked. Naughton opened the passenger door of his truck, and Bradley climbed in.

He got in the driver's side and looked at Bradley, who was looking out the passenger window. "Are you sure you want this?"

When she turned to look at him, he knew he didn't have to ask again. Her face was flushed, like it had been earlier, and her breathing was labored.

"I just want to forget about the fire and the wine my aunt and uncle lost. I want to forget about Trey and Calder, even if it's just for a little while. Don't you, Naughton?"

"More than anything."

"Let's go, Naughton. Please."

"Tell me what you want, Bradley."

She leaned over and put her hands on him. "You, Naughton. I want to see you." Her fingers fumbled with the buttons on his shirt. "And then, taste you." She ran her tongue along his collarbone, and he thought he'd explode. He took her hands and moved them away from his body.

"We're five minutes from my place, and while I drive, I want you to tell me every single thing you want me to do to you when we get there."

Naughton hoped Bradley would talk. He didn't think she would, that she'd be too embarrassed or too shy to say the things out loud he knew were swirling inside her, but she surprised him.

15

"I want everything with you, Naughton." She touched her breasts through her clothing. "Your mouth on me here, and your fingers…"

"I want to see you," he whispered. "Let me see you."

Bradley's hands fumbled with the buttons on her shirt until it was open to her waist, exposing her creamy, white flesh and the pink lace of her bra.

Naughton reached over and pulled the cup of her bra down until her breast popped over its tightness and he could see her pretty, pink nipple.

"Show me, use your fingers. Show me what you want me to do to you."

She teased the pink bud with her own hand, until it puckered, making his mouth water. He shifted in his seat, adjusting his jeans to give himself room to accommodate her effect on his body.

Naughton pulled through the gates of Butler Ranch and waited while the big barn doors opened so he could pull his truck inside.

When Bradley's fingers touched the lowest button on her blouse, Naughton put his hand on hers. "Leave it. I have to see you."

He led her to the house through the back door—the one closest to the barn—and once they were inside, pushed her up against the kitchen counter.

Bradley's blouse hung loosely at her sides, her creamy flesh illuminated by soft moonlight. She was the most perfect woman he'd ever seen. Every fantasy of every woman he'd ever imagined fell away as his desire for her exceeded his every expectation. With her trapped between his body and the counter, he pulled her other breast free of the confining cup.

He lowered his mouth, teasing her tender flesh with his tongue. When she arched in response, his body fit perfectly into the molded contours of hers.

"Tell me more."

When she toed off her shoes, he mirrored her actions and waited while she took a ragged breath. Bradley slid her hands down her torso releasing the button on her jeans. Naughton slid his hand beneath hers and lowered the zipper while Bradley pushed the heavy denim barrier keeping his skin from touching hers over her hips and down to the floor. Her deft fingers settled on the waistband of his jeans, and they repeated the dance of hands until his jeans lay on the floor on top of hers.

Naughton's lips dragged from her mouth to the spot just below her ear. "Tell me what's next, Bradley. Nothing else happens until you tell me."

She could tell him, if only her brain would slow down enough to form words. *Everything.* That's the only word she could force from her brain through her vocal cords, and it was the truth. She wanted everything from him, and she wanted it everywhere.

Bradley took Naughton's hand and led him out of the kitchen. When they reached the bottom of the stairs, he folded his arms, and his eyebrows came together.

"The sauna," she murmured. She would've missed his smile if she'd blinked; his frown returned instantly.

"I want to feel your skin against mine."

"More, Bradley. What else?"

She leaned forward, whispering even when there was no one else to hear. "I want you inside me, Naughton. Don't make me wait any longer."

He let her lead him up the stairs and into his bathroom. She shrugged her top down her arms and eased Naughton's shirt from his shoulders as he stood still, letting her take the lead. His boxer briefs were next. She tapped his leg and he stepped out of them. Instead of lowering her panties, Bradley took his hands and guided them to do it for her. His fingers trailed along her skin, leaving chill bumps in their wake.

Naughton leaned back, keeping one hand possessively on her waist, while with the other, he opened a small closet door she hadn't noticed before. Without taking his eyes from hers, his hand moved back and forth, until his fingers found their treasure, and he let out a deep breath.

She smiled. "Relieved?"

"You have no idea."

Bradley opened the sauna door while Naughton fiddled with its control panel, and then opened his hand so she could see the condom wrapper in his palm.

"Bradley. Tell me. Do you want this?"

"Now, Naughton. Put it on."

She led him into the sauna, and pushed him down on the warm wooden bench, straddling him and wrapping her legs around his waist. When their bodies joined, it was as if they were made to. Bradley put her arms around Naughton's neck, rubbing her stiff nipples back and forth across his rock-hard chest.

"God, you feel good, baby," he breathed.

He gripped each side of her face with his hands and thrust his tongue into her mouth, matching the rhythmic movement of their conjoined bodies. One hand moved from her face to her bottom. He held her still as his body stole control from hers. His other arm snaked around her waist, holding her as close to him as she could get, and then, when her skin was touching his everywhere it could, they came together in an explosion of force Bradley hadn't known existed.

"We were made for this," he whispered after he had caught his breath. "Your body and mine, there could never be a more perfect fit."

Bradley put her palms on either side of his face and kissed him so hard, she took his breath away. Already he wanted her again. He stood, lifting her with him, and carried her into his bedroom. He gently lowered her onto the fluffy comforter, and then leaned forward, ravaging her mouth once more before he left her there alone and went back into the bathroom.

She heard the sauna door open and close, followed by the closet door she'd heard him open earlier. He came back to where she waited, having disposed of the first, but with more condoms in hand.

"Tell me what you're thinking…" he said again.

"I need more of you."

"You can have more whenever you want, Bradley. All you ever have to do is ask."

Naughton reached for his phone, to silence the annoying buzz of the alarm that sounded far too early. Bradley, nestled beside him, tightened the arm she had wrapped around his waist and opened her eyes. "It's still dark."

"Close your eyes and go back to sleep, sweetheart," he whispered.

"What time is it?"

"Three, and I wish I didn't have to, but I have to get out in the vineyard."

It didn't matter what had happened last night at Jenson, he had to focus on the harvest here, or Butler Ranch would lose fruit when they could least afford to.

Bradley climbed out of bed, stretched, and yawned. "I have to go get my clothes."

"They're right here," Naughton pointed at where he'd set them on the chair.

She picked up her shirt. "I'll just throw this on for now."

"Bradley?"

"What?" She stood before him, naked, her shirt dangling on her finger. If only he didn't have to pick today, but he did.

"What are you doing?"

"We're picking."

"*I'm* picking."

Bradley, still naked, dropped her shirt on the floor and put her hands on her hips. "No, Naughton. *We're* picking. I work for Butler Ranch, remember? If you're worried about my aunt and uncle, I plan to go see them later this morning. In the meantime, we have fruit to pick, so I'm going to go to the winery and get my clothes."

Many wineries had locker rooms, with showers, off their main building, Butler Ranch included. After being in the field, picking all day, or even in the winery, clothes were often drenched in grape juice and caked with dirt. The locker rooms gave the workers a place to hose off their rubber work boots, change their clothes and either discard them, a common practice, or put them in tagged laundry bags.

A service, much like a restaurant's linen service, came in to collect the bags of soiled clothes and returned them the following day, after they'd been commercially laundered. In preparation for the harvest, Bradley had brought clothes from her aunt and uncle's, and put them in her locker.

Naughton walked over to where Bradley stood, picked her up, set her on the bed, and smiled. "I'll go get your clothes, sweetheart. Locker number?"

"Twelve, but I can go."

He leaned over and kissed her. "While I love having you naked in my bed, I have to draw the line at anyone else, here at the ranch, seeing what's mine."

Bradley grinned. "Yours?"

"That's right, sweetheart. You're all mine."

"What about you? Do I get to claim exclusivity rights too?"

"Already granted, Bradley." He narrowed his eyes and looked deep into hers. "I'm serious about this."

She sat up, leaning over first to switch the bedside light on, and then rested back on her elbows. "Naughton, I—"

He leaned forward again and covered her mouth with his, stopping her from saying another word. He pulled back and rested two fingers against her lips. "I'll go get your clothes, and then we'll talk. Okay?"

She nodded.

—:—

Bradley got out of bed, turned the water on in the shower, and opened the linen closet door, looking for a towel. She guessed the only shelf that looked as though things weren't in their exact right place was the one that held the condom packets now on Naughton's bedside table.

She brought the soft and fluffy towel up to her nose and breathed in the scent that had come to represent Naughton to her. The linen closet, like the walk-in one in his bedroom, was lined with cedar, a scent that, to her, was all man.

She dropped the towel, climbed into the steamy shower, and lathered her body with soap that smelled of sandalwood. This scent too was all Naughton— powerful and rugged, like the man himself. When Naughton's arms were around her, she felt like that was exactly where she was supposed to be. He didn't even have to be touching her, as long as he was near, Bradley felt safe.

Having spent a couple of hours with Trey last night, the difference in how she felt was more pronounced. She'd never felt secure with Trey, that she could be herself or relax. She perpetually felt on edge. She hadn't realized before how exhausting it was to be with him. Having overheard everything he'd said, made it obvious why she felt the way she had. He had never been interested in her; he'd only wanted her aunt and uncle's land. She shook her head, wishing she'd never met Trey Deveux.

She closed her eyes to concentrate on the feel of the water trickling down her body and let the steam of the shower soothe her. Even when the shower door opened, she didn't startle. The hands that wrapped around her and covered her breasts, and the lips that kissed her neck were already familiar ones.

"I hope you don't mind, I made myself at home," she said.

"Mind? Never."

He turned her around, and she looked into his eyes. "Naughton, I—"

"Shh." He touched her lips with his finger. "Later."

She understood. All too soon, they'd have to step outside the world they'd cocooned themselves in last night, and face both what had happened at Jenson, along with whatever else Trey and Calder were plotting.

"Where are we picking today?" she asked.

"What's left of the Sauv Blanc and the Chard. If we finish before dawn, we'll move over to the smaller vineyards that are higher up."

"Marsanne and Roussanne?"

Naughton smiled. "And Viognier."

She was about to turn the water off when Naughton gripped her neck and brought his face close to hers. "I need you to promise me something."

She nodded.

"Let law enforcement do their job. Stay away from Trey."

When she tried to look away, his hold on her tightened. "Bradley?"

"I know."

She'd gone to the ladies' room last night, and then disappeared. Trey had to know she'd heard the conversation between him and Calder. What he would do next was anyone's guess.

The last thing she expected, however, was to see him outside Naughton's door at three a.m.

—:—

Naughton held the door open for her, but as soon as he saw Trey waiting in the darkness, he moved in front of Bradley, shielding her from him.

"You're trespassing," Naughton snarled.

"I need to talk to Bradley." Trey tried to move around Naughton, but he cut him off.

"Get off our land or I'll call the sheriff."

"Hold on a minute—"

"The sheriff it is." Naughton was placing the call when Trey knocked the phone from his hand.

"What's going on here?" asked a voice in the darkness. It sounded so much like Kade that Naughton expected him to appear instead of Maddox when he walked closer.

"Call the sheriff, Mad. We have a trespasser, arsonist, and thief on our land."

"Is that what you think?" Trey looked at Bradley.

"Don't talk to her, talk to me." Naughton moved so Bradley was behind him. "Go inside, sweetheart."

Relieved when he heard the door open and close, Naughton reached down to pick up his phone.

"I knew she'd be here," Trey hissed.

"Thanks, Bill," Naughton heard Maddox say as he turned back around to face them. "Sheriff's on his way."

"I need to talk to Bradley."

Naughton wanted to pound Trey Deveux into the ground, and he would before he'd let the bastard anywhere near Bradley. "You have ten seconds to get in your car and get the hell off our property," Naughton seethed. He moved toward Trey, fists clenched.

"I'll leave, but this isn't over."

"Sounds like a threat to me. Does it to you, Naught?"

"Sure does, Mad. Maybe we should detain him until Bill gets here."

Trey stepped back to where his car sat parked, got in, and sped down the main drive, throwing stones and dirt behind him.

Naughton heard his front door open and turned to speak to Bradley. "He's gone."

"He threatened you. I heard him."

Maddox held up his phone. "The sheriff overheard it all. At the very least, we'll get a restraining order in place. If he sets foot on Butler Ranch or Jenson Vineyards, Trey Deveux will find himself in county lockup."

Bradley shivered and Naughton put his arm around her waist. "You don't have to be afraid of him. We have eyes and ears everywhere."

—:—

None of them heard or saw the person standing in the darkness, close enough to hear every word they spoke. Yes, there were eyes and ears everywhere, far more than they knew.

16

At daybreak, Naughton called Bradley's cell and asked her to meet him in the Viognier vineyards. Before she could tell Brodie where she was going, he held up his own phone.

"I'll drive you up," he yelled over to her.

Bradley hadn't been without a Butler brother within twenty feet of her all morning. Maddox had led her to one of the Sauvignon Blanc vineyards first thing, while Naughton took a crew to another. As soon as Brodie arrived, he stayed with her while Maddox led another group over to the first Chardonnay vineyard they'd pick today.

"It's fine, Brodie. I can get there on my own."

"We're done here anyway."

They weren't, but close enough that the crew they'd been working with could finish on their own.

"Where's Peyton?" she asked, climbing on the back of the four-wheel ATV Brodie was walking over to.

"At her parents' with the boys."

"We're all on edge, and I feel like it's my fault," she confided in him.

"You didn't start this, Bradley. Calder did, and from what I've heard, Deveux had a hand in it too. You're an innocent bystander."

She shrugged. "Still."

Brodie shook his head.

The words she had heard Trey say to Calder played over in her head all morning while she picked grapes.

The land is worth it, always has been, particularly if we can add more along Adelaida Trail.

She hadn't let herself think about that part of what he'd said last night, but now, memories of things that had happened in the last four years came flooding back to her.

Trey knew, when they met, that she had a tie to Jenson Vineyards. In the first few minutes, she'd told him she was Charlie and Jean's niece. Had that been the only reason he'd pursued her all along? Was that why he had put so much pressure on her not to go back to Cornell for graduate school, and then earlier this year, pushed her to take a job with her uncle rather than accept an offer from a Napa winery?

Keep your eye on the prize, brother. And she ain't it.

What a fool she'd been. No wonder she'd always felt like she wasn't good enough for Trey because, in his eyes, she wasn't.

You have to work for Jenson. It's your heritage.

Had he realized the land would never be hers, so instead, sought to ruin her aunt and uncle financially and force them to sell? What else did he and Calder have planned? She knew they wanted more land on Adelaida Trail, and after the fire and what had happened last night at Jenson, Bradley believed there was nothing they'd stop at to get it. How many other wineries were they planning to target?

"There she is." Naughton walked over when Brodie stopped the ATV at the end of a row of Viognier. He kissed her cheek, and then looked at her hands.

"Where are your gloves, Bradley?"

She didn't like to wear them when she picked for the same reason she'd never want to rely on machine harvesting. Grapes were fragile. If she touched each cluster with her fingers, held it in her hand, she could feel their weight and intuitively know whether it was heavy with juice or if a few of the grapes had been compromised. Subsequently, her hands were covered with scratches and cuts.

Naughton brought her right hand to his lips and kissed each fingertip, and then her palm. "You wouldn't wear them if I asked you to, would you?"

Bradley shook her head.

Naughton smiled and put his arm around her shoulders. "Let's take a walk."

Brodie waved behind him as he left on the ATV. "Where's he going?" she asked.

"To call the harvest, at least for a few hours. It's getting too hot to keep picking."

She agreed. Now that they were harvesting rather than salvaging grapes after the fire, what they picked and when wasn't as urgent.

"I thought we'd go see Charlie and Jean."

"I talked to Aunt Jean a little while ago."

"How are they doing?"

"Okay. She said Uncle Charlie has been on the phone all morning, talking to the police and insurance adjusters. She told me the police didn't have any leads on the guys who did it."

"I heard from Alex that Gabe and Trevino felt pretty bad that they weren't able to catch them."

Bradley shook her head. "I hate this."

"Me too, sweetheart."

"I asked, and my aunt said there really isn't anything they need my help with right now."

"Are you ready for triage then?"

"Does that mean we're crushing today?"

"Yep."

The last vestiges of sunrise could be seen on the horizon, but any fatigue she might have felt dissipated when she heard they'd crush today.

Under normal circumstances, freshly-picked clusters of grapes would come into the winery to be sorted for quality. In France, that process was called triage, directly translated—selection.

Bradley wouldn't know until she got to the winery whether they'd sort what they'd picked a couple of days ago first, or keep that in cold storage. It would be up to Maddox to decide.

Once he had, she along with several other workers would line both sides of a conveyor belt, and separate the good fruit from the inferior, removing unripe, diseased or damaged grapes, along with any leaves that weren't weeded out in the field.

In her last year at Cornell, the enology department had tested a system that was being used for triage in the Bordeaux region of France. The grapes still moved along a conveyor belt, but instead of human sorters, an optic sensor recognized any grape that didn't have the desired size, shape, or color, and then a blast of air separated it onto another belt used for waste.

Like machine harvesting, Bradley didn't trust the optical system. She'd been on the team that evaluated the grapes that had been sorted out as inferior, and found there to be a high percentage of good grapes that were thrown out with the bad.

However, when it came to crushing and destemming, Bradley was all for the modernized approach. The days of foot-stomping died out before she was born, and she was glad it had.

After being sorted, the conveyor belt would move the clusters into large, automated crusher-destemmers, which would destem the grapes and then break the skins open, exposing the fruit's juice and pulp.

White grapes typically went directly from there into the press, which separated the juice from the skins.

For red wines, depending on the varietal and the winemaker's preference, the stems, seeds, and skins stayed with the fruit and were pressed off later, sometimes after a few hours, sometimes after as long as a month. The longer the stems, seeds, and skins stayed with the juice, the higher the tannins in the wine would be. Tannins were what gave wine like Cabernet Sauvignon its characteristic dryness.

—:—

Naughton watched Bradley as she got lost in thought on their way back to the winery. He wished he could climb inside her brain and go for the ride her thoughts were taking her on.

There wasn't anyone he knew who worked in the wine industry that didn't love this time of year. It was filled with worry, even without something as catastrophic happening as a fire. But it was also filled with excitement and joy. Every varietal they harvested had the potential to yield or become an integral part of a great wine.

This time around, it felt different though. Year after year, he and his brother partnered in bringing in the harvest. Naughton grew the grapes, Maddox made wine with them. It was still exciting, still fraught with worry, still a magical journey, but having Bradley with him accentuated all of it. It was more exciting, more magical with her here.

He'd noticed little things about her the last few days, like how she refused to wear gloves when she picked. He remembered the first day they met, and they walked through her uncle's vineyards. Bradley's fingers had trailed along the leaves and grapes. It made sense now that she'd want to touch them, feel them, know them, and learn from them.

Last night her fingers had trailed along his skin the same way, as though she was learning the feel of him, inch by inch. He leaned over and kissed her neck just below her ear, and she stopped walking.

"What was that for?"

"Being you."

Bradley kissed him back, and when Naughton lifted her with his hands on her bottom, she wrapped her legs around his waist. That's how Maddox and Alex found them moments later, with their mouths and tongues locked together.

"Oh, Lord," Naughton heard Alex say. As much as he didn't want to release Bradley, he did. When she slid her way down his body, he wondered how angry

Maddox would be if he whisked her away for an hour or so. As it was, he turned her to face them, her back to his front, wrapped his arms around her waist, and rested his chin on her shoulder.

Alex climbed off the ATV and walked over to where they waited. "I was hoping to kidnap Bradley so she could help me with tomorrow's dinner, but it looks like you've got your own plans."

Naughton smiled. "I do, but we're both going to have to step aside and let Maddox take our girl."

"Who are you?" Alex teased.

Naughton shrugged. He shocked himself, hearing his words come out of his mouth.

"Why does Mad get dibs on her?"

"Because more than anything, Bradley wants to get her hands on those grapes. Am I right?" said Naughton.

Bradley turned around, kissed Naughton's lips, and then eased out of his hold.

"Sorry, but Naughton's right. I know I offered to help, but—"

"Stop, I was teasing. There's little that could come between my Mad-man and me these days, except maybe if I stole you away during crush."

Naughton watched Bradley climb on the back of the ATV with his brother after Alex said she'd prefer to walk back with Naughton. He'd give anything to feel her behind him on his motorcycle, her body crushed against his while they explored the rolling hills of the wine country. It would be days before they'd be able to get away like that, but only hours until he'd have her back in his bed, and that was better than any motorcycle ride he could take her on.

"You are long gone, aren't you, Naught?"

He looked at Alex but didn't answer.

They walked along in silence for a few minutes, until they rounded a bend and could see the charred vineyards where the fire had gone through. Naughton stopped walking and sat on a boulder along the side of the dirt road that wound its way through their land.

"How long have you and Maddox been together?"

"Is that a rhetorical question? You probably know better than I do."

"I'm serious."

"Twenty years."

"I've known Bradley a little over a week."

"What's your point?"

He shook his head. "It's crazy."

"You're falling in love with her."

"It's crazy," he said again.

"It isn't, Naughton. Not at all. I've loved Maddox since the day I met him, and he says he feels the same way. We were both too stubborn to admit it, and we almost lost each other."

"I've never felt this way. Not even close."

"Trust it, Naught. She's one of the good ones, and not only that, she's it for you."

"What if she doesn't feel the same way?"

Alex took her sunglasses off and looked into the clear, blue sky above them. "Hey, Kade," she said. "Can we get a little help down here, please?"

17

It was dark outside, otherwise, Bradley had no idea what time it was, and she was too tired to do as much as pull her phone out of her pocket to look. Maddox had gone in search of his phone to call Alex. He'd told her he'd be right back, and they'd talk about the next day's schedule.

If she didn't smell of dirt and hours-old grape juice, she'd find a corner to curl up in and sleep. Instead, she let her eyes drift closed for just a moment.

"Hey, sleeping beauty," she heard Naughton say at the same time she felt his fingers run through her hair.

"I'm a mess," she said when she opened her eyes. "Hi," she added when he smiled at her.

"Hi, angel."

The way Naughton looked at her melted her heart. She couldn't imagine anyone looking at her the way she'd seen Maddox look at Alex, or Brodie look at Peyton. When he reached under her knees, put his other arm around her waist, and picked her up, Bradley felt certain she was dreaming.

"Rest your head on my shoulder," he told her. She wrapped her arms around his neck and let her eyes drift closed again. When she felt a breeze, she opened them. "Wait, Naughton. I can't leave. Maddox is coming back to talk to me about tomorrow."

"He knows where to find you," he said and kept walking.

Bradley tried to wriggle out of Naughton's arms, but he only tightened his grip. "I'll put you down once we're inside."

"Inside where?"

He somehow managed to unlock and open the back door of his cottage, and set her on her feet once they were in his kitchen.

"I'm a mess," she said again when he palmed her cheek and ran his thumb over her lips.

"Let's get you out of these clothes," he murmured, pulling her shirt over her head. Bradley looked down; even her bra was dirty.

"Have you talked to Charlie or Jean?" he asked, gently guiding her to the chair by the table, and when she sat, he pulled her rubber boots off, and then her socks.

"I talked to Aunt Jean again this afternoon. She said they're doing okay."

"Are they picking?"

Bradley smiled. "Not yet. She said another week at least."

"Hmm. Looks like I'm going to win our bet." He smiled and nuzzled her neck.

"We never bet."

"Sure we did. We just never said what we were wagering. I know what I want, though."

"That isn't fair. You already know you've won."

Naughton cupped her face with his palm. "We want the same thing, sweetheart. Don't we?"

Before she could answer, he covered her mouth with his, and then ran his hands up her legs until he reached the button on her jeans. "Stand up for me, angel," he breathed.

She loved his terms of endearment—sleeping beauty, angel, even when he called her sweetheart. Like with the way he looked at her, each time he used one, she melted a little bit more.

"You're so sweet to me," she whispered, resting her hands on his shoulders. "You've got to be as tired as I am."

He pulled her jeans and panties over her hips and tapped each leg for her to step out of them. She was standing naked except for her bra when she heard Maddox at the front door.

"Open up, Naught. I need to talk to Bradley."

She reached for her clothes, but Naught grabbed her arm and swung her up over his shoulder.

"What are you doing?" She pounded on his back. *"Put me down,"* she shrieked and laughed all the way up the stairs. By the time Naughton deposited her on the edge of his bathtub, tears were rolling down her cheeks from laughing so hard.

Naughton was laughing too, but when she looked into his eyes, they both stopped. The heat between them spread as he palmed her cheek with his right hand and turned the water on with his left.

"Climb in whenever you're ready. I'll be back as soon as I get rid of my brother."

"Naughton?" she said as he was walking out of the bathroom.

"Yeah?"

"Thank you."

Instead of walking out the door, he turned around and knelt in front of her. "Hell with Mad," he muttered before he covered her lips with his.

Between the two of them, he was out of his clothes before Maddox pounded on the door for the third time. Naughton reached into the pocket of his jeans that were now on his bathroom floor and jabbed the screen with his finger. "Go away," he growled when Maddox answered Naughton's call. "I'll have her call you later."

Through the phone, Bradley could hear Maddox's laughter before Naughton disconnected the call. He threw his phone on top of his jeans, unfastened Bradley's bra, and added it to his pile of clothes.

He climbed into the tub and held her hand in his to help her do the same. Bradley waited until Naughton adjusted the temperature and lowered himself into the water before she sat between his legs and rested her back against his chest. His arms snaked around her waist, pulled her closer to him, and then he reached over to turn on the jets.

As the water swirled around her body, Bradley couldn't remember a time she'd felt as content as she did resting in Naughton's arms.

She traced a heart pattern on his thigh with her fingertip. "You're so good to me." When he didn't say anything, she leaned over and turned her head so she could see his face. His eyes were closed, and his head rested against the stone behind him. "Naughton?"

He raised his head and opened his eyes, looking so deeply into hers. She shifted further and brought her palm to his cheek. "You make me feel…I can't describe it. I've never felt this way."

He nodded, so she continued. "I've never doubted that I'm loved, but since my mom died, I've never felt so…cherished." Her eyes filled with tears, and when she tried to look away, he held her face in his hand so she couldn't. "Does that sound crazy?" she asked.

"Not at all."

Naughton wished he could bring himself to speak as freely as Bradley had. As he'd told Alex, he'd never felt this way either. How could he tell a woman he'd known for such a short amount of time that he loved her? That was the only word that came close to describing the way he felt. She said he made her feel cherished. She made him feel so much more—alive, yet calm, tranquil almost, as though whatever had been missing in his life, whether he'd known it was or not, was resting her body against his.

"Have you eaten?" he said instead, and Bradley laughed.

"Naughton, there's only one thing I'm hungry for, and it has nothing to do with food."

He kissed down the side of her neck as he covered her breasts with the palms of his hands. He squeezed and then stroked her skin, circling her nipples.

Bradley dug her fingers into his thighs. "That feels so good," she moaned. "You can do that as often as you like."

"Yeah? You won't mind if I sneak up behind you in the vineyards and run my hands all over your body?"

"As good as what you're doing feels, I wouldn't care where we were."

He moved his hands to her arms and rubbed her muscles, then up to her shoulders. The more he massaged her body, the deeper she sank into him, as though every inch he touched turned to putty.

Not so for him, though. The more of her skin he laid his hands on, the bigger he grew and the harder he got. She shifted so he rested between the cheeks of her bottom, and it was his turn to moan.

"I need to be inside you, sweetheart," he whispered. Bradley reached over and pressed the button to turn off the tub's jets, and then flipped the drain lever so it opened. She shifted then, so she was on her knees facing him, and wrapped her arms around his neck. "There's no place I'd rather have you be," she murmured before she kissed him.

Naughton opened his mouth and grasped the back of her neck, holding her close as he deepened their kiss. Everything he couldn't bring himself to say, he put into his hands, his mouth, his body, somehow hoping she'd feel it.

"Are you real?" he asked. "Can this be real?"

—:—

He said it so softly, Bradley could hardly hear him, but she understood why he'd asked. She felt the same way. How could this possibly be real? They hadn't even known each other long enough for this to count as the honeymoon phase, where they agreed on everything, wanted to do the same things all the time, and always looked picture perfect. In fact, Naughton had seen her at her worst on more than one occasion.

Side by side they rested on his bed, studying each other. She'd probably already said too much, and now it was Naughton's turn. If he didn't have anything to say, she wouldn't either.

Naughton closed his eyes and ran his hands over her body, as though he was memorizing every curve. As tired as she was, as much as she wanted to close her eyes too, she didn't. Instead, she studied the subtle changes in his expressions as he explored her nakedness.

Naughton wasn't Bradley's first lover, but there were few that had come before him. Now that she knew Trey's motivation for wanting to be with her, she better understood the sporadic nature of their physical relationship. His indifference had added to her feelings of inadequacy, when all along he'd never truly been attracted to her.

Being with Naughton was like swinging to the opposite end of the spectrum. When he ran his fingers down her arm, chill bumps followed in their wake. It was as if love traveled from his body to hers whenever and wherever he touched her.

When he'd touched almost every inch of her with his hands, he started over again with his lips. He ran his tongue down the crevice between her breasts while his fingers pinched then soothed her nipples. Bradley was on the verge of an orgasm from that intimacy alone.

The farther he trailed down her body, the closer she got to exploding under his touch.

"Come for me, angel," he whispered when his hands and lips reached the apex of her legs.

Her molten need for him reached a climax, and she arched into his touch. "Please, Naughton," she begged.

"Tell me what you need, Bradley." The warmth of his breath re-ignited her already fiery desperation.

"You. I need you inside me. Now, Naughton. Please."

He entered her then, thrusting deep, and filling her emptiness completely. With Naughton inside her, Bradley felt complete. He had said the words himself last night—*your body and mine, there could never be a more perfect fit.*

—:—

Maddox sent Naughton a text saying Hawks took a crew out already to pick the Viognier, and asked him what was next.

We'll walk at three, he answered and then added, *with Bradley.*

Of course with Bradley, Maddox responded.

She slept soundly, her head resting on his chest and her arm around his center. There hadn't been a woman in this bed before her, and if he had his way, there wouldn't be one after her either.

Naughton heard Kade's voice inside his head as he drifted to sleep. "Feed the white wolf, brother."

When the alarm sounded, Naughton felt as though he'd just closed his eyes. This time he'd set it for two, but only so he'd have an hour with Bradley before he had to share her with the rest of the world.

"I never called Maddox last night." Her eyes were still closed, and her voice was heavy with sleep.

"I'm the boss today anyway."

Bradley opened her eyes and smiled. "Does Maddox know that?"

"I'm the harvest boss. His shift doesn't start until you get in the winery."

"So, boss-man, what are we picking today?"

"I'm gonna let you decide."

Bradley sat straight up and pulled her legs under her. "Really?" Her eyes twinkled and her smile stretched across her entire face. In that moment she reminded Naughton of his niece, Spencer, and the way she'd looked last Christmas morning.

"Yes, really." He leaned forward and kissed the tip of her nose.

"What's close?"

He shrugged and winked.

"Are you serious, Naughton? You're really going to let me decide? I mean—"

"Yes, Bradley. Now please go back to the excited girl you were two minutes ago and quit doubting yourself."

She leaned over and fell against the pillow, back to smiling. "How do you know me so well?"

This time when he kissed her, he went straight for her mouth. As their tongues caressed one another, Naughton rolled so Bradley was on top of him.

"My turn to tell you what I want you to do."

"Cuz you're the boss?"

"Yep."

—:—

"Where to?" Maddox asked Naughton when they met him on the edge of the vineyard. Brodie was there too, yawning while he waited on the ATV.

Naughton turned to her and waited too. When she looked at Maddox, he smiled. Bradley thought it was his most endearing trait. When Maddox smiled, it was as though he and the person he smiled at shared a very happy secret.

"I'm gonna like this," he said, rubbing his hands together.

"What's happening?" Brodie had stretched out on the seat of the ATV, using the front of it as a very uncomfortable-looking headrest.

"Naughton's letting Bradley decide what we're picking today."

Brodie yawned again. "Let me know when she's made up her mind."

"He's no fun," Maddox said. "So where to?"

"Merlot," she answered.

"Merlot," Maddox called over to Brodie.

"I heard her. I'm right here," he mumbled.

The first vineyard Bradley wanted to check was close enough that they could walk. Brodie drove ahead on the ATV, saying they'd need it later anyway.

Naughton wove his fingers with hers and it felt like the most natural thing in the world. The smile hadn't left Maddox's face, and now he was whistling.

"You crack me up," Bradley said to him.

"You sound like Alex. Who says 'crack me up' anymore?"

"We do, because we're the cool kids," she answered.

Maddox looked past her at his brother. "It's good to see you happy, Naught."

"Good to feel happy."

Maddox's eyes opened wide, and he shook his head. "Damn, Saint John, you must be heaven-sent to get my little brother to admit he's happy."

"What are we going for?" Naughton asked when Bradley stopped at the first row of Merlot vines.

She looked at Maddox.

"Your call. What should we make this year?"

Bradley looked over the grapes in the first row. Most appeared ripe. First, she tasted a couple, and then used the refractometer to measure the Brix, or sugar levels. Farther down the row, she tasted again, and farther still, took another set of measurements. From there, she walked several rows over and repeated the process while all three Butler brothers waited with folded arms.

"I don't know about you," she heard Maddox say to Naughton, "but I'm loving this."

"Bordeaux," she said finally.

"So we pick?"

Bradley handed the refractometer to Naughton, who took it but set it near the ATV.

"Wait. You're not going to…"

Naughton shook his head.

"But…"

Maddox pulled a radio out of his back pocket. "We're starting with Merlot this morning, boys. Bradley's making us a fine Bordeaux this year."

There were two basic styles of Merlot, and which they chose to make determined when they'd pick.

Traditionally, Merlot was a primary grape used in the French Bordeaux-style wine, along with Cabernet Sauvignon, Cabernet Franc, Petit Verdot, Malbec, and Carménère.

The second of the two styles required a later harvest, which would give the wine enough body to stand on its own. Those wines, typically one-hundred percent Merlot, were high in alcohol, lush, and fruity, but lacked the complexity of other wines made from a single varietal.

While she and Maddox said they were making a Bordeaux, they couldn't call it that, because by law, only wines made in that region could bear the name.

They could call it a Meritage, which was the same basic blend, but recently Bradley heard more and more winemakers refer to the blend as a Claret, which was a term the British coined for a wine made in that style.

Maddox stood between Naughton and her and put an arm around each of them. "We're gonna have so much fun! I can't wait to see what the next few years bring both to Butler Ranch and Demetria."

Bradley looked at Naughton, trying to gauge his reaction. He smiled, which had to mean he agreed, didn't it? What a dream that would be, to work in the vines with him, and Maddox too, of course.

She still couldn't believe he entrusted her with such an important decision. Surely Naughton didn't do it because of his romantic interest in her. He hadn't even checked her measurements or given his opinion. Joy surged inside of her; no one had ever believed in her the way Naughton did, not even her uncle.

When Maddox walked over to talk to Brodie, Bradley crept up behind Naughton and put her arms around his waist. She rested her head against his back. "Thank you," she said.

He turned in her arms. "You know what you're doing, Bradley. You were born to do this."

"You really believe that?"

"I wish you could step outside of yourself and see how good you are. You're intuitive, like it's in your blood. I said once before, you and I are going to make amazing wine together." He looked over at Maddox. "I love my brother, and I've always loved making wine with him, but with you, it'll be nothing short of magic."

"Naughton, I…"

He waited, but she couldn't bring herself to say the words. He'd think she'd lost her mind, but in reality, all she'd lost was her heart.

"Finish what you were going to say, Bradley," he murmured.

"I…don't know how to thank you for giving me this opportunity."

"You're welcome. Maybe later I'll get you to tell me what you really wanted to say."

18

They picked the Merlot until ten when the heat of the day got too intense, and then Naughton walked Bradley back to the winery.

"We aren't crushing today," she said.

"Maddox told me."

"I think I'll go home for a little while then."

"I'll drop you off on my way to Demetria."

Naughton and Hawks were going to Demetria to bring the horses back, but that wasn't the only reason. There were two things Hawks had told him he wanted to talk to him about when they got there. He only elaborated on one, but Naughton could guess the other.

Later this afternoon, Alex and Peyton, along with his two sisters, Skye and Ainsley, their parents, plus Alex's mother, and Peyton's parents were hosting the dinner at the Los Caballeros winery to thank everyone who came out to help after the fire.

The Spanish-style meal would be served throughout the afternoon and evening to allow for vineyard owners, winemakers, and their employees to come when they could get away from the harvest or crush.

"What time do you want to go to Los Cab later?" he asked.

"I'm not sure. I want to ride over with Uncle Charlie and Aunt Jean."

Naughton was uncomfortable with the idea that she wouldn't be with him or either of his brothers.

Bradley cupped his cheek with her palm. "Stop scowling," she teased. "Uncle Charlie is just as good a bodyguard as you and your brothers are."

He wouldn't apologize for worrying about her. Now that he'd found her, the idea of losing Bradley was more than he could let himself think about.

After he had dropped Bradley off at home, Naughton followed Hawks to Demetria, each of them towing a trailer for the horses. Since it was the easiest place to load, they pulled behind the house, where Hawks had been keeping his truck.

From where they had parked, he could see inside through the wall of windows that looked out over the vineyards. While he didn't like the fact that it sat so close to the main road, he loved the way it had been designed.

It was a single story, set up with an open floor plan, like a loft. Lena Hess had lived in the house until a couple of months ago, and before that, her mother and father had lived in it.

Maddox had told him Lena's mother had Parkinson's disease and her father designed the house to accommodate her as the disease progressed.

The land Kade had deeded to them, originally belonged to Lena's grandparents on her mother's side, whose family name was Demetrius. When Lena told his brother and him that the estate had originally been called Demetria, they immediately knew that's what they'd name it.

Most people in the valley referred to it as the Hess Estate. Hess was Lena's father's surname, but even she didn't know how, when, or why people started calling it that. Her father had always planned to replant the vineyards and make wine on the estate after he retired, but her mother's illness thwarted his plans.

It had been two years since Parkinson's took Lena's mother's life and her father left the estate. When Kade first brought Naughton to see it, he hadn't said how he came to own the four hundred acres he'd deeded to his brother and him, and Naughton hadn't asked. He assumed Kade had somehow managed to purchase it, but with a four-million-dollar price tag, it was difficult for Naughton to comprehend how.

Lena had also told Maddox there were another two hundred hectares that sat unused. That land had been for sale, and the Calder family had been bidders. That was how Rory Calder had discovered the Avilas had stored wine in Demetria's caves.

Even though the caves were on land owned by Maddox and Naughton, he'd made it his business to explore every acre that had once made up the estate.

When Lena confronted him about it, Calder divulged that he knew she'd secretly been married to Kade years ago. If Lena hadn't agreed to go along with Calder's plans, he'd threatened to expose the marriage to Naughton's family, knowing they were unaware of the union. It wasn't until Maddox uncovered the secret on his own that Lena could escape Calder's blackmail scheme.

Maddox believed there were more secrets Lena held, and for a while, seemed determined to uncover them. Naughton hadn't felt the need to, until the other day when he saw his father in Harmony, and then when Hawks told him he'd seen their father here with a woman.

"What do you want to do first?" Hawks asked.

"Tell me what you wanted to talk to me about, and then we'll load up the horses."

They walked over to the picnic table by the creek, and Hawks told him what he'd learned about the fire. Johnny Vatos, the man Hawks had grown up with, was, in fact, the person in custody accused of arson, and not a migrant farm worker as the sheriff had told the Butler family.

"I still don't understand why the sheriff thought he was a migrant worker."

"He gave them his given name, Juan, and pretended he didn't speak English. Once they fingerprinted him though, it wasn't long before they knew exactly who he was."

"I don't get it."

"I don't either, and he's not confessing anything other than he was the one that set the fire."

"Did he say why?"

"He says he wanted assurance that his family would be taken care of."

"By starting the fire? That doesn't make sense. He's telling you why he's going down for it, but not the reason he started it," said Naughton, and Hawks nodded.

"Johnny has aged twenty years to the five since I've seen him. I doubt I would've recognized him if I passed him on the street."

"Think he'll change his mind?"

"No way. Johnny will go to his grave with the name of whoever paid him to do this."

Barring any other evidence, Johnny's refusal to confess more than his involvement would leave law enforcement with nothing else to go on. Vatos would spend the rest of his life in jail, and whoever had paid him off would walk free and have every opportunity to do more damage.

"Did you hear about Jenson?" Naughton asked.

Hawks nodded. "Heard it was bad."

"They lost every vintage back ten years."

"Damn."

"Yep, and it was the good stuff," Naughton told him.

"Does insurance cover somethin' like that?"

"It does, but it'll be years before they can build their stock back up, which means years before they can release anything but the young varietals."

Hawks shook his head. "What's happening to our valley, Naught? It's like it's cursed."

Not a curse as much as a few greedy bastards who'd stop at nothing to get their hands on land that would otherwise never be offered for sale. If the wine conglomerates were behind this, the way Naughton thought they were, they'd soon learn that the owners of the wineries in the collaborative would rather turn their operations into dairy farms than sell.

"Naught?"

"Yeah."

"There's somethin' else."

He nodded.

"Your father was back, with the woman."

"When?"

"Early this morning. I almost ran into them when I walked outside on my way back to the ranch, but I stopped when I heard voices."

"Could you hear what they were talking about?"

"Only part of it. The woman kept insisting she see 'him'."

"Who?"

"Neither said. But your father did say that she knew she couldn't. He told her to stop asking."

"Anything else?"

"Yeah. They saw the lights on in the house. Your father told her it was too risky for them to meet here again."

"Anything else?"

"Nothing else I could hear."

Naughton leaned forward and put his head in his hands. "Did you see her?"

Hawks nodded. "It was dark, so I didn't get a good look."

Naughton got up from the table and took the path into the woods that would lead him to where the horses were. What he needed now was a long ride on Huck. Time to think, and time not to think.

—:—

"How are you coping?" her aunt asked.

"Me? I'm worried about how you and Uncle Charlie are doing."

"I'm not sure it's hit us fully yet. Charlie has been on the phone most of the day again today. Earlier this morning the alcohol tax bureau rep called to say he'd be here tomorrow."

"I didn't think about that." The inventory Jenson had lost was worth a significant amount of money. Her aunt and uncle would be getting a substantial refund on their tax bond. "Word travels fast, doesn't it?"

"We live in a tight community, so yes, it does. We've had so many offers of help already."

"What kind of help?"

"Grapes, juice, wine to blend. Help with the harvest in case it becomes too much for us to manage."

"Just like everyone helped after the fire."

Her aunt nodded. "Tell me what's going on with you and Naughton."

Where did she start? "We're getting to know each other."

"And?"

Bradley shook her head. "It's crazy."

When her aunt didn't ask what she meant right away, Bradley thought she could leave it at that.

"Are you in love with him?"

"I hardly know him."

Her aunt opened her arms, and Bradley stepped into her embrace. "You know him, sweetheart, better than you know most anyone else."

"I don't know…"

"Yes, you do. Let it happen, Bradley. Go with it. Let yourself love him, and let him love you back."

"What if he never does?"

"Love you?"

Bradley nodded.

"That ship has sailed, my darling girl."

"How could that be? We don't know each other, Aunt Jean," Bradley insisted.

"It's a terrible segue, I know, but your father is coming for a visit."

"He is?" Bradley reached for her phone, but it wasn't in her pocket. "I haven't talked to him in a couple weeks. Not since I told him about the job offer from Butler Ranch."

"He spoke with your uncle."

"When?"

"When did he speak with your uncle, or when is he coming?"

"Both."

"Your uncle called and told him about the fire at Butler Ranch."

"When will he be here?"

"Tomorrow morning."

"What about my saying Naughton and I don't know each other reminded you to tell me my father was coming?"

"It's one of the reasons for his visit. Your dad wants to meet him."

"Why?"

"Ready to head over?" her uncle asked, coming into the kitchen.

"I was just telling Bradley that her father will be arriving tomorrow."

"Yes. He is," Uncle Charlie sighed.

It was no secret that her father and uncle had never seen eye to eye—particularly since her mother died. Bradley knew that Uncle Charlie had argued several times on her behalf, advocating for her to spend summers with them. Her uncle had also argued with her dad about her pursuit of a field of study he was adamantly opposed to.

"Where is he staying?"

"With us," Aunt Jean answered. "Where else would he stay?"

She didn't know. This would be the first time he visited ever, as far as Bradley knew. Later, she'd try to remember to ask her aunt why she'd said her father wanted to meet Naughton.

"Let's go," her uncle said, holding the door open for them. "We'll drive over."

Bradley reached again for her phone, remembering it wasn't in her pocket. "I'll just grab my phone," she told them, and ran upstairs to get it. She checked her bedroom and bathroom, looked all around, but didn't see it. The last time she remembered having it was when she was at Butler Ranch. She'd probably left it there.

"Can we swing in to the ranch?" she asked when she got in her uncle's car. "I think I left my phone there."

When Uncle Charlie pulled up to the gates and stopped, Bradley climbed out. "I'll grab it and meet you over there," she told him.

He nodded and her aunt waved. "See you shortly."

Bradley was glad for a few minutes alone so she could process her father's impending visit. Fortunately, it was harvest season, and she wouldn't have to come up with an excuse as to why she couldn't spend much time with him. It had been awkward between them since she was a teenager. Other than her attending Cornell, his alma mater, they'd never found another shared interest.

She wished she could remember more about her mother. Aunt Jean was willing to tell her stories about their antics as children and teenagers, but her aunt had few stories to tell after her mother and father were married. Not even about their wedding.

"They eloped," Jean had told her. "Your grandparents didn't even know they were engaged."

"Why not?" she remembered asking.

"We didn't know much about your dad. I'd only met him once before your mom announced they were married."

Bradley opened the winery door and slipped inside to look for her phone. She was almost to the locker room, where she assumed she'd left it, when she heard voices.

"I have to see him," she overheard a woman's voice say. She couldn't hear the man's voice well enough to know what he said in response.

"I don't care." The woman's voice got louder. "He needs to know, and I refuse to leave until I see him."

Bradley heard footsteps heading in her direction, and ducked behind the door. When she heard the footfalls pass, she waited until the winery door closed before she went to her locker, found her phone, and was ready to leave. She stayed in the locker room a few more minutes, just to be sure the people she'd heard talking were gone.

What had the woman meant when she said she wouldn't leave without telling *him*? Was she talking about Naughton, and if so, was she someone he'd been involved with?

19

Naughton saw Jean and Charlie Jenson walk over to where Alex and Peyton's mothers were chatting. Why wasn't Bradley with them?

Charlie looked up and walked over to Naughton.

"I thought Bradley was coming with you," Naughton said.

"She left her phone at your winery, but she should be here shortly."

"Huh." He'd been specific. Either he'd pick her up, or she could ride over with her aunt and uncle. Those were the only two options. Why didn't Bradley simply do as he asked?

Charlie put his hand on Naughton's shoulder. "It'll be okay, Naught. You can wait another five minutes."

He couldn't, actually. Every minute she wasn't with him was sixty seconds too long. He walked away from Charlie and called her cell. When she didn't answer, his irritation turned into concern.

Where are you? he texted.

Again, no response, so he took the dirt trail that went from Los Cab to Butler Ranch to look for her.

She was coming out of the winery door when he walked up.

"Hey, you," he said.

She put her hand on her heart. "You startled me."

"I was worried about you."

"I left my phone." She held it up.

"That's what your uncle said."

Bradley looked away and folded her arms.

"What else happened?"

"What do you mean?"

Naughton put his hand on her nape and squeezed. "Something's bothering you."

When she tried to move away from his grasp, he slid his hand to her arm. "Stop," he said. "Tell me what's going on?"

"I overheard something…" she began.

Naughton cupped her cheek with his palm. "Tell me what you heard, Bradley."

"I heard two people talking. A man and a woman."

"Who?"

"I have no idea."

"Can you describe them?"

"I didn't see them; I just heard them."

"What did they say?"

"The woman said she needed to talk to 'him.' She told the man he couldn't keep her away from whoever he is, any longer."

Interesting. Hawks said the woman kept insisting she see "him." Was he the person she wanted to see?

"Did you hear anything else?"

"She said it was time you knew, and that she wasn't leaving until she saw you."

Naughton had no idea what that meant.

"Naughton, do you…did you…"

"What are you trying to ask me, Bradley?"

"Is there someone?"

Ah. Now he understood her question. She assumed the woman was someone he'd been involved with. While that was possible, it was unlikely. He hadn't been a monk, but he hadn't been a player either. He couldn't think of any woman from his past that his father would have reason to talk to, let alone keep from talking to him.

"No, Bradley. There isn't."

"She was insistent, Naughton."

"I think I know who this mystery woman was talking to, and it's time I tracked him down."

"Who?" she asked.

"My father."

—:—

Naughton held her hand as they walked back to Los Cab. She hadn't said a word since she told him what she'd heard, and she hated what she was thinking instead of saying.

After Trey's betrayal, knowing he'd never really been interested in her, she was consumed by self-doubt. As she told her aunt, she didn't really know Naughton Butler. Was he telling her the truth when he said there wasn't someone from his past, or even his present?

He seemed troubled as they walked. His grip on her hand was tight, and he hadn't said any more than she had.

"I need to find my brothers," he told her when they got to the table where Alex and Peyton were sitting.

"Okay."

"Bradley, look at me."

She didn't want to, but she did anyway.

"I won't lie to you. I'm not lying now, and I never will."

"I know," she said, lying herself. The truth was, she didn't believe him. When he leaned down to kiss her, she turned her head.

She saw the hurt in his eyes, but she couldn't help the way she felt.

"I'll be back as soon as I can." He walked away, leaving her feeling worse.

"Have a seat." Alex patted the chair next to her. "What's up with you two?" she asked.

"Nothing."

"Liar," Alex said, smiling.

"I overheard something."

"What?"

Bradley told Alex the same story she'd told Naughton, and when she got to the end, she believed even more strongly that he wasn't telling her the truth.

—:—

"Where's Da?" Naughton asked his brothers.

"Last I saw, he and Ma were talking to Ainsley."

Naughton looked over to the table where Ainsley sat, talking to their other sister, Skye.

"Maybe they're with the grands," Brodie said.

"There," said Maddox, pointing to a patch of grass where his mother sat with Skye's kids. She held the baby, Kade, on her lap, while Spencer circled them, tapping her grandmother and brother on the head every time she went around.

Naughton didn't see his father anywhere.

"There's Da," said Brodie, pointing toward the path Naughton and Bradley had just walked.

"I can't wait any longer, Mad," said Naughton.

"Has something else happened?"

Naughton told Maddox and Brodie the story Hawks had told him and what Bradley overheard.

"Who do you think this mystery woman is?" Brodie asked.

"No idea, but I'm about to find out."

Maddox and Brodie followed Naughton who intercepted their father before he could get to their mother.

"Da, we need to talk," he said. Naughton didn't expect his father to nod, or agree, but that's what he did.

"Soon," his father answered.

"Now, Da."

"No, not now. Soon, Naughton, I promise, but not now," he said before walking away.

"What now?" Brodie asked.

Naughton shrugged. "No idea. Mad?"

Maddox shrugged too. "He knows you know something, or that we all do. We can't force him to tell us what's going on."

"I'm hungry," Brodie groaned. "And since it doesn't appear Da is going to do it, we have a lot of people to thank on our family's behalf."

Naughton agreed, and followed his brothers table to table, shaking hands, and expressing their appreciation. Every so often, he'd glance at their parents. His mother was completely taken with her grandbabies, but every time Naughton looked, his father was looking at him, not his grandchildren.

He glanced at Bradley every so often, too. She was watching him with the same expression on her face as his father's.

—:—

"Somethin's up," said Alex. "Look at them." She pointed in the direction Bradley was already looking.

"They're hiding something," said Peyton. "All of them." She looked over at Laird and Sorcha. "I wonder if they know." Both Alex and Peyton looked at Bradley.

"What?" she asked.

"It's complicated."

"I get it." She stood to leave, but Peyton put her hand on Bradley's arm.

"Don't go. What we're referring to has nothing to do with Naughton."

"But whatever it is, you can't talk about it in front of me."

"Has Naughton told you much about Kade?"

"Not really."

Peyton looked at Alex, who shrugged.

First Trey, now Naughton. Even Alex and Peyton were keeping something from her. It was time for her to leave. She'd had enough of secrets.

"I'll be right back," she said to them, knowing full well she wouldn't be.

—:—

"Where did she go?" Naughton asked Alex. He'd looked away to talk to someone, and when he'd looked back, she was gone.

"She didn't say, but she did say she'd be right back," Alex told him.

"How long ago was that?"

Alex looked at Peyton, and they both shrugged. "I don't know. Maybe five minutes," answered Alex.

Naughton rubbed the back of his neck.

"Settle down, Naught. She'll be right back." She tugged on his arm.

Maddox joined them. "What's his problem?"

"Bradley is *missing,* " she smirked.

Naughton's eyes met his brother's, and neither smiled.

"It was a joke," Alex punched his arm.

"Not a funny one, sweetheart." Maddox put his arm around Alex and pulled her close. His eyes didn't leave Naughton's though.

Naughton walked away from the table, sent Bradley a text, and held his breath, hoping she'd respond.

Where are you?

It took her a couple of minutes, but she answered.

Home. Not feeling well.

What's wrong?

Need some rest. Turning my phone off.

He didn't feel well either, but it wasn't because he needed rest. He needed Bradley, and he couldn't explain the feeling he had that she just took a huge step away from him.

"What's up?" Maddox asked.

"She left."

Maddox nodded his head.

"You're not surprised."

"It's time you told Bradley everything, Naughton. And I mean everything—the stuff about Kade and Lena's marriage, even the stuff we can't explain."

"Why?"

My guess is she's feeling the same way we do about Kade. She knows there's more going on than meets the eye, and every time one of us changes the subject or avoids answering her questions, she knows we're hiding something."

"What good will it do to tell her? These aren't her problems, Mad."

"They will be, little brother. Trust me on this."

"Do you think she's in danger?"

"No, Naughton. I think she's in love."

It had only been five minutes since Bradley had last looked at the time, but it felt like five hours. She'd tried to sleep, but couldn't be still long enough for her body to give in to its fatigue.

Naughton. He was all she could think about. She hated the way she'd left, especially after turning away when he'd tried to kiss her. The man had been nothing but good to her, and what had she done? Essentially punished him for Trey's lies and deceit.

She grabbed her phone off the nightstand and sent him a text. *I'm sorry,* she wrote and watched the screen, waiting for him to answer.

I am too, he wrote.

Where are you?

About to go for a ride on the bike.

Before she could think of what to say next, another text came over from him.

Wanna go with me?

More than anything.

Bradley was waiting on the front steps when Naughton drove up on his motorcycle. She ran over to where he stopped, and waited until he killed the engine and took his helmet off before she threw her arms around him.

"I'm so sorry," she whispered.

Naughton set the helmet behind him and put his arms around her waist. "There's nothing for you to be sorry for."

"I left…and…"

"I have a lot to tell you."

"You do?" Oh, God. What? Had she been right? Was there another woman in his life?

"Yep, and none of it is what you're thinking."

She nodded and waited for him to explain further.

"We're going for a ride on the bike, and then I'll tell you about my brother Kade."

Alex and Peyton had asked if he'd talked to her about him. When she said he hadn't, they'd clammed up. "Okay," she murmured.

Naughton unclipped the second helmet from the side of his motorcycle and handed it to her. She put it on, and when he'd done the same, she climbed on behind him and put her arms around his waist.

"Ready?" she heard him shout, and she nodded.

—:—

Naughton loved the feel of her behind him on his bike. He'd been craving it for days. With her arms around him, he took the back roads as far as he could before driving out to the highway. He drove all the way to the beach, trying to figure out how to tell her about Kade. He had no idea where to begin.

He parked the bike along Moonstone Beach Drive and waited while Bradley climbed off and set the helmet on the ground before he did the same.

He pointed across the road to a restaurant and then at the beach.

"Let's walk," she said, without him needing to ask. They'd gotten a few hundred yards before he stopped.

"Mind if we sit?" he asked.

She shook her head and sat next to him on the sand.

"My first memory of Kade," he began. "I think I was five—which would've made him eleven—was right here on this beach."

"What were you doing?"

"All I remember about that day was him doing handstands. He told me it didn't hurt when he fell and landed in the sand. His arms, even then, were so strong."

Naughton looked out at the ocean. "He wasn't for this world," he murmured.

"What do you mean?"

"He was bigger than our little valley. Christ, he was bigger than the planet. Kade was meant to do so much more than grow grapes or make wine. My big brother was meant to save the world." Naughton's eyes filled with tears, and he didn't care if Bradley saw them.

"You miss him a lot," she said, cupping his cheek with the palm of her hand.

"Kade was in the military, and every time he left for a mission, I knew there was a chance he wouldn't come back, but I always believed he would."

He shrugged. "When he didn't, I was blindsided. I couldn't believe he was dead. I still can't. I keep expecting to see him, walking on this beach, everywhere. I expect to see Kade everywhere I look."

Tears slid down his cheeks, and he tried to wipe them with his shoulder.

"It doesn't feel like he's dead, Bradley. Does that sound crazy?"

She shook her head. "No."

"Kade had a lot of secrets. Some we've uncovered, and some, I believe, we're about to."

"Is this about the conversation I overheard?"

He nodded. "You aren't the only one. Hawks did too. That's how I knew it was my father you'd heard, because Hawks saw them."

"Who was your father talking to?"

"That's the part we don't know. It was too dark for Hawks to get a good look at her. And you didn't see them at all."

"I'm sorry."

"Don't be. I'm glad you didn't. I mean…I don't know what I mean."

"It's okay."

"My brothers and I asked Da about it when you were sitting with Alex and Peyton."

"What did he say?"

"He said he'd tell us, but not yet."

"Was that it?"

"Pretty much."

Bradley looked out at the ocean.

"What are you thinking?" he asked.

"I don't know. This really isn't any of my business."

"I want it to be."

"What do you mean?"

"I want you in my life, Bradley, and that means I don't want there to be secrets between us."

"I don't like secrets," she murmured. "That's why I left."

"I knew that. Not right away, though. Maddox pointed it out to me."

Bradley laughed. "He did?"

"Yep. Do you want to know why?"

"Sure."

He'd offered, now he had to tell her.

"If you don't want to tell me—"

"See, that's the thing. No secrets, right?" he said.

"Right."

"He said I should tell you all of it. Everything we knew about Kade, even the stuff we didn't, the unexplained stuff. When he said it I didn't agree, I told him these weren't your problems."

"What changed your mind?"

"It was something else he told me."

"Naughton," she smiled. "Just say it."

"He told me you're in love with me."

20

The lump in her throat she had expected wasn't there. Not even a little discomfort in her tummy. Naughton said the word "love," and her body floated into the warmth of the feeling. He said Maddox had told him she was in love with him, and as crazy as it sounded in her head, hearing the words spoken didn't sound crazy at all.

"Bradley?"

She turned to him and smiled. "I won't deny it, Naughton."

He leaned forward and covered her mouth with his. His kiss was gentle, loving. Instead of waging battle with urgency and heat, their tongues stroked and caressed.

"I won't deny it either," he murmured and smiled.

But who would be the first to say it? She felt it, but for whatever reason, she wasn't ready to say the three little words she'd never spoken to anyone other than her family.

"I've always worried that I'm too much like Kade."

"In what way?"

"He held so much inside, afraid to confide in any-one. I know he loved Peyton, but I'm not sure he ever told her. I don't want to be like that, especially with you, Bradley."

"You aren't."

"How do you know that?"

"Because you talk to me, Naughton. More than you realize. The other day, Alex said something to me, about you not being a talker. I disagreed with her. It's when you don't talk to me that I know something's wrong. But it's more than your lack of words. I can see it in your face. I can feel it in your body. It's *hard* for you not to talk to me."

"You don't think it's crazy?"

"Of course, I do. And yet, it feels so right, doesn't it?"

"Nothing has ever felt as right as being with you does."

"I feel the same way, Naughton."

"I need to tell you more about Kade."

She nodded, waiting for him to find the words.

"There are times it feels as if Kade is still alive, or like his spirit is hovering all around us. Even dead he's controlling the course of our lives."

"What do you mean?"

"Brodie and Peyton were the first. It was like he brought them together. Even when they fought it, it was as though he put his hand on them and guided them back together. He left this box that he wanted Brodie to give to Peyton, but she didn't want it."

"Why not?"

"I guess she didn't want to feel the pain of losing him all over again. She and Brodie eventually opened it together, and inside, there was a letter from Kade."

"What did it say?"

"Kade told her that he'd never been the right man for her, but Brodie was. There was a ring that had belonged to our grandmother, inside the box. She'd given it to Kade, telling him that, when he met the woman who was supposed to wear it, he'd know. In his letter, he told Peyton that he'd known since the day he met her that she was that woman, but it had taken him a long time to realize he wasn't the man who was supposed to give it to her."

"Wow. So it was like he knew Peyton and Brodie would be together before he died."

"Exactly. They'd never even met."

"Brodie and Peyton?"

"That's right." Naughton scrubbed his hand over his face. "He brought Alex and Maddox together too."

"What do you mean? I thought they'd been together for years."

"They were, but it was only after Kade died that they finally admitted the extent of their feelings to each other."

Naughton looked out at the ocean. "I knew about the land Kade gave Mad and me, but I didn't tell Maddox about it. Just like he said in his letter to Peyton, he told me I'd know when the time was right."

"How?"

"He wanted me to wait until Mad and Alex realized they loved each other. A lot of shit went down with them, and for a while, I didn't think they'd ever realize it, but Kade never doubted they'd end up together."

"So, then you told him?"

"Indirectly."

Naughton said Kade told him where to find the property deeds and an envelope to be given to Maddox, through their parents, when Naughton believed the time was right.

Naughton took a deep breath and turned to her. "The other day, Maddox asked me what Kade had wanted for me. I told him I didn't know."

When his eyes filled with tears, Bradley put her arms around him and squeezed. It was a long time before Naughton spoke again, but she waited, knowing that when he was ready, he would.

He leaned into her and rested his face on her shoulder. His tears seeped into her shirt. "I miss him so much. And I don't understand why he didn't…"

"I understand, Naughton. I really do."

It was the way she felt about her mother. One day she was gone, and she hadn't left anything behind. Bradley was a twelve-year-old girl who never heard her mother's loving words again. There were no notes, no letters, no messages—only deafening silence in a home that no longer felt like one.

Naughton wiped away his tears. "I'm sorry."

"What for?"

"Losin' it."

"Please, don't apologize for sharing your feelings with me."

Naughton nodded. "There's more."

He explained that when everything went down with Los Cab, Lena Hess asked Maddox to meet her at Demetria. She had cleared Naughton's name and exposed Calder that night, but she also let it slip that she and Kade had secretly been married years ago.

"When Maddox left that meeting, he saw my truck parked in the woods near the creek, but I hadn't left it there."

"Who had?"

"We still don't know."

"Someone took your truck?"

"Yeah, and by the time Mad asked me about it, they had brought it back. So I had no idea what he was talking about when he asked me why I'd been at Demetria."

"Oh, boy," she sighed. "This is crazy."

"I know." Naughton took another deep breath before continuing.

"I have my theories about who may have driven my truck that night."

"You do?"

"I told you that Hawks saw my father talking with a woman at Demetria. At first Mad and I thought it might be Lena, but now I don't think it was. I think it was whoever you heard him talking to. What we don't know is who she is or why she wants to talk to me."

"She said there was something you needed to know."

He shook his head. "More secrets."

"Is there anything else?"

"About Kade?"

She nodded.

"Only really weird shit that no one can explain."

"Like what?"

"Like everyone thinking they've seen him. Except me, of course." Naughton's eyes filled with tears again. "You must think—"

"I don't think anything Naughton except that you miss your brother. The same way I miss my mother."

"Thank you for that."

She smiled and waited for him to continue.

"Maddox thought he saw Kade at the house I saw Da go into."

"Really?"

Naughton nodded. "Before that, our ma said Kade paid her a visit, and so did Peyton, even Brodie said Kade helped him stay alive after the plane crash."

Bradley's eyebrows went up.

Naughton told her about Brodie's disastrous trip to Argentina, and how, while they all thought they were dreaming when they "saw" Kade, it was Peyton's story that was the most difficult to explain since, in it, Kade told her things she couldn't have known.

"Lang's story bothered me the most."

"Lang?"

"Sorry. Lang is Peyton's ex-husband. He was trying to get custody of their two boys, and Maddox and I thought we'd change his mind. When we got there, he told us that Kade had already been to see him."

"This is eerie."

Naughton was quiet again, looking out at the ocean.

"I'm not gonna lie to you, Bradley. There have been plenty of times I've been pretty pissed off that he hasn't come to see me."

Naughton laughed, but Bradley understood what he meant.

"I would feel the same way."

"You would?"

"Of course."

Naughton turned his body so he was facing her. "Why?"

"Because you miss him, because you feel left out."

He shook his head. "Nail on the head, darlin'. Mad said he felt the same way. Especially when he was so broken up about Alex. We all used to go to Kade for advice."

"There's something I remember the therapist saying after my mom died. She told me that when I wanted to know what my mother thought about something, I should ask her."

"Have you?"

"All the time."

"Does she answer?"

"Never." Bradley laughed. "But I can usually figure it out on my own. Which is the point. Deep down I know what she'd say. Or at least, I think I do. It's harder since I was so young when she died."

Naughton nodded. "The hard part for me is how much we're discovering that seems so out of character for our brother. Like the property. Kade never would've taken someone's land in a divorce settlement. It just wasn't the kind of man he was."

"You think there's more to it."

"There's gotta be."

They sat quietly for several minutes before Naughton spoke again.

"Still think you're in love with me?"

"More than ever."

"Yeah, me too."

21

"Ready to head back?" he asked, wishing they didn't have to.

"Whenever you are. Although, I would like to check on my aunt and uncle. *Oh.* There's something I need to tell you."

"Yeah?"

"Um…my father is coming to visit."

"You don't sound happy about it."

"It's just…it's awkward. We don't have a lot in common, especially since I work in an industry he detests."

"Your dad doesn't like wine?"

"It goes way beyond wine. He doesn't approve of alcohol in any form."

"Were you raised Mormon or something?"

"No." She smiled, but then her expression changed. "My mom was killed by a drunk driver."

"God, Bradley. I'm so sorry. You told me and I forgot."

"He was very opposed to me becoming a wine-maker. I have Uncle Charlie and Aunt Jean to thank for backing me up. I mean, I knew they supported and encouraged me, but I doubt I knew the extent."

"When will he be here?"

"Tomorrow."

"That soon?"

"Uncle Charlie called and told him about the fire."

"He's worried about you."

"Yeah. There's more, Naughton." She laughed. "Now I sound like you."

He laughed too.

"He wants to meet you."

"And I want to meet him."

"That's nice and all, but, no offense…"

"None will be taken."

"I don't know how he even knows about you, let alone why Aunt Jean told me one of his reasons for wanting to visit is to meet you."

"It doesn't matter, angel. Whatever your father wants to know, I'm happy to tell him. No secrets."

"He never met Trey."

That didn't make Naughton unhappy. He'd like to forget Trey Deveux ever had a role in Bradley's life. He'd like her to forget it too. It wasn't just jealousy—although there was a lot of it—it was more that he'd hurt her, and every time Bradley thought about him, there would be a part of her that would blame herself for whatever bad had happened and still might.

"What are you thinking about?" she asked.

"You're not responsible for Deveux's actions."

"How do you know me so well?"

He shrugged. He just did. He couldn't explain it any better than she could explain how she could see so deep into his soul. That was honestly how he felt, like Bradley knew his inner turmoil and, somehow, reached in to soothe it.

"I don't know which came first, or if it happened simultaneously, but I just do, Bradley. I know you, and I love you." The words flowed out without him being able to stop them, not that he would've if he could have. He'd promised no lies and no secrets. He loved her, and not telling her so would be keeping a secret.

"Naughton, I—"

"You don't have to say it just because I did."

She folded her arms and glared at him.

"Sorry. Finish what you were going to say."

She put the palms of both her hands on his cheeks and kissed him. She stroked his lips with her tongue until he opened to her. As their tongues tangled, Bradley pushed him back on the sand and deepened their kiss. And then she stopped, pulling back to look in his eyes.

"I love you, Naughton."

He put his hand on her nape and drew her back so his lips could reach hers again, giving back the kiss she'd just given him.

"Should we take this party home?" he asked a few minutes later. It would soon be dark, and once the sun went down, it would be chilly right on the water.

"Yes, please."

When they climbed the steps back up to where his bike was parked, Naughton realized he hadn't seen her get something to eat earlier at Los Cab.

"Hungry?"

She smiled and nodded. "Starving."

"Ever been to the Sea Chest?"

"I haven't."

"You're in for a real treat, then, sweetheart."

Bradley pulled her phone out of her pocket and swiped the screen. "Should I call Maddox, or at least check in with him?"

"He knows you're with me, and with the dinner at Los Cab, nothing is happening in the vineyards or at the winery tonight."

"You're sure?"

"I know this doesn't feel like a normal harvest or crush, and that's because it isn't. On the other hand, half the westside hasn't started picking yet. Right, Bradley?" he smirked.

"Yes, Naughton," she smirked back.

—:—

"Sleepy?" he asked when they got back to Butler Ranch.

"Yes and no."

Naughton kissed her neck. "Same."

"What time are we picking tomorrow?"

"Three too early?"

"You're the boss." Bradley smiled.

"What time does your father get in?"

"I have no idea." Her aunt had said morning but not a specific time. "I should call my aunt." She pulled her phone out and realized it was later than she thought. "I'll wait until tomorrow."

"Whatever you want to do, angel."

"I like that."

"That I'm so agreeable?"

"That you call me angel."

Naughton pushed her up against the door that led from the barn to his cottage and trailed kisses from her neck to just below her ear. "You are my angel, Bradley. Maybe I have heard from Kade. Maybe he sent you to me."

—:—

Naughton silently cursed the alarm when it went off at two. They hadn't gone right to sleep last night, and even when they had, he'd woken up, unable to resist making love to her again.

Instead of waking her up now, he reset the alarm for two-thirty and closed his eyes, but sleep didn't come.

Even without the impending visit from Bradley's father, today was going to be a big day. Tonight the Westside Winery Collaborative was scheduled to meet, and he suspected it might take a while.

As she had at the last meeting, Alex advised the members that she hadn't included Tablas Creek when she sent out the meeting announcement. From what Naughton gleaned, no one wanted a representative from the Calder family's winery in the collaborative, let alone at the meeting.

"Naughton?" Bradley groaned.

"Yeah, angel?"

"Don't we have to get up?"

"Twenty-five more minutes."

When she murmured, "Thank God," Naughton expected her to close her eyes. Instead, she threw off the sheet and blanket and covered his body with hers.

"Hope you don't mind if I keep you from going back to sleep."

"You're the boss, sweetheart. At least for the next twenty-five minutes."

Forty-five minutes later, they threw on their harvesting clothes and were headed into the kitchen when Naughton's phone pinged.

"What?" he barked at Maddox, who only laughed. "Just checkin' to see if you're lettin' my assistant winemaker come to work today, little brother." Naughton disconnected the call without answering.

"Coffee first, then Maddox."

"Don't get me fired."

"Hey, now. There's a good idea. If he fires you, then I can hire you, and he'll have no say in where you are and when."

"Nope, sorry. I draw the line at working for my boyfriend."

"Your boyfriend, huh?"

Naughton ran his fingertip down her cheek when they turned pink. "I like bein' your boyfriend."

He watched as she opened the cupboard where he kept his French press and filled the tea kettle with water. He busied himself getting out cups, and milk from the refrigerator, so he didn't embarrass her again by staring. As she passed him to put the kettle on the stove, she kissed his cheek. If his life could be just like this forever, he'd be in heaven. He looked up at the ceiling, wondering again if maybe Kade had truly sent Bradley to him.

—:—

Bradley wiped the sweat from her brow with the bandana she kept in her back pocket. It was only nine in the morning, and it was already over ninety degrees. Temperatures were predicted to hit one hundred and fourteen by mid-day. Worse, according to the forecast, the extreme heat would last through the weekend.

With weather like this, sugars would soar in the fruit still on the vine, and without the temperature dropping enough at night, flavor development would lag. This was exactly what Trey said had been happening up north. Naughton may be known in the industry as the vine whisperer, but even he couldn't do anything about this kind of heat.

Now the question was, what would he do? Would he gamble, hoping cooler temperatures would return and force the grapes back into balance? Or would he pick, fearing the sugar levels would get so high that it would jeopardize fermentation?

She'd picked almost another row when her phone pinged with a call from her aunt.

"Hi, there. I was going to call you around ten."

"I figured with this heat, you'd take a break soon."

"I'm waiting for Naughton to call it."

"Your uncle has been fretting all morning."

"What's he leaning toward?"

"Letting it hang. You know your uncle."

Bradley smiled. Naughton would probably do the same.

"He's off to pick up your father."

"Oh, no. You should've called me. I could've gone."

"You're picking, we aren't. It's okay. Charlie didn't mind."

"He can't stand my dad."

"I wouldn't go that far, and honestly, Bradley, I think it's the other way round."

"You said Dad wants to meet Naughton, but how does he know about him?

"I'm not sure, to be honest. Your uncle must've said something, although he wouldn't admit to it when I asked."

Maybe she wouldn't bring it up, then. If her father didn't ask, there was no reason to introduce Naughton to him.

"When does his flight land?"

"It landed a few minutes ago. My guess is they'll be back in less than an hour."

"I should probably be there…"

Aunt Jean laughed. "Yes, Bradley, you should."

She couldn't decide who to call first, Maddox or Naughton, so she texted them both. A few minutes later, her phone pinged with Naughton's call.

"Hey, angel. I was just getting ready to call you."

"I'm sorry to do this, but my father never visits."

"It's okay. I'm getting ready to call it anyway. It's so damn hot. You want to meet me at my place, or do you want me to come get you?"

"I can walk home. It's not that far, Naughton."

She didn't hear anything on his side of the call and wondered if maybe it had dropped. "Naughton? Are you still there?"

"I'm here."

"What's wrong?"

"Nothing's wrong. I just misunderstood."

Oh, God. Did he want to come with her? She was trying to spare him, but instead had she hurt his feelings?

"Where are you?" she asked.

"Twenty-four. I guess I'll see you—"

"I'll warm the shower up. Or maybe it would be better if I didn't. A cold shower would feel pretty good right now."

"Bradley…"

"I'm sorry, Naughton. It didn't occur to me that you'd actually *want* to meet my dad."

"Of course I do."

"Then you better get a move on. Edgar Saint John does not like to be kept waiting."

"Edgar, huh? Something tells me I shouldn't call him Ed."

"Uh, no. That would not be a good idea, unless you're after his bad side."

Bradley adjusted the water until it was more room temperature than warm. Its briskness both cooled her overheated body and jarred her awake. She and Naughton hadn't slept much the night before, and this morning, when he had offered to let her sleep, she couldn't keep her hands off him.

When she was close to him, his body drew hers like a magnet. She heard him moving around the bathroom and found herself giddily waiting for him to join her. What she'd told him earlier was true; her father did not like to be kept waiting. On the other hand, maybe it was time she learned to put the other man in her life first.

"I'm waiting," she called out in a sing-song voice.

"What are you waiting for?"

"My boyfriend to wash my back. Or my front. Well, both actually."

He opened the shower door, still fully dressed. "I wasn't sure…"

He tried to back away when he realized what she was doing, but she was quicker than he was. Bradley pulled him into the shower with her and closed the door behind him. She pushed him up against the stone wall and ground her mouth into his.

"Good thing I dropped my phone on the bed," he said when she took a breath and looked in his eyes.

She smiled. "Didn't think about that."

Naughton spun her around and pushed her up against the wall the way she'd had him. "Tell me what you want," he said, as she felt him unfastening his jeans.

"You. Inside me. Don't make me wait any longer."

Before she finished her sentence, Naughton lifted her between him and the wall and slid inside her.

"God, you feel good," he groaned. He turned around, separated himself from her body, lowered her onto the built-in bench, and opened the shower door.

"Where are you going?" she asked.

"You feel too good, angel. I love not having anything between us, but I need to grab a condom."

"It's okay, Naughton. I mean, I have an IUD. You know, birth control …" She didn't want to think about the reason behind her needing it and ruin the moment, but as Naughton's eyes bore into hers, making her feel uncomfortable, she mumbled, "Never mind." She got up, trying to push past him. Instead of letting her, he picked her up again, pushed her back against the wall, and thrust as deeply as he'd been before.

"I can't…think…about you…with anyone…else," he said with each push. "You're mine, Bradley." He ran his tongue up her neck to her lips. "All mine."

"Naughton—" she cried, loving his possessiveness.

"Say it."

"I'm yours, Naughton. And you're mine."

He thrust once more and held her still except for the inside of her body clenching his.

He lowered her legs but kept her pinned between him and wall. He ground his mouth against hers the way she had with his. With her tongue and lips, she said the words she longed to say out loud. Naughton pulled away, his eyes boring into hers like they had before.

"I love you," he said. "I love you, and I'm never going to stop loving you."

Between her physical exhaustion, anxiety about seeing her father, and the roller coaster their lovemaking always took her on, Bradley's emotions sprang to the surface, and her eyes filled with tears. She put her hands on either side of his face and looked into his eyes. "I love you, Naughton, and I'm never going to stop either."

"We're going to be late," he said a few minutes later.

"I don't care," she told him. "Ed can wait."

22

Bradley didn't seem nervous, but Naughton was. He'd never met anyone's father, not in this context anyway.

"Stop it," she whispered when they walked into her aunt and uncle's house.

"What?" he whispered back.

"Scowling. He doesn't bite."

She smiled, and he did too.

When Bradley introduced them, Naughton had to admit Edgar Saint John reminded him of himself. He made little eye contact, and saying their handshake had been awkward was being generous.

Naughton caught Charlie's eye. He was standing out of Edgar's view, smiling. He was enjoying this, the bastard.

"So, Naughton…you and Bradley," Charlie began, and Jean swatted him.

"I made some tea," she said before he could finish whatever he was going to say. "I'd suggest we sit outside, but with this heat…"

Instead, Jean led them into the living room. Naughton stood next to the chair where Bradley sat, brushing her arm with the back of his hand.

Edgar didn't have much to say, so Naughton was relieved when Charlie brought up the harvest.

"What's your plan?" Charlie asked. "Pick or wait?"

"Wait."

Bradley looked up at him and smiled.

"What?" Naughton asked her.

"I knew you'd wait," she said.

"Oh, yeah? What would you do, Bradley?"

"Wait."

"You're probably wondering what they're talking about," Jean said to Edgar.

"I'm assuming they're referring to whether it would be more beneficial to pick now before sugar concentrations make fermentation impossible, or wait to see if the pH levels adjust with cooler temperatures."

No one in the room spoke. All eyes were on Bradley's father, who sat stiffly in what looked to be a comfortable chair.

"What would you do?" Naughton asked him.

"I'd wait, of course." Edgar smiled at their easy acceptance.

"Why of course?" Naughton tried to encourage him.

"This close to the Pacific Ocean, the odds that the temperatures will, in fact, drop far outnumber the odds it won't. If you pick now, you're assured a poor year, comparatively speaking. If you wait, there's a very good chance it'll be one of your better vintages."

Edgar turned to Charlie. "If you wouldn't mind an outsider's opinion, I'd like to discuss your options for futurities given your recent losses. Contrary to what you may think now, the loss, while devastating, may result in positive shifts in sales that you wouldn't expect."

"Supply and demand," murmured Naughton.

"Exactly."

"You're what sells, Charlie. You're the rock star. People love your wine in the same way fans love a band's music. Their expectations are entirely dependent on you, not on any particular juice." Naughton looked down at Bradley, who nodded.

"I agree, Uncle Charlie."

"Look at the startups who are already selling out vintages," Edgar added. "It isn't because of the wine, it's because of the winemaker."

"You've done research," Charlie commented.

"I am an economist, Charlie," Edgar said in a tone that made Naughton laugh.

Edgar turned to him. "It isn't the commodity. It's the market. You understand that, don't you, Naughton?"

"Yes, sir."

Edgar nodded. "I thought you might."

—:—

Bradley pinched the outside of her leg where her hand rested. She did it twice, and then a third time. She didn't wake up. She looked over at her aunt, who winked.

"Help me bring some snacks in?" Aunt Jean said.

Bradley jumped up. "Yes, please," she said, and then flushed at her bizarre reaction. Naughton put his hand on her arm, leaned over, and kissed her before she left the room and met her aunt in the kitchen.

"Was the tea spiked?"

"No, sweetheart." She laughed. "But I do feel as though I'm watching a movie play out in our living room.

"It's bizarre, right? My father is so…interested."

"His comments were unexpected. Although, I think your father is trying to figure out a way he can participate in the life you've chosen for yourself even though he doesn't approve of the *commodity*."

"Am I crazy, or are they alike?"

"Oh, sweet girl. You are not the least bit crazy."

"Naughton and Dad, right?"

"Yes, Naughton and your father."

"But—"

Aunt Jean put her hand on Bradley's shoulder. "They are alike in the best possible way, Bradley. Not in the worst. Celebrate it."

"Hell, that was outta nowhere," said her uncle, joining them in the kitchen. "They're head-to-head, deciding the future of the universe, or maybe just the Westside Collaborative." Uncle Charlie laughed and shook his head. "When I was leaving the room, I heard Naughton invite your dad to the meeting tonight."

"What?"

"You heard me."

"Did Dad accept his invitation?"

"I think he did."

"Oh, Lord." Bradley sat down in the kitchen chair, realizing she sounded just like Alex.

"We better go back in," said her aunt.

"Snacks?"

"Oh, right. Thanks for reminding me."

Aunt Jean opened the refrigerator and pulled out some fruit and cheese.

"Here, Charlie, make yourself useful and slice this."

"Yes, dear." He winked at Bradley. "I may have to give Naughton some pointers on the ways of the women in your family."

Aunt Jean put her arm around Bradley's shoulders. "You're the spitting image of your mother at your age."

"I am?"

"Your aunt too," said Uncle Charlie, who set his knife on the counter and left the room.

"Where's he going?"

Aunt Jean shrugged and smiled. "Who knows?"

After a couple of minutes, he was back, holding a picture frame. "You probably haven't seen this in several years. When you were younger, you'd ask to see it all the time."

He handed her the photo taken the day he and Aunt Jean got married. Bradley's mother had been Jean's maid of honor, and in the photo, her aunt and her mother were head-to-head, smiling.

She sat down and studied the image. She couldn't remember how long it had been since she'd last seen it.

At least twelve or thirteen years. She ran her fingertips over her mother's face.

Uncle Charlie was right. She hadn't realized how much she looked like her mom and her aunt.

"You're a lot like her in other ways too," said her father, who was standing in the doorway.

Bradley turned and looked at him. "How?"

"Your sense of humor. Your kindness. Your humility."

"Thank you," she murmured.

"The way you love," he added, startling Bradley and probably her aunt and uncle too.

"We married a month from the day we met. It might have seemed crazy to some, but we didn't care." Her father looked at Aunt Jean. "That's why we eloped. We knew what we were doing. We knew it was right, and we didn't want anyone to try to talk us out of it."

Bradley looked at Naughton, who was standing behind her father. "When it's right, you know it," he murmured.

Her dad turned around. "Yes. Exactly."

Uncle Charlie cleared his throat. "I hear you're coming to the meeting tonight," he said, leading her dad and Naughton back to the living room.

"Wow," Bradley whispered, thankful for a chance to breathe.

"Charlie to the rescue. He's pretty good at changing the subject when he senses a conversation is getting awkward."

"It's like I don't even know him."

"Your father?"

Bradley nodded.

"Time to, I'd say."

—:—

An hour before it was scheduled to begin, Alex changed the location of the meeting. Instead of meeting at Stave, she wanted to meet at Los Cab. Her turf, she'd told Maddox and Naughton when they asked why. "No one comes in that we don't want in," she said.

Naughton sat with Bradley's father not far from where she was helping Alex and Peyton call the collaborative members about the location change.

He'd learned a lot about her in the last few hours. Once Edgar started talking about his only child, he hardly took a breath between stories. There were stories about Bradley's mother too.

"I've missed a lot," Edgar confided in Naughton. "For many years I believed the light in my life had gone out. It was unfair to Bradley." Edgar looked at his daughter, and then at Charlie and Jean. "They raised her."

"They helped, but she's your daughter."

"Yeah?"

"Definitely. She's a lot like you."

Edgar cringed, but then smiled. "Thank you, Naughton."

An hour later, Alex called the meeting to order after making sure a representative from every collaborative member, except Tablas Creek, was in attendance.

"I'm sure you're all aware of what took place at Jenson Vineyards Monday night."

There were murmurs from those in attendance, most conveying their outrage and sympathy for Charlie and Jean.

"We believe that the person or people behind the vandalism at Jenson, and the fire at Butler Ranch, are the same as those behind the events that took place here, at Los Cab."

There was no reason for Alex to explain what had happened, everyone knew and empathized. Naughton knew that most had miscalculated their inventory, and thus threatened their bond, at one time or another.

"We also believe there is further imminent threat to Los Cab, Butler Ranch, and the other vineyards and wineries on the westside, and that is my reason for calling tonight's meeting."

Alex explained that a collaborative member had overheard a conversation between Rory Calder and Trey Deveux, and the specific things that were said.

"Why haven't they been arrested?" asked Bob Dunning. "If someone overheard them mention Jenson, isn't that proof enough?"

Maddox spoke up. "You know it isn't, Bob. As much as we wish it were."

Dunning's property was on Adelaida Road, bordering Los Cab on the south.

"It should be," Bob muttered.

Naughton lost track of the rest of the conversation, focusing on Bradley instead. She watched and listened while the members talked. With every word spoken, he saw her take more and more on her shoulders.

There was someone else who caught Naughton's eye. The man sat near the door that led from the entryway into the main tasting room and wasn't someone he recognized.

"Who's that?" he asked Charlie, motioning to the man.

"I think he's from Murray," Charlie answered. "New guy. Can't remember his name."

Naughton looked first at Maddox, and then at Brodie. He motioned toward the man, and they both nodded.

Alex asked about the harvest, and the members took turns saying who was harvesting what and when. There were many who found themselves in the same position as Jenson and Butler Ranch, including Los Cab.

"It's a gamble," Gabe, Alex's oldest brother and head winemaker, commented. "But what I'm hearing is that more of you are gambling too."

Heads around the room nodded. The closer the winery and vineyards were to the ocean, the greater the chance cooler temperatures would return at least in the evening. The members whose land sat farther east were taking the most risk.

Naughton saw that Edgar was scribbling on a notepad. He was anxious to hear his take on the meeting once it was over.

"What can we do to stop Calder?" one of the other vineyard owners asked. "I can't be the only one who feels certain he's behind the crime wave."

"I heard he has a connection to the Mumm family," said someone else. "Those bastards swooped into Napa in the seventies and practically stole the land they built and planted on."

Naughton saw Bradley's head shoot up.

"I heard that too," said someone else. "The Deveux family is as cutthroat as they come. Does the youngest have a connection to someone here, other than Calder?"

There were murmurs, and a few members turned to look at Charlie and Jean, but no one said anything about Bradley's connection to Trey.

"The Deveux family and the Calders are more than connected," someone else added. "They're related. By marriage."

"What's this?" asked Maddox.

"Some say it was an arranged marriage. One of Rory's brothers married one of the Deveux daughters."

Naughton doubted Bradley knew anything about the connection, or she would've mentioned it. Catching her eye across the room, she appeared stunned.

The man Naughton had noticed earlier remained quiet. He looked around the room but didn't engage in conversation. He also didn't introduce himself to anyone. The collaborative was like a family—many of its members had known each other for generations. The man from Murray's presence was like someone attending a family reunion and not making any attempt to meet the family.

"The impact this has had on the Westside, and the rest of our little valley, has been devastating," said Alex. "Like many of you, I grew up here. It's always been a place where we felt safe leaving our doors unlocked and the keys in the ignition of our ranch vehicles at night. I can't accept that our community is turning into a place where we can't trust our neighbors."

Maddox joined Alex at the podium and put his arm around her. "I'm sure all of you want to stop the wave of attempted hostile takeovers that, as Alex said, threaten our way of life. The only way we can send the message that we aren't interested in having our vineyards eaten up by big wine conglomerates is to stand together."

The crowd at the meeting were on their feet, like an angry mob ready to do battle with the monster from the forest. The level of the volume of conversation had risen to the point where Alex would have a hard time getting the attention of the members in order to finish the meeting.

Naughton looked over to where Bradley was and saw through the crowd that she remained seated. He caught the eye of each of his brothers again, making sure they were still surveying the room, watching for anything out of the ordinary to happen. A minute later, he looked back to where Bradley had been sitting, but she was no longer there. He scanned the room to see if she was talking to anyone, but he couldn't find her.

"Where'd Bradley go?" Naughton asked Charlie.

"I don't know. Just saw her a minute ago. Maybe she's in the restroom," he answered.

Time stopped then, as Naughton saw the back of the man from Murray. He was moving too fast to simply be leaving. Something felt off. He waved his arms at his brothers and pointed to the door.

Brodie reached it first, and when he did, broke into a run. Naughton ran too, charging through the front door, right on his brother's heels.

"Check the bathroom!" he shouted back at Maddox "Make sure Bradley is either in there or back in the tasting room."

Naughton saw the tail-end of a black SUV driving away. "Did you get the plate?" he asked Brodie.

"Wasn't one."

A few seconds later, Maddox came running out the door, Charlie and Edgar behind him. *"Bradley's gone, Naught. No one can find her."*

23

Naughton couldn't focus. He had to chase the vehicle he saw leaving, but where were his keys? Where had he parked the truck?

"Let's go, Naught!" he heard Maddox yell from his SUV, jarring him out of his paralyzed state. Naughton ran over, got in, and saw Brodie was already in the back seat. Maddox peeled the tires down the dirt drive, not even waiting for him to close his door.

He looked back and saw Charlie Jenson and Bradley's father in the car behind them.

"They're going north; we're going south," explained Brodie. "They have a description of the vehicle. Bradley's father is the point of contact, so am I."

What was wrong with him? He heard Brodie's words, understood the plan, but he couldn't *think.*

"No one saw her?" he asked.

"No one. Alex and Peyton had everyone looking for her. There were only two places she could've been, Naughton."

Maddox turned right out of Los Cab and took Adelaida Trail all the way to the highway.

"Anything yet?" Maddox asked Brodie.

"Not yet," he answered. *"Wait! I just got something from Gabe,"* he shouted. "He said they caught sight of a black Suburban, no plates, on Hidden Valley Road!"

Maddox slammed on the brakes and spun the SUV around. "Where is he now?"

"Near Vineyard Road."

"They're headed to Tablas Creek!" said Naughton, snapping back to reality.

"You're right, Naught. Brodie, call Charlie," Maddox barked. "Have him take Tablas Road."

If the SUV was headed to Tablas Creek Winery, this would mean, between the three of them, they'd box the SUV in.

"Where's Trevino?" Maddox asked.

"Hang on," said Brodie.

"Who else is out looking for her?" Naughton asked while they waited.

"Everyone, Naughton."

When they pulled into Tablas Creek, Naughton saw Charlie and Edgar were already there. Mad's

SUV hadn't come to a complete stop before Naughton jumped out.

Charlie walked toward him. "Gabe got here first. The sheriff's on his way."

"Where is she?"

"In there." Gabe pointed to a storage building next to the winery. "He's got a gun, Naught."

Naughton charged forward, but Maddox stopped him with a tight grip. *"What the fuck?"* he yelled. *"Let me go."*

"Listen to me, Naughton! Did you hear Gabe? Whoever has Bradley has a gun."

Naughton heard his brother's words, but he couldn't process them. *Who* had her? How did they know there was a gun? Why was everyone standing around doing nothing? He stood, unable to move, staring into his brother's eyes, willing him to give him answers.

"We think it's Calder who's got her," said Charlie, motioning to where Trey Deveux stood, pacing frantically, talking on his cell phone.

When Naughton made a move toward Trey, Maddox grabbed hold of his arm again. "Wait," he said, only loud enough for Naughton to hear.

The sheriff pulled up behind Mad's truck. "The SWAT team is on their way," he told them. "They know there's a hostage situation."

"I know nothing about this," Naughton heard Deveux say to the sheriff. "This is all on Rory. Things got out of hand. I tried to stop him."

"From doing what?" Naughton seethed. "Setting our vineyard on fire? Or kidnapping Bradley?"

Trey shook his head. "It wasn't supposed to go this way."

Maddox stepped forward. "What *way* was it supposed to go, Deveux?"

"It was all about money. That's it. Like what went down at Los Cab. The plan was to uncover vulnerabilities, and then leverage them to get owners to sell. That's it."

"Bullshit," Naughton spat.

Maddox put his hand on his brother's shoulder.

"They're here," said the sheriff, pointing toward the tactical vehicles that were pulling up in the driveway. "Sergeant Akins is the unit commander. I need to brief him on what we know so far." The sheriff motioned for both Gabe and Trey to follow him.

"Naughton," Maddox said. "Come on. Let them do their job." Naughton followed his brothers back to the barricade the team had just put into place.

"The hostage negotiator is trying to reach him now," the sheriff explained when he came back to where they stood.

"What does he want?" Maddox asked.

"That's unclear at the moment."

Naughton paced, clenching and unclenching his fists. If something didn't happen soon, he'd explode, and when he did, he'd charge into the building where Calder held Bradley and kill the sonuvabitch with his bare hands.

—:—

Bradley's head was pounding, and her mouth felt as though she hadn't had hydration in weeks. The last thing she remembered was coming out of the ladies' room and finding Jason Calder waiting just outside the door. He must've hit her over the head with something because she didn't remember anything after that.

From where she lay on the concrete floor, her hands and feet bound, she could see Jason pacing as he yelled into his phone.

"She recognized me. What the fuck was I supposed to do?" she heard him yell. *"Get your ass over here and help me straighten this mess out."*

She wouldn't have realized who he was if someone at the meeting hadn't mentioned that Trey's sister had married Rory Calder's brother. She'd met them both briefly and had completely forgotten their connection.

"None of us would be in this mess if you hadn't fucked up in the first place. Dad sent me here to fix things, so the way I see it, this is your problem."

Bradley heard a door open near the back of the winery and watched as Jason spun around, leveling the gun in the direction of the noise she'd heard.

"Drop it or I'll shoot you, and I don't miss," she heard a deep voice say. There was an eerie calmness to the man's words that chilled her to her core. She couldn't get a good look at whoever was speaking but heard a quick succession of cracks before she saw Jason Calder fall to the ground.

"No!" she tried to scream, but no sound came out.

Seconds later, she heard doors burst open again and could see people in tactical attire run into the winery from the opposite direction.

Two men ran straight to her while two others checked Calder. "He's dead!" one of them said while others ran through different parts of the building.

"Are you Bradley?" the one nearest to her asked.

She nodded, still unable to find her voice.

"I'm Ty, and I'm gonna check you out while my buddy here gets you out of these ropes. While we do that, can you tell me what happened in here?"

"He shot him," she whispered.

"Who?"

"One guy came in through the back and shot him, right before the rest of you came in from the other direction."

"Can you describe the man who came in through the back?"

"I couldn't see much, but he was dressed like you are."

She overheard the tactical team yell something about another gunman, and more footfalls running through the winery.

A voice came through the radio the man kneeling next to her had attached to his gear. "All clear?"

"Interior clear," he responded.

"Bradley, can you tell me what month it is?" he asked while he checked the pulse in her neck.

"September."

"Good. This will be bright for just a couple of seconds," he said before he shined something in each of her eyes. "Can you move your right index finger for me?"

"Good," he said, and then asked her the same thing about her left hand.

"My head hurts." Her voice was getting stronger.

"I bet. Looks like you've got a pretty good bump on your noggin. Do you want to try to sit up?"

She did, with their help, and then the same man asked her a few more questions about whether she knew where she was and if there was anywhere else on her body she was hurt. Finally, they asked her if she could stand and helped her to her feet.

"Let's get you out of here," one of the men said.

She closed her eyes as they led her past where she'd last seen Jason's body. She didn't know whether it had been moved, but if it hadn't, she didn't want to see it.

Once they were outside, Bradley could see Naughton a few feet away, behind a barricade. When her eyes met his, he jumped the fencing and ran over to her.

"I need you to stay back," someone said, trying to intercept him.

"He's all right," she heard the sheriff say. "But, Naughton, let them do what they need to do."

She reached out for Naughton, who pushed his way through and put his arms around her.

"I was so scared," he whispered.

"I was too," she answered.

He pulled back and looked in her eyes. "Did he hurt you?"

"Just my head hurts right now."

He brushed the hair away from her face. "*Jesus. I'm so sorry, angel."

Naughton turned to the sheriff. "How much more tonight, Bill? Can't she answer your questions in the morning?"

The sheriff stepped away to talk to someone who was also in tactical gear. "What more do you need from her tonight?" Bradley heard him say.

"My guys have scoured the area and have no leads on the gunman."

The sheriff walked back over to her, and the other man followed. "Bradley, what can you tell us about the person who shot Calder?"

"As I said before, I couldn't see much." She looked at the other man standing behind the sheriff. "He was dressed like you are."

"Your dad is here," Naughton told her.

"Will they let him over here?"

"Bill?" Naughton said to the sheriff, who looked at the sergeant.

"I think we're done for tonight," he said. "But we'd like to see you tomorrow and get an official statement. We can come to you."

"Let's get you home." Naughton picked her up from the floor with a swoosh of force so powerful, she lost her breath. Once they were on the other side of the barricade, he set her on her feet.

Her dad put his arms around her and kissed her forehead. "I'm so glad you're safe," he said.

"Thanks, Dad. I'm sorry I put you all through this scare," she said, looking at Uncle Charlie and Naughton's brothers.

"I want to get her home," Naughton said to her father. "You can come to the house."

Her father cupped her cheek with his palm. "Do you want me to come tonight or in the morning?" he asked.

Before she could answer, Naughton did for her. "Let's give Bradley a few hours to rest. We'll see everyone in the morning. Okay?"

Her father nodded, and Naughton led her to an SUV. "Mad?" she heard him ask.

"We'll get a ride with Charlie or Gabe," Maddox said, handing him the keys, and kissing Bradley's cheek. "Get some rest, Saint John. We'll see you tomorrow, okay?"

"Thanks, Maddox," she answered, and then looked at her father. "I love you, Daddy."

His eyes filled with tears. "I love you too, sweetheart."

—:—

Bradley didn't speak on the way home, and Naughton was relieved she didn't. Until he had her safe inside his cottage, he couldn't hear or even think about what had happened tonight. As it was, he had to grip the steering wheel with all his might to keep his hands from shaking. He had never been so terrified in his life.

He looked over at her, now and then, as he drove the back roads to Butler Ranch. Her head rested against the seat, and her eyes were closed. When he saw she had her left hand outstretched, he wove his fingers with hers. She opened her eyes then and squeezed his hand.

He parked as close to the front door of the cottage as he could get, and then came around and to her side, lifting Bradley in his arms. He carried her inside but didn't stop. He kept going, climbing the stairs, until he could gently set her on his bed. She lay back, and he stretched out next to her, touching her body with his in every place possible.

His fingertips caressed her cheek as they laid side-by-side, staring into one another's eyes.

"You're safe now," he murmured when she shuddered.

"I was so scared," she said so quietly he could barely hear her.

"Me, too."

She leaned forward, and he met her lips with his, kissing her gently, reverently, with as much restraint-filled love as he had in him. Part of him wanted to devour her, but she needed him to nurture and cherish her now, so that's what he did.

"I love you so much," he murmured.

"I love you, Naughton."

She closed her eyes. "Do you…"

"What?"

"Want to know?"

"Only if you want to tell me."

"Not yet."

Naughton kissed both her eyelids, the tip of her nose, and her forehead before his lips settled back on hers.

"I want you," she pleaded.

Naughton slowly unbuttoned her blouse, trailing kisses as he did. When her blouse hung open, he ran his lips down her tummy until he came to the waistband of her jeans. He unfastened them and gently tugged them until they came off. "Let me," he said when she went to unfasten her bra. She rolled far enough that he could reach behind her and pull it away from her body.

He stood then, and took off his clothes, watching as her eyes surveyed his nakedness. "Are you sure?" he whispered.

She nodded and held her hand out to him. "Please, Naughton."

24

The bed was empty when Bradley opened her eyes. It was light out, and she could hear Naughton talking to people downstairs.

She threw the covers aside, found where she and Naughton had left her clothes, and dressed. She felt sluggish, and if Naughton had still been in bed with her, she could easily have gone back to sleep.

Before she reached the bottom step, she heard Naughton say, "What do you mean you don't know who the other gunman was?"

"It wasn't one of our team," she heard someone say as she rounded the corner to find Naughton, her father, the sheriff, and another man—who looked vaguely familiar—sitting in the living room.

When he saw her, Naughton stood and met her near the doorway.

"Did we wake you?" he whispered.

She shook her head. "You weren't there…"

"I'm sorry, angel."

Her father stood and put his arms around her when Naughton stepped aside.

"Good morning, sweetheart," he said.

"Hi, Dad."

"Good morning," said the sheriff, standing and motioning for her to take a seat. "Do you remember Sergeant Akins?"

"That's right. I remember you from last night."

The sergeant nodded. "Sorry to bother you this early, ma'am, but we do have a few more questions."

"You don't have to talk about it until you're ready," said her father.

Naughton nodded. "Your father's right. If you're not ready, they can come back when you are."

"It's okay, but I don't remember much. I went to the ladies' room…" She put her hands to her pounding temples.

"I'll get you a glass of water," said her father, walking out of the room and toward the kitchen.

"What happened after you went to the ladies' room?" the sergeant probed.

"Give her a minute," Naughton snapped before she had a chance to answer.

Bradley put her hand on Naughton's arm. "I'm okay," she murmured. "I heard you say something about the other gunman?"

"Can you tell me what you remember?"

"I came out of the restroom, and Jason was standing there—"

"Jason?" Naughton asked.

"Let her finish," said Bradley's dad, handing her the glass of water.

Naughton looked at her, and then at the two men questioning her.

"The person who was shot wasn't Rory, Naughton. It was his older brother," explained the sheriff. "But like her father said, let her finish."

Naughton stood and grasped the back of his neck.

Bradley reached her hand out to him.

"I'm sorry." He sat next to her and held her hand in his.

"Before I knew what was happening, he hit me over the head with something. That's all I remember until I woke up in the building at Tablas Creek."

Bradley took a drink of water. "I hadn't been conscious long when I heard Jason, on his phone with Rory—"

"Where the hell is he?"

"We'll get back to that." The sheriff leveled his eyes at Naughton. "Let the sergeant finish his questioning, Naughton, or I'll ask you to leave the room."

"Go on, ma'am," said the sergeant.

"Jason just kept yelling, and that's when someone burst through the back door."

"Can you describe him?"

"I couldn't see much, but he was dressed like the rest of you were last night."

"Anything else?"

"His voice. I remember it was deep and kind of gruff."

"Do you remember what he said?"

"Every word. First, he told Jason to drop the gun, and then he said, 'I'll shoot you, and I don't miss.' That was it."

Bradley felt Naughton tense up.

"What are you thinking, Naught?" asked the sheriff.

Naughton shook his head. "Nothin'."

Bradley couldn't say what exactly she was feeling, but something told her Naughton was lying.

The sergeant handed Bradley his card. "If you think of anything else, give me a call."

"I'll walk you out," said the sheriff.

"Can I see her now?" Bradley heard her aunt say when the sheriff opened the front door.

"Come in, Jean," he said. "You too, Charlie."

Bradley stood when she saw her aunt and uncle come inside. Aunt Jean ran over to her, and Bradley sank into her embrace. She ran her hand over Bradley's hair as she cuddled her, humming something that reminded Bradley of her mother.

"Have a seat," Naughton said, motioning to where he and Bradley had been sitting.

Aunt Jean led Bradley over to the couch and held her for a long while after they sat, her nestled between her aunt and uncle.

"I wanted to come last night," said Aunt Jean. "But your father and Charlie talked me out of it."

"She needed rest," said Naughton.

"She needed you," said Jean, smiling at him.

—:—

A few minutes later, the sheriff came back inside. "Bradley, Naughton, I'll give you an update on what else we know, and then I'll leave you to your families," he said, motioning toward the other room.

"It's okay, you can tell us all," said Bradley.

"Trey Deveux gave us a signed, detailed confession last night, including the names of the men that opened the taps at your place," he said to her uncle. "Trey has proof that Rory Calder was behind most of it, which he was willing to share with us as long as we gave him a deal."

"What kind of deal?" Naughton snarled.

"He's still going to jail. For how long will be determined by how much he helps us moving forward."

"Were the two men who opened the taps arrested?" asked Charlie.

The sheriff nodded. "And we have enough evidence to hold them and get a conviction."

"What about Vatos?"

"Whether Rory paid him to set the fire or not doesn't change anything. He'll still be charged with arson," the sheriff explained.

"And Rory?" asked Charlie.

Naughton moved forward, sitting on the edge of the couch.

The sheriff cleared his throat. "As Bradley said, the man who abducted Bradley—and who was subsequently shot—was Jason Calder, Rory's older brother. He's been positively identified."

"Dammit, Bill. Quit stalling. What about Rory?" Naughton demanded.

"We're looking for him."

Naughton shot off the couch. "You're *looking* for him?"

"Rory Calder is now considered a fugitive."

"Jesus Christ." Naughton left the room, but came back a couple of minutes later.

Naughton knelt in front of Bradley and put his hand on her cheek. "You're moving in here with me."

"Yes, I am. And Naughton, I'm never leaving."

"Call Hawks tonight and have him get in touch with the labor contractor. He can decide how much help he needs. And don't pick anything new; just finish what we started." Naughton said to Maddox before he and Bradley went to bed. It had been a long day, between the sheriff and SWAT commander's questioning, and Bradley's family and his wanting to see her, talk to her, make sure she was okay and he was too.

"Anything else, boss?"

"Yeah, don't call me. I'll call you."

Maddox put his hand on Naughton's shoulder. "You take what you need, Naught. I don't think you ever have before."

"I need her," he murmured and let Maddox pull him into a hug.

"Yeah, you sure do," his big brother said.

Naughton rolled over and groaned when he heard someone knocking on his front door. It was daybreak, but since Maddox knew he and Bradley wouldn't be in the vineyard today, he had no guess as to who would come calling at this hour.

When whoever it was wouldn't go away, Naughton stepped into his jeans and padded down the stairs, ready to tear into the person at his front door.

"D'ye no ken I'm knockin'? Sheesh," his mother said and smacked his head when he opened the door.

"Good morning, Ma," he kissed her cheek, and then followed her into his kitchen. "Why are you here so early?"

She waved her hand at him. "I brought the food."

Naughton watched as she unloaded a basket full of bacon, sausage, baked beans, and skillet bread. "You dinna have eggs?"

"I have eggs, Ma."

She glared at him until he took them out of the refrigerator.

"Cold eggs." She shook her head.

Naughton stood behind her and put his hands on her shoulders. "Why are you really here, Ma?"

She pulled a handkerchief from the sleeve of her blouse. "Don't you get me started again." She spun around and cried into his shoulder. Between her sobs, she spoke, but Naughton didn't understand a word of the Gaelic she used when she was upset. After a minute, she pulled back, walked over, and lit the stove.

He reached up and lifted the cast iron skillet from the hook above his stove and watched while his mother cooked eggs.

"*D'ye no ken* I have no favorite," she began, waving the spatula at him. "But if I did…" She stopped to blow her nose in the handkerchief. *"Bhiodh e thu fhèin."*

He understood so little of her ramblings when she was like this, but in this case, he knew exactly what she'd said. From the time he was a little boy, she'd told him he was her favorite. Every time she did, even now, he figured she said it, at one time or another, to all her children.

"I have to go," she said abruptly. "Your da will wonder where I've run. But first," she took his hand and opened his palm. "This is for you."

"What is it, Ma?" he asked when she placed the felt pouch in his hand and closed his fingers around it.

"Bho mo mhàthair." Her eyes filled with tears again, and she was out the door before Naughton had a chance to look inside the pouch, but he figured it was the way she wanted it. Whatever she'd given him was from her mother. He opened the pouch and peeked inside. When he saw its contents, he knew exactly what it meant and what he'd do with his grandmother's gift.

Bradley was awake and sitting up in bed when Naughton came back upstairs.

"Good morning, my angel," he said before he dropped his jeans and climbed in next to her.

"Something smells really good."

"Ma brought breakfast."

"Oh." When Bradley smoothed her hair, Naughton smiled.

"She's gone now."

He pulled Bradley close and put his head down on the pillow while she rested hers on his chest. "I meant what I said last night about you moving in with me."

"I meant what I said, too."

"You're never leaving, huh?"

"Nope. Not unless it's with you."

"You love like your mother," he whispered, remembering what Bradley's dad had said.

She nodded.

"And I'm a lot like your father."

She smiled. "All the best parts."

He looked into the eyes of this woman, who he knew as well as if they'd already spent a lifetime together. A lifetime in less than fourteen days. The quantity of time meant nothing. The quality of it meant everything.

"Do you believe in soul mates?" he asked.

"I do now," she answered and smiled.

"Seriously."

"I am serious, Naughton. I don't think I did before I got to know you and your family. When I saw how Maddox and Alex were together, and Brodie and Peyton, I knew, then, it was real. I told you that since my mother died, I haven't felt so cherished. It's more than that; I know what love is now, Naughton. True love. The kind of love that lasts beyond a lifetime. I can't imagine spending a day of my life without you."

He leaned forward and kissed her—one of those soul-melding, deep, passionate kisses they shared whenever their lips met. He'd never known a kiss could be so intense. It wasn't just about covering her mouth with his, their tongues stroking and caressing, it was about a love so pure, it forever altered the course of his life.

"Do you have any idea how much I love you?" he asked.

"I do, Naughton. I feel it every time you touch me. I see it in your eyes every time you look at me, and I hear it in every word you speak."

"I have a business proposition for you?"

"You do?" She laughed.

"It means you're going to have to tell Maddox you can't work for him anymore."

She smiled. "And why is that?"

"Because you and I are destined to not only make a beautiful life together, we're destined to make extraordinary wine too."

"Are you offering me a job, Naughton?"

"I'm offering you a life, Bradley. One spent with me. You and I will take this land so lovingly cared for by my parents and their parents before them, and the legacy will live on, in us, and our children and grandchildren."

Her eyes filled with tears. "I accept your offer with my whole heart."

Naughton opened the hand hiding the contents of the pouch from his mother and slipped the emerald ring, which had been his grandmother's, on Bradley's finger.

"Marry me too?" he whispered.

"Yes, I'll marry you too. I love you, Naughton."

"I love you so much, Bradley." He kissed her again and again, as he intended to do every day and every night from now on. "I'm thinking it'll be a short engagement."

"I agree."

"The final day of the harvest?"

"Yes," she said as he rolled her under him and joined their two bodies together forever.

Epilogue

Naughton walked through the rows and rows of Cabernet Sauvignon, cursing the vines. These were the only vineyards left to be harvested, along with a small amount of late harvest Zinfandel, and it was as though the grapes were refusing to fully ripen.

He didn't care if they weren't ready to pick; Friday would be the last day of this year's harvest regardless, because he simply couldn't wait any longer to make Bradley his wife.

Naughton, his family, and the employees of Butler Ranch always had a big party when the tractor brought in the last grapes picked. It was a tradition Maddox started a few years ago after spending a year working for wineries in Europe. This year, though, the celebration would be the most important of his life because it was when he and Bradley would be married.

Tonight, her aunt and uncle were hosting dinner at Jenson Vineyards for the two of them to discuss the final arrangements for the wedding. Her father, his parents, Maddox, Alex, Brodie, and Peyton were invited, too.

Their wedding would be small, limited to family only, and would take place right outside the winery, on the edge of the vineyard.

Edgar Saint John had called Naughton, earlier today, telling him he was anxious to discuss the futurities market for both Butler Ranch and Jenson Vineyard wines. Instead of having that conversation this evening, Naughton suggested that they meet the following day.

"Right, right," Bradley's father had said. "Tonight is about your marriage to my daughter."

His future father-in-law was making every attempt to get to know Bradley better by way of learning as much as he could about the industry she'd chosen for her career. Sometimes his overzealousness bordered on awkward, but understanding where he was coming from, Naughton couldn't help but cut him some slack.

Edgar was right, though, about the potential for Butler Ranch and Jenson Vineyards to turn their misfortune into financial gains.

Higher than average yields for the last three years had left many wineries on the westside with excess inventory. Los Cab had come close to losing their bond with the alcohol tax board because of it, when Alex's brother Enzo, who was responsible for tax compliance, hadn't updated their numbers.

Now, with yields far lower, the demand for their wine would increase and prices would likely rise. It felt wrong to take advantage of the fire and vandalism, but however the market reacted was out of their control.

If he was a praying man, he'd ask God to keep the forces determined to ruin his family, and those around him, away. Bradley had already suffered enough, both recently and earlier in her life. She deserved a wedding—and a life—filled with happiness and celebration.

"Hey, Naught. Got a minute?" He'd been so lost in thought, Naughton hadn't heard his brother Maddox pull up on one of the vineyard's ATVs.

"What's up?"

"I want to ask you something."

Naughton followed as Maddox walked to the same place outside the caves where he and his brothers confronted their father last month. The foreboding feeling Naughton had in the pit of his stomach strengthened. Why did he have to sense something bad was about to happen this close to the wedding?

"There are a couple things…" Maddox began.

Naughton waited for his brother to continue although every second increased his anxiety level. He wanted to yell at him to get on with it, but Mad was never quick about anything, especially something important he had to say.

"I was wondering if you'd be my best man."

Naughton's sigh of relief was audible. That was what his brother had been agonizing about? Had he been that nervous before he asked Brodie the same question? Maybe.

"Of course, Mad. I'd be honored."

"It would mean a lot to me, and it would complete the circle."

"What's that mean?"

"You asked Brodie, Brodie asked me, and now I've asked you."

A second sigh of relief escaped Naughton's lips. He'd hoped Mad's feelings wouldn't be hurt that he'd asked Brodie to be his best man instead of him.

"That isn't why I asked, though, Naught. There isn't anyone I'd want beside me when I marry Alex more than you. After all, you've been beside us since the beginning."

"I'm just glad you figured it out."

"Me, too."

"There's something else."

When Naughton gripped the back of his neck, Maddox pulled his arm down. "It's a good thing, Naught. At least I hope you'll see it that way."

"Would you please just get on with it?"

Maddox laughed. "Yeah. Sorry." His brother rested his hands on Naughton's shoulders and looked him in the eye.

"Remember when you said you wished you knew what Kade wanted for you?"

He nodded.

"Have you figured it out yet?"

Naughton shook his head and held his breath, waiting for his brother to continue.

"You'll know soon enough." Maddox stood.

"That's it? You've got to be kidding."

Maddox slapped Naughton on the back. "I promise it won't take as long for you to learn your fate as it took me to learn mine."

"I can't believe this. Are you really going to drop that on me, and then walk away?"

"Believe it, brother." Maddox laughed and climbed on the ATV. "Hey, I forgot to mention that Ma invited Ainsley to come tonight. Skye and Mac, too."

Naughton better call Bradley so she could let her aunt know. "Are they bringing the kids?" Sky and Mac had two. Spencer, who was almost four, and her baby brother, Kade, who had been born in July.

"They weren't going to, but Jean told them they should."

"Did you hear about the houseful your aunt and uncle are having tonight?" Naughton called Bradley and asked after Maddox left to go back to the winery.

"Aunt Jean is so excited. She said she always wanted a big family, but since she and Uncle Charlie never had kids, she didn't think she ever would. I'm pretty sure they intend to adopt your family, Naughton. Every one of you."

"They may change their mind once they see us all together."

"I'm looking forward to meeting your sisters."

It was hard to remember, sometimes, that Bradley hadn't been a part of his life for very long. It seemed like he'd known her forever, instead of just a couple of months.

"Are you nervous about tonight?" she asked.

He wasn't. Not at all. Asking Bradley to marry him hadn't been a choice, it was just meant to be. "Are you?" he asked rather than answering.

"Not at all. Is that weird?" When she laughed, Naughton felt all the tension and worry he'd been feeling leave his body. As long as he was with Bradley—and he intended to be until his dying day—whatever the world threw at him, he could handle. Without her, he'd be lost.

"I love you," he murmured.

"I love you, Naughton. I can't wait to be your wife."

"What time do you want to leave this afternoon?"

"Probably around one. I'm almost done with the paperwork Maddox handed off to me, and then I have to run home and change."

He and Bradley were going to the courthouse in Paso Robles to get their marriage license, and then to pick out wedding bands.

"You need to get the rest of your stuff moved into my place."

"I *have* been a little busy."

"Well, get at it, woman."

She laughed. "So bossy. I may have to rethink working for you instead of your brother."

"I told you once you'd never work for me."

"I remember, so what do we do?"

"We work together."

Naughton checked the time. He had about twenty minutes before Bradley was due to meet him at the house, so he stopped at the winery to see if Maddox had any firm numbers about the amount of juice that had been adversely affected by smoke taint.

When he took a shortcut through the tasting room, he saw a woman standing just inside the door.

"Who are you?" he asked. "We aren't open yet."

"You must be Naughton," she said.

"I didn't ask who I am, I asked who you are," he barked, a feeling of *déjà vu* washing over him.

She stepped forward and held out her hand. "I'm Quinn."

Naughton folded his arms. "Quinn who?"

"My last name's Hess although, recently, I've discovered that on my birth certificate it's listed as Butler."

"Who the hell are you?"

"I'm your oldest brother's secret, and I have a lot to tell you, *Uncle* Naughton."

Naughton was reeling. Was this, or *she,* what his father, or Lena, had been hiding?

"Have a seat," he said, motioning to a stool at the tasting bar.

"You haven't been easy to get an audience with."

"You're here now. Start talking, Quinn."

"I'm not sure where to begin…"

Naughton heard someone walking through the winery and remembered he was supposed to meet Bradley at the house in just a few minutes. He didn't know what the hell to do. He had to find out who this woman was and if she really had a connection to Kade.

"Before you get started, I have to make a phone call."

She nodded, and he went behind the bar and through a door to the storage room to call Bradley.

"Hey, there," she answered. "I was just looking for you."

"Something's come up, and I need to change our plans. We'll have to go into town tomorrow."

"Naughton, what's wrong? I don't like the sound of your voice."

He scrubbed his hand over his face, unsure of what, or how, he should tell her.

"Where are you?" she asked before he could answer.

"In the tasting room."

"I'll be right there."

He looked through the window of the door that separated the storage and tasting rooms, and studied the woman who'd introduced herself as Quinn. There was definitely a resemblance to Lena, but she didn't look much like a Butler.

Her hair was a very pale straw color, and her eyes were dark brown. There was nothing in her facial features that resembled anyone in his family either, and she was tall and thin, more like Peyton and Alex than his sisters or mother, who were all petite.

Quinn looked up at the same time Naughton heard another door open. He went into the tasting room and saw Bradley walking in, followed by Maddox.

"Who's this?" Maddox asked, walking over to meet her.

"I'm Quinn," she said before Naughton could preface her introduction.

"What's your last name, Quinn?"

"As I was just telling your brother—"

"Hess," Naughton said before she could continue.

"Interesting." Maddox studied her. "Any relation to the Hess family we know?"

Naughton opened his mouth to answer, but this time, Quinn interrupted him.

"Lena Hess is my mother."

"I'm Bradley. I'm Naughton's fiancée."

Quinn shook Bradley's hand but kept her eyes on Naughton. Evidently, she'd gotten the message he didn't want her to say anything about Kade or her connection to his family.

"It's nice to meet you, Quinn," said Maddox. "We don't know your mother that well and had no idea she had a daughter."

"I've been away…until recently. First, boarding school, and then college."

"Fall break?" Mad asked. Every so often his eyes met Naughton's, who knew full well what his brother was up to.

"Something like that."

"We haven't seen your mother since…when was the last time we saw Lena, Naught?"

"Late June, early July, from what I remember."

"That's actually why I'm here…about my mother." Quinn's eyes shifted from Naughton to Bradley. "But I can see this isn't a good time."

"It isn't, actually. Bradley and I have an appointment this afternoon."

"Maybe I can help you," Maddox offered.

"Thanks, but…I'll, uh…be in touch." Quinn picked her purse up from where it sat on the bar and turned to leave.

"Wait," Maddox spoke before Naughton could. "How do we get in touch with you?"

While it was Maddox she was answering, Quinn looked at Naughton instead. "You don't. I'll get in touch with you."

"What was that all about?" Bradley asked after Quinn walked out.

"I'll explain on our way into town." Naughton walked over and kissed Bradley's forehead. "I need a minute with my brother first, though."

"Of course. I'll…wait at the house?"

"Thanks, angel." Naughton smiled and leaned forward to kiss her lips. "I promise I won't be too long."

Naughton and Maddox both waited for the door to close behind her.

"Think she's Da's secret?"

"And Kade's."

Maddox raised an eyebrow.

"When she introduced herself to me, she said she'd recently discovered her birth certificate says Butler, not Hess."

"Ho...lee...shit."

"Right."

"Think we shoulda just let her walk outta here?"

"Probably not, but I didn't know what else to do."

"I hope she doesn't wait too long to get back in touch."

"I don't think she will. I got the impression she needs our help, didn't you?"

"Sort of. For me it seemed more like she needed *your* help."

Naughton thought so, too. He just hadn't wanted to say it, hoping his instincts were wrong. "Why just me, though? It doesn't make sense."

"No idea, brother." Maddox shifted his weight from one leg to the other. He probably didn't realize it, but it was one of his tells.

"You've got something to tell me. What is it?"

"Alex and I had dinner with Noah Ridge a couple of weeks ago. I was going to wait until after the harvest and your wedding to tell you."

"Tell me what—that you had dinner?"

Maddox shook his head. "It appears that our big brother had a connection to Rory Calder."

Naughton sat down when his head started spinning. "So it was personal."

"What's that?"

"When Calder framed me for turning the Avilas in to the tax bureau, I felt like it was personal."

"The plot thickens with Quinn wanting to talk to you and not me."

"Bradley's waiting…" And with news that Calder had a connection to his family, Naughton didn't like the idea of her being alone, ever.

"Go on, then. There's nothing we can do about Quinn now." Maddox laughed.

"What's funny?" Naughton didn't see a damn thing humorous about the situation.

"We should've invited her to dinner tonight. That would've been interesting."

"You're a sick *sonuvabitch* sometimes. You know that?"

"So Alex tells me."

Naughton took his time, walking from the winery to his house, trying to decide what he should and shouldn't tell Bradley. He hated hiding anything from her, but did she need to know anything about Quinn now? On the other hand, they'd promised not to keep secrets from each other and he had to honor that.

Just as he was about to put his hand on the doorknob, the door opened.

"It was her," Bradley said, her eyes wide. "That's who your father was talking to in the winery."

Naughton gently pushed her back into the house and closed the door behind him. "What makes you so certain?"

"Her accent mainly, but her voice too."

"I didn't pick up an accent."

"It was very faint, but if you'd ever lived in New York, you'd recognize it immediately."

"Let's sit down." Naughton led her into the living room and pulled her down next to him on the couch. "Before you walked in with Maddox, Quinn told me that she has reason to believe my brother Kade was her father."

Bradley gasped. "You had no idea?"

"That he had a daughter? Hell, no." Naughton put his arm around Bradley's shoulder and pulled her close to him. "There's more."

Bradley pulled back and looked into his eyes. "What?"

"I don't know if you remember, but when I told you about what went down with me, Calder, and Los Cab, I said that it felt personal."

She nodded.

"After you left just now, I was talking to Maddox, and he told me he'd recently learned that Calder and Kade had some kind of connection."

"What?"

"The connection? Mad didn't elaborate, but I can guess."

"You can?"

"Sure. With Kade's line of work, inside of the military or out, it isn't difficult."

"What do you want to do, Naughton?"

"I'm not sure what you're asking. Do you mean right now? What we'd planned to do. Go into town and get our marriage license."

"Do you think we should delay the wedding?"

It was Naughton's turn to gasp, but he held it inside. "Why would we do that?"

"I don't know…everything that's happening."

"Not on your life, Bradley." As soon as he said the words, he regretted them. He wouldn't bet on the life of the woman he loved, literally or metaphorically. "If anything, I want to marry you sooner."

"Why?"

"Because I want you with me, by my side, forever and ever."

"I'm by your side now, Naughton."

He cupped her face and lowered his mouth to her lips. Part of him was afraid she'd turn away, but she didn't. Bradley held still while Naughton brushed a line of kisses from her lips to her cheek, and then her brow, and back down again.

She stood and held her hand out to him. "Come with me, Naughton."

He followed her up the stairs and into his bedroom, their bedroom now. His hand slid to her shoulders as she reached for the waist of his shirt that was tucked into his jeans.

Naughton was impatient. He moved her hand away, unfastened his jeans, and let them slide off until they were half-hitched on his legs before he kicked them off.

Her clothes were next. They both pulled and pushed until she was as naked as he was. He twisted his body so she landed on the bed beneath him.

Once the heat had been ignited, Naughton couldn't wait another minute to be inside her. It was frenzied, fast, and hard, but Bradley seemed to need it that way as much as he did. He stopped moving and brushed her hair away from her face, so he could look into her eyes.

"Don't make me wait, Naughton," she pleaded, arching into him.

"Shh, now," he said to her. "There's no need to hurry, angel. We have the rest of our lives."

She flicked her tongue against his lips and started moving again, enough that Naughton lost his resolve and pounded into her, hearing his own raw groan as her warmth pulsed around him.

"I love you, Bradley," he whispered before an intense explosion ricocheted through his body and mind. She made a humming sound that vibrated through her body into his, and Naughton knew her climax had been as powerful as his was.

He bent his head and caught her lower lip, biting it gently, and then sucking it into his mouth. Her fingers dug into his shoulders as her hips began to rock again. When she tried to kiss him, he wrapped his fingers in her hair.

"I want to watch this time," he told her, rolling his hips with hers. He felt her tighten around him a second time as he fought to hold himself back until her tremors subsided. Blood roared in his ears as he once again lost his resolve and thrust into her over and over, until he could no longer move.

He must've fallen asleep, but woke up when Bradley pulled him out of bed and into a hot shower. "What time is it?" he asked, his voice heavier than he'd expected it to sound.

"A little after three. We can still make it downtown," she said as she drizzled shampoo into her hair. "Unless you'd rather wait."

He moved her hands away and massaged her scalp. "Turn around." With her back to him, he trailed the suds from the shampoo down the front of her body.

"I guess you'd rather wait," she murmured.

"Nah, I'm just gettin' you clean before I make you my wife."

"Naughton, we're not getting married until Friday. I hope you know I plan to shower again between now and then."

"Yeah, well, I have somethin' else in mind."

Keep reading for a sneak peek at the next book in the Butler Ranch Series—
Mercer's Vow!

He's a bodyguard with an alpha mentality.
They call him intense and stealthy.
She calls him off-limits.
We call him Mercer Bryant.

Mercer Bryant made a promise—one he intends to keep—even if it kills him. He would do anything for his partner. Keeping secrets and fulfilling promises goes with the territory. His current mission: discreetly protect Quinn Sullivan at all costs. As a former CIA operative, Mercer knows his way around violent and undercover operations. Protecting the independent and fiery Quinn keeps him on his toes. But, she wants nothing to do with him or his mission.

Hellbent on delivering on his vow, Mercer takes on the enemies responsible for his partner's disappearance—but there is more on the line. Keeping Quinn safe means letting down his guard and letting her into his heart. Suddenly, Quinn sees Mercer for more than just the man next door. Now, she needs to accept that there is only one man to keep her alive: Mercer Bryant.

1

Quinn stood and stretched her legs, deciding—finally—to let her friends know she was leaving. When she turned away from the water, she caught a glimpse of someone who looked familiar, but she couldn't place him.

The gravel pathway she walked wasn't well-lit, so she could see the man standing with his shoulder up against the stone archway that separated the concrete surrounding the home's pool from its gardens, better than he'd be able to see her.

As she got closer, she was certain she recognized him from her apartment building, but what on earth was Mr. Bryant doing here? She knew she seemed like a snob for wondering.

She remembered feeling the same way the day he moved into the only other apartment on her floor. Initially, she thought he worked for the moving company but found out differently when she got on the elevator with the rest of the movers at the end of the day.

"I haven't met my new neighbor yet," she'd said. "I hope he didn't work you too hard today."

"No ma'am," one of the men had answered. "Mr. Bryant helped."

After seeing him that day, even from a distance, she'd been surprised the board had approved the sale. He looked like someone who should grace the cover of a SEAL romance novel, not that she read them, but still—he screamed military.

Creeping closer, she realized how much taller he was than she'd thought. Quinn fanned her face at the hard outline of his muscular back. Did the man really need to wear a shirt that tight?

It seemed as though he was looking for someone, but rather than making his way through the crowd, he stayed on the periphery.

Quinn hadn't decided whether or not to say hello, when he turned and looked straight at her.

"Hi," she murmured.

His eyes scrunched and then widened in recognition. "Hello," he answered.

In the light from the party, Quinn noticed that his hair, which she thought was brown, was more of a sandy color and, as she got closer, that his eyes were a light shade of hazel, like toffee.

"Mr. Bryant…" What could she say that wouldn't offend him? Her first inclination was to ask what he was doing there.

"It's Mercer."

Quinn's cheeks flushed. "I'm sorry, Mr. Mercer."

"Just Mercer."

Oh. Mercer was handsome. Very handsome, in fact, with a body that sped up her heart rate. His tight, black, v-neck shirt emphasized the muscles on the front of him as effectively as the back, and his arms were rock-solid.

Her first impression, that he was a military man, stuck. He kept his hair neatly trimmed, but his groomed, medium-stubble beard ruled him out as being active duty. Didn't it?

She shook her head at the memory she didn't realize she carried with her. It had been years since she'd spent time with her grandparents, not since she left for boarding school, but one memory remained of her grandfather talking about his days in the Marines.

She'd asked him what the word "jarhead" meant, and he'd told her it had nothing to do with the high and tight haircut he'd still sported, but had more to do with a Marine's willingness to follow orders without question.

"Our heads are hard, but sometimes empty," he'd joked.

They'd talked about beards that day too, because her grandmother had teased that his would hardly pass muster.

"What are you doing here?" The question slipped out, even though she'd decided, a minute ago, it would be rude to ask.

"Meeting friends," he answered almost too quickly, as if he'd anticipated the question. "You?" he added.

"With friends, although…" Quinn liked that he kept his gaze steady and didn't finish her sentence when she hesitated. "I was thinking about leaving."

"Me too," he murmured.

"I was about to call for car service, if you want to share a ride," she offered.

"I have a car."

Oh. Did that mean he was offering her a ride or declining her invitation to share one?

He turned to leave, but looked back when Quinn didn't follow. "Coming?" he asked.

"I should probably let my friends know…" Again, he didn't finish her sentence. "I guess I could just text them."

He nodded and motioned for her to follow.

"Here we are," he said, stopping next to a sleek convertible that reminded Quinn of a bullet.

"Nice car," she said after he'd opened her door, waited for her to be seated, and then closed it behind her.

"Thanks. It isn't mine."

"No?" Interesting. Maybe the apartment wasn't either, although Quinn hadn't seen anyone else come or go. "Whose is it?"

"Belongs to a friend."

"It's nice that your friend lets you use it." Quinn ran her hand over the supple, dark-colored leather. "What is it?"

"A Jaguar Series One E-Type. Uh…sixty-two."

He answered as though he expected her to know what that meant. Jaguar was the only part of it that sounded familiar. Having lived in and around New York City for the last fourteen years, cars hadn't been something she had reason to learn much about. She'd never even learned to drive.

Quinn relaxed in the comfortable seat of the Jaguar, shifting her focus from the man next to her to the warm summer breeze on her face.

"Cold?" he asked, once he picked up speed on the highway.

"It feels good. Although…maybe a little."

Mercer reached behind her seat and pulled out a blanket. "Mind if I leave the top down?"

Quinn snuggled under it. "No. It's fine. What about you? Do you have a jacket?"

"I don't get cold," he answered.

"Ever?"

"Not in the summer."

"Hmm."

Mercer turned and looked at her when she didn't continue. "Yeah?"

"Nothing."

He smiled. It was the first time she'd seen him do anything but frown. "You have a nice smile."

He looked away, as though he wasn't used to the compliment. "You do too," she heard him murmur.

She studied him longer than she should have. He probably felt her lingering gaze, but he didn't acknowledge it. Who was this man? And how did someone who looked as though he was under thirty, and had probably served in some branch of the military, afford a two-million-dollar apartment in the heart of Manhattan? Quinn supposed he could be a trust-fund kid, like she was, but he didn't appear to fit that bill either.

Who in the hell was this man?

About the Author

USA Today and Amazon Top 15 Bestselling Author Heather Slade writes shamelessly sexy, edge-of-your seat romantic suspense.

She gave herself the gift of writing a book for her own birthday one year. Fifty-plus books later (and counting), she's having the time of her life.

The women Slade writes are self-confident, strong, with wills of their own, and hearts as big as the Colorado sky. The men are sublimely sexy, seductive alphas who rise to the challenge of capturing the sweet soul of a woman whose heart they'll hold in the palm of their hand forever. Add in a couple of neck-snapping twists and turns, a page-turning mystery, and a swoon-worthy HEA, and you'll be holding one of her books in your hands.

She loves to hear from my readers. You can contact her at heather@heatherslade.com

To keep up with her latest news and releases, please visit her website at www.heatherslade.com to sign up for her newsletter.

MORE FROM AUTHOR HEATHER SLADE

BUTLER RANCH
Kade's Worth
Brodie's Promise
Maddox's Truce
Naughton's Secret
Mercer's Vow
Kade's Return
Butler Ranch Christmas

WICKED WINEMAKERS
FIRST LABEL
Brix's Bid
Ridge's Release
Press' Passion
Zin's Sins
Tryst's Temptation

WICKED WINEMAKERS
SECOND LABEL
Beau's Beloved
Cru's Crush
Bones' Bliss
Snapper's Seduction
Kick's Kiss

ROARING FORK RANCH
Roaring Fork Wrangler
Roaring Fork Roughstock
Roaring Fork Rockstar
Roaring Fork Rooker
Roaring Fork Bridger

THE ROYAL AGENTS
OF MI6
Make Me Shiver
Drive Me Wilder
Feel My Pinch
Chase My Shadow
Find My Angel

K19 SECURITY
SOLUTIONS TEAM ONE
Razor's Edge
Gunner's Redemption
Mistletoe's Magic
Mantis' Desire
Dutch's Salvation

K19 SECURITY
SOLUTIONS TEAM TWO
Striker's Choice
Monk's Fire
Halo's Oath
Tackle's Honor
Onyx's Awakening

K19 SHADOW OPERATIONS
TEAM ONE
Code Name: Ranger
Code Name: Diesel
Code Name: Wasp
Code Name: Cowboy
Code Name: Mayhem

K19 ALLIED INTELLIGENCE
TEAM ONE
Code Name: Ares
Code Name: Cayman
Code Name: Poseidon
Code Name: Zeppelin
Code Name: Magnet

K19 ALLIED INTELLIGENCE
TEAM TWO
Code Name: Michelangelo
Code Name: Reaper
Code Name: Typhon
Code Name: Rogue
Code Name: Hornet

PROTECTORS
UNDERCOVER
Undercover Agent
Undercover Prince
Undercover Infidel
Undercover Savior
Undercover Assassin

THE INVINCIBLES
TEAM ONE
Decked
Edged
Grinded
Riled
Smoked

THE INVINCIBLES
TEAM TWO
Bucked
Irished
Sainted
Hammered
Ripped

THE UNSTOPPABLES
TEAM ONE
Furied
Merried
Vexed
Inked
Jagged

COWBOYS OF
CRESTED BUTTE
A Cowboy Falls
A Cowboy's Dance
A Cowboy's Kiss
A Cowboy Stays
A Cowboy Wins